An Un

"Will you marry me and take me with you to North Dakota?" I blurted the words out so fast my head was spinning. I anxiously waved the fan as I waited for his response. I couldn't bring myself to drink the punch, so I just held it, hoping I wouldn't spill it since my hand was beginning to shake.

His head shot up and he looked at me, shocked. "I must be dreaming," he whispered.

I sat still, not daring to speak another word. I figured since he loved me, he would agree to my request. However, his response surprised me.

"I don't think it's a good idea. As much as I would love to take you with me, you would be doing it for the wrong reason."

"You love me. You will treat me well."

"But you will be doing this to get away from Kent and Rebecca. It wouldn't be right."

Panic flashed through me. "Why couldn't I learn to love you? Just because you've loved me first, it doesn't mean I won't come around to loving you."

"You love Kent."

"Now. But that can change." Couldn't it? Was I destined to love Kent for the rest of my life?

***

Falling In Love With Her Husband

Falling In Love With Her Husband

Ruth Ann Nordin

Falling In Love With Her Husband

V 1.0
Rewrite of *Todd's Bride* and *Ann's Groom*

Cover Photos at www.dreamestime.com and www.istockphoto.com.

Ruth Ann Nordin Romance Books
http://www.ruthannnordin.com

PRINTED IN THE UNITED STATES OF AMERICA

Dedicated to Barb McDonald, a woman with a good heart and a great common sense approach to life. Your friendship has been a blessing to me.

Dear Reader,

This is a rewrite of my two books, *Todd's Bride* and *Ann's Groom.* Most of the content is what you'll find in the other two books. I wrote *Todd's Bride* first which was written in Ann's point of view. However, I liked Todd so much that I wanted to write his point of view as well. So I wrote *Ann's Groom* a couple months later. I still wasn't satisfied with the final product. I wanted to combine them into one book instead of having two separate books telling the same story. The result is *Falling In Love With Her Husband.*

Sincerely,
Ruth Ann Nordin

Other Romances by Ruth Ann Nordin
(in chronological order)

Regency Collection
The Earl's Inconvenient Wife
Her Counterfeit Husband
A Most Unsuitable Earl
His Reluctant Lady

Nebraska Historical Romance Collection
Her Heart's Desire
A Bride for Tom
A Husband for Margaret
Eye of the Beholder
The Wrong Husband
Shotgun Groom
To Have and To Hold
His Redeeming Bride
Isaac's Decision
Kent Ashton's Backstory (Prequel to Catching Kent)
Catching Kent

South Dakota Historical Romances
Loving Eliza
Bid for a Bride
Bride of Second Chances

Montana Historical Romances
Mitch's Win
Boaz's Wager (coming soon)

Native American Romance Series
Restoring Hope
A Chance In Time
Brave Beginnings
Bound by Honor Bound by Love

Virginia Historical Romance Series

An Unlikely Place for Love
The Cold Wife
An Inconvenient Marriage
Romancing Adrienne

Other Historical Romances

Meant To Be
Falling In Love With Her Husband

Omaha Contemporary Romances

With This Ring, I Thee Dread
What Nathan Wants

Florida Contemporary Romances

Substitute Bride

Across the Stars Series

Suddenly a Bride
Runaway Bride
His Abducted Bride

Chapter One
Todd's Point of View

Virginia
September 1899

I still remember the day I realized I loved Ann Statesman. It was a year ago. My parents took the whole family to her house to celebrate her sixteenth birthday. Since I wasn't allowed to bring Alex along, I figured it was going to be boring with no one but our parents and my sisters there. I would have brought another one of my friends had they been able to come along, but they were busy. When we got to her house, I sat in the parlor, bored out of my mind, while the girls all giggled and talked about stuff only girls would be interested in. I tuned these topics out fairly well.

As I was staring out the window, Ann walked up to me. "Would you like to play the new game my parents bought me for my birthday?"

Anything to get away from the mindless chatter appealed to me, so I nodded and followed her to her bedroom. Ginny, one of the servants in her household, was with us, so there was no way anyone would think we were doing anything improper. Her bedroom was a typical girly bedroom but somehow, it didn't seem so bad compared to what my sisters' bedrooms were like.

She handed me a deck of cards. "The game is called Solitaire. Are you familiar with it?"

I shook my head.

"It's a game you can play by yourself." She shuffled the deck and set seven cards out in a row on her desk. I watched as she continued to set the cards out. Some were faced up and some were faced down. As she did this, she explained, "Since I'm an only child, I don't receive games that are for two or more players. This card game is fun and can be tricky. If you make a mistake, you have to hope you'll get to use the necessary card again."

"Why are you doing this for me?" I had to ask it. Usually, she didn't notice me.

She smiled at me.

I blinked. Since when did she look pretty?

She handed me the rest of the cards. "It can't be fun for you to sit in the parlor and listen to us talk about clothes and jewelry. I know our parents are close and wanted to spend the day together, but it's hardly any fun for a boy to be surrounded by girls. Also, I was the one who insisted that Creepy Alex wasn't allowed to come. I'm sorry, Todd, but I just can't stand him. He thinks his pranks are funny but I don't."

I shrugged. "I guess he's not for everyone."

"I had hoped that maybe one of your other friends would be able to come. Simon and Jeff are actually nice. It's too bad that didn't work out. So I thought if you could play an interesting game away from the rest of us, it would help pass the time."

"Thank you."

She spent the next five minutes teaching me the rules of the game, and I was intrigued by it.

"I will let our parents know that I invited you back here so they won't bother you until it's time to eat," she said.

"Would you like me to stay here, Miss Ann?" Ginny asked her.

Ann looked at me for a moment before turning back to the servant. "No. I trust him."

That was when I fell in love with her. From that moment on, I sought her out whenever she was around. I found that I was able to have a good conversation with her as long as we were alone, with a servant quietly watching. Being wealthy with servants following us all over the place, we grew up used to it. But the times when I could talk to her without one of my sisters, our parents or a friend with us was rare. Most of the time, I had to listen to her and Agnes talk. I stayed as long as I could tolerate the conversation. On several occasions, I attempted to change the topic, but Agnes dominated the room so I gave up and left. As much as I loved to sit and look at Ann, I could only handle so much female talk.

I spent hours staring at her picture. It was the only one I had of her. It was taken on her sixteenth birthday. She gave Agnes a copy. I wanted to ask for one too but was suddenly too nervous around her, so I offered to buy Agnes' copy.

"Ann's my dearest friend," she said. "If I sell this, it'll be like I'm selling my friendship. I can't do that."

I didn't hide my disappointment. "It's just one picture. You have others of her."

"True but this is her most recent one." She paused and gave me a careful look. "Do you love her?"

I shook my head. "Of course not." Like I would ever admit such a thing to my sister!

She didn't seem convinced. To her credit, she didn't give me a hard time about it. "I'll tell you what. I'll ask her for another picture."

"You're not going to tell her why, are you?"

"I should. It might be the first step to her becoming my sister by marriage."

"I just want her picture. I don't want to marry her." At sixteen, I wasn't thinking that far off into the future.

"I'll get the picture and I won't tell her why."

As soon as I got the picture, I framed it so it would stay in good condition. As the year passed, I often gazed upon it and recalled the day she taught me Solitaire.

It was easy to admire her dark hair, fair complexion, brown eyes, and hourglass figure. I couldn't think of a single thing that was wrong with her. Well, that wasn't entirely true. She did have one flaw. She didn't love me.

***

My last attempt to get Ann's interest came in October when we were seventeen. She came down with a fever and was unable to attend school, so I volunteered to take her homework to her. This was my chance to talk to her without Agnes being around.

Monday through Thursday, I visited with her in her bedroom. Ginny stayed in her room while I discussed the class lessons for the day and recorded her answers to the questions on our homework. Even when she was sick in bed, she was beautiful. Her disheveled hair and runny nose did little to discourage me. It was nice to see her without her jewelry, fancy dresses and hats on. We mostly made small talk, and I thought she was beginning to enjoy my company. I know the more I learned about her, the more I loved her. She wasn't sure what she wanted to do after we finished school in May.

"I suppose it will be time to get serious about looking for a husband because I have to," she said thoughtfully. "I hate to say it but sometimes being wealthy isn't much fun. You have to do what others expect you to do. For once, I would like to do something that isn't proper." She glanced at Ginny and smiled. "I often tell Ginny that one of these days,

I'm going to let my hair down and go outside without a hat or a parasol."

I grinned. "I wouldn't mind seeing that."

"Oh, I know it isn't a big thing as far as the rules go."

"Who says you have to do something drastic? Sometimes just doing something small can help when we live under the expectations of our parents."

"So you do understand."

More than she realized. That was one of the reasons I went along with some of Alex's pranks. They were harmless and funny. I didn't want to mention him though. I wanted to keep the atmosphere pleasant.

"What are you going to do, Todd? Are you going to college or start working?"

I hesitated to answer her question. I was seriously considering moving to Jamestown, North Dakota to be a farmer. Alex's aunt and uncle, who lived in Fargo, told me many stories about farming and North Dakota whenever they came for a visit. They also sent him pictures, which he showed me.

Finally, I answered, "I'm not sure yet."

"Tell me. Do men have the same pressure to marry that women do?"

I thought over her question. "No. At least, I don't. We do feel pressured to find a suitable job."

"So we have our own pressures to deal with. How do you cope?"

"By dreaming of what I want to do."

"Really? What is that?"

Did I dare tell her? I wanted to, especially since I was hoping to ask her to marry me and go with me when we finished school. But with Ginny there, I decided not to mention it. I didn't know how much servants talked amongst themselves and did not wish my parents to discover my possible plan. The only person I trusted with the information was Alex who faithfully kept my secret and helped me find out more about farming and North Dakota.

"It's alright. You don't have to tell me," she said. "I can understand the need for a secret."

Again, she amazed me.

"I suppose we should discuss my homework," she stated before she sneezed into her handkerchief.

"God bless you," I whispered. Even when she sneezed, she was pretty.

"Thanks."

We turned to the homework.

When Friday came, I wore my best suit. It was a medium gray color with a dark blue tie. I even paid attention to how I combed my hair. This would be the day I would ask her if I could court her. Since we had some pleasant conversations over the week, I was hopeful that she might start to see me in a more romantic light. I didn't want her to think of me as just Agnes' older brother.

When I arrived at her house with her books, my heart pounded loudly in my chest. I rang the doorbell and waited for her servant to answer. I followed George into the parlor and smiled at the sight of her. She wore a gorgeous dark green dress and had her hair neatly pulled back with a dark green bow. I didn't dare hope she dressed nicely for me.

Ginny took my hat and coat.

"You look like you're feeling well," I greeted as I set her books on the table.

"I do. Thank you." Ann motioned to the chair. "Will you sit down?"

I sat in the chair while she sat on the sofa. Of course, I wished that I was sitting next to her but knew it wouldn't be proper until I was courting her, and even then, I wouldn't sit too close.

"My fever is gone, though I still have a stuffy nose," she reported. "I do appreciate your keeping me current on my school work."

"It was either come here or work at my father's bank." That wasn't really the reason I was doing it, but I didn't feel ready to say the truth yet.

"Are you ready to start that so soon?"

I sighed as I thought about working there. "Apparently."

"I take it that it doesn't please you. You should be able to have the job of your choosing after you graduate, so your time at the bank will be temporary."

"We'll see." The truth was, if she showed any interest in me, I would seriously consider staying in Virginia and working at my father's bank, but I didn't want her to feel responsible for such a decision. After a few moments of awkward silence, I said, "We got a new student today."

"Really? Who?"

"Kent Ashton. He just arrived two days ago from New York."

Her eyes lit up. "New York? How impressive."

I frowned. A lot of the young ladies in class thought Kent was exciting. Did I really have a chance next to someone who was obviously more charming and sophisticated than I was? "Yes. Many girls seem to be taken with him. Alex had to welcome him the only way Alex could." It wasn't my intention to bring Alex up but I hoped to get off the topic of Kent.

"Oh no!"

"You know, Alex may be a prankster but he's harmless. He's not all bad."

She rolled her eyes. "Alex is so childish. When are you going to get tired of his foolishness? I hope Kent doesn't assume everyone is as ill-mannered as Alex."

I stiffened. "I admit that Alex does joke a little too much, but he is a good friend."

I thanked the servant who brought me a cup of hot cocoa.

"Personally, I think he's a bad influence. If I hadn't dumped sand all over him when we were ten, he never would have left me alone. I hope Kent will teach him a lesson."

I grinned as I recalled the day Alex and I were so bored in class that we threw pebbles in her hair until she got fed up and poured a jar of sand all over us. "I must have taken two baths that night to make sure all of that sand was off of me."

She chuckled at the memory, her mood brightening. "It was kind of funny."

"Everyone in class learned not to mess with you after that. Oh, Agnes wanted me to give you her letter. She wanted to come but I felt it was best that she wait until you're healthy. I don't want her to risk getting sick."

"Tell her I miss her," she replied as she took the letter. My heart rate increased as our fingers lightly touched. "So, what homework do I need to do?"

I wanted to say something more but decided to go over her homework.

After an hour, I stood up to leave. "I will see you on Monday. I'm glad you're feeling better."

"Thank you again for bringing me my homework so I don't get behind in school."

I shrugged. "It wasn't a bother."

Ginny brought me my hat and coat. I slipped them on and hesitated. Would it be appropriate to ask her if I could court her?

"Is there anything else?" she wondered.

Suddenly, I realized I couldn't do it. "No. I better go."

And so I left with a lot I wanted to say but couldn't.

Chapter Two
Ann's Point of View

On Monday, I entered the classroom.

"Ann, may I say something?" Todd Brothers asked as I passed him.

I stopped, not because I wanted to but because it would be rude if I didn't. I clutched the books to my chest and waited. He wouldn't say anything in front of the entire class. Would he? I had the sinking sensation that he wanted to court me and hoped to make sure the conversation regarding it never came up.

He stood up from his desk. He smoothed his hair and adjusted his tie. "I'm glad to see you made it."

I shrugged. "It was either come here or stay bored at home, staring at the walls." It was a dumb joke but it was all I could think of. I glanced at my seat, which was a couple of rows from him.

"Did I upset you Friday when I talked about Alex? I know he bothers you."

"You're his friend. I expect you to mention him from time to time." I sighed. "I suppose he shouldn't irk me so. I mean, it's not like he does anything to me. No one else seems to mind his pranks. It probably doesn't help that I keep calling him Creepy Alex either."

He chuckled. "He calls you Scary Annie."

I frowned. "I'm not scary."

"Well, you did hit him with a broom once."

I giggled. "That was funny, wasn't it?"

"Good for you," someone interrupted. "I think Creepy Alex is an apt term. However, I can't imagine you being scary, even if you did come after me with a broom."

I paused and turned around so I could see the person who spoke. Dark brown hair, clear green eyes, and a great smile. This had to be Kent. And he was handsome! I imagined someone from New York would be fascinating but he put all of my fantasies to shame. I thought he was rude to listen to what Todd and I said, but since he set his books on the desk in front of Todd, I realized he couldn't help but overhear if that's where he had to sit.

"I'm Kent Ashton." He kissed my hand.

I stared at him, bewildered that he could be so bold. That must be how New Yorkers were. Bold and charming. I cleared my throat. "Todd told me you came here last week."

"Yes. My family moved here from New York."

"I know. He told me that too."

"We can always talk later when your family comes over to see mine," Todd said.

Remembering Todd, I looked at him. "What?"

His smile faltered. "Never mind. I just wanted to apologize for mentioning Alex on Friday."

"Oh. It's alright. I wasn't upset with you."

He nodded and sat down.

Blushing, because Kent still had his beautiful green eyes on me, I shyly said that it was nice to meet him and walked to my desk. I had no idea what to say to him. He was much more sophisticated than me. To my surprise, he followed me.

"May I hang your coat in the back of the room?"

My heart skipped a beat. "Uh…" None of the young men had offered to do that before. But Kent was from New York. Maybe young men did that kind of thing there.

"I promise I won't run off with it," he teased.

I laughed. "I know."

Feeling somewhat awkward and aware that Debbie and Rachel watched me with amused expressions, I took my coat off and handed it to him. I watched as he put it on one of the hooks.

He returned to me. "I hope you don't think I'm overstepping my bounds, but I think you're the best looking lady in this room." Then he went to his seat.

My eyes grew wide. He was definitely bold! I numbly sat down and stared ahead at the front of the room where the teacher was getting the day's lecture ready. Kent Ashton was better than I thought he'd be. The teacher stood up to speak, so I turned to my books and got my things ready for the day.

***

Kent turned out to be very charming and attentive. He seemed to care for me and we did have fun talking about how creepy Alex was whenever he pulled another one of his silly pranks. I spent Saturday afternoons in my parlor listening to Kent tell me how exciting New York was. He even brought pictures of New York and of the people he knew there. It sounded better than Debbie claimed it to be.

"If we get married, I'll take you there so you can see it for yourself," he once said.

When December came, he asked my father if he could court me, and my father said no. This was the second time he refused to let Kent be with me. Greatly upset, I confronted my father about it that night at dinner.

"Your mother and I don't trust him," my father replied. "He's not what he appears to be."

"Have you met his parents? You always told me that I should judge a man by his parents."

"Ann, I am the voice of experience and wisdom. You have to trust my judgment."

"No one else is appealing to me, Father. I have been paraded through this town in front of countless bachelors who are only interested in my dowry. And a couple of those men were old enough to be your age. What kind of life am I going to have if I'm confined to a loveless marriage? All these men care about is what I can give them instead of who I am."

My mother sighed. "What about Todd?"

"We've already had this discussion. I don't want to marry him."

"Ann," Father began, "marriage is more than fleeting emotion. It is best built upon a foundation of friendship. You aren't looking at things clearly. Kent may be charming but there's something wrong with him. Todd, on the other hand, is stable, trustworthy, and loyal. You can be sure that he won't do anything to harm you."

"What proof do you have that Kent would do that?"

He stared at the fork in his hand. "I don't have proof. I just have a bad feeling about the boy."

My mother nodded. "You should consider Todd. I see the way he looks at you during church and when we're at the Brothers' home. He loves you. Why, a boy like that will treat you as you deserve to be treated. What you and Todd need is to spend time together."

"I spent time with him in October. He's alright but he's not... Well, to be frank, he's not exciting."

My father set his fork aside. Picking up his pipe, he looked at me. "So you are opposed to Todd?"

"Yes! I don't love him."

"Alright. Your mother and I will speak with Kent's parents so we can get a better idea of what he is like."

He kept his promise and both he and my mother concluded that his parents were respectable people, so they allowed the courtship. I was ecstatic. Kent did mention marriage and the possibility of checking Europe out on our honeymoon. He said he had an uncle in Ireland who could give us a personal tour. He even brought over brochures and pictures. He frequently told me I was pretty and bought me little gifts for no reason at all. He also took me to symphonies and the theatre.

Debbie, Rachel and Agnes sat with me and planned out my future wedding. Agnes would be my maid of honor while Debbie and Rachel would be my bridesmaids. They were excited for me and it was fun to look forward to the future instead of dreading it.

***

Then April came.

"Miss Ann, Mr. Ashton's here to see you," Ginny announced.

I turned from my bedroom mirror in anticipation.

Ginny giggled.

"Do I look alright?" I asked her. I wore a dark blue satin dress. He liked the color blue the best.

"You look as beautiful as usual. Come along. It wouldn't be right to keep him waiting."

I took a deep breath to calm my nerves. When I entered the parlor, my heart raced with excitement. "Good afternoon, Kent," I greeted warmly as I approached him. "It's good to see you. Will you sit down?"

"No thank you, Miss Ann."

Surprised by his formality, I stood awkwardly. Out of the corner of my eye, I noticed Ginny shrug, just as bewildered as I was. I waited for him to speak but he refused to look at me. I knew something was wrong, so I took great care in asking my question. "Did you have a bad day?"

"No. I...I have to tell you something," he mumbled, staring at the lace curtains on the other side of the room.

I was afraid of what he had to say, so I didn't press him to continue.

He sighed loudly. "I don't know how to tell you this."

I remained silent. Part of me needed to know while another part wished to remain ignorant. At last, I asked, "Is someone in your family ill?"

"No, nothing like that."

By now, I was squirming. When I could not stand the awful silence anymore, I demanded, "What is it?"

"I cannot call on you again."

"What?" I dumbly asked.

"I love Rebecca Johnson, and I intend to marry her."

"How...When...?" I couldn't manage to finish my question.

"It just happened. I didn't plan it. I don't think anyone can plan things like this," he hastily explained.

Before I could reply, he walked to the front door. "I hope there won't be any hard feelings between us. I'll see you in church tomorrow. Good-bye, Miss Statesman."

And just like that he was out of my house and out of my life. I didn't know how long I sat in the chair, staring blankly at the wall in front of me. All I kept wondering was how he could claim to love me one day and claim to love someone else the next. Ginny sat by me. I took small comfort in her presence. I appreciated the fact that I didn't have to talk to her. I wished to be alone with my thoughts for a while.

When dinner came, I went through the motions in a stupor. I ate dinner outside on the veranda with my parents but I didn't participate in their conversation. I wasn't hungry so I kept moving the food around on my plate.

"Ann, my dear, what's wrong?" my mother asked.

I took a deep breath. My parents didn't like it when I cried. Tears were not allowed in front of others. I braced myself. "Kent came by today, and he announced his engagement to Rebecca Johnson."

"He's going to regret it someday," my father softly replied.

"Oh my dear Ann, is there anything we can do to help you?" She put her arm around me and gave me a gentle squeeze.

I battled with my sense of grief and humiliation. They had warned me. I felt like such a fool for not listening to them.

"I want to be alone right now. May I be excused?"

"Of course you may," my mother said. She quickly wiped the tears welling in her eyes.

Her concern for my emotional welfare made me grateful for her. I could tell by the look in my father's eyes that he also grieved for me. Even if they were most likely glad for the ending courtship, they didn't show it because they loved me. Their support and concern gave me a calm deep in my heart.

That night, I fell asleep as soon as my head hit the pillow, and I woke up refreshed and eager for church. The reality of Kent and Rebecca didn't sink in until I saw them sitting together at church. He leaned over and whispered something in her ear. She laughed so loud that I could hear her from across the room.

I felt faint. I leaned on my parents for support. Don't cry, I repeated to myself.

"He has nerve," my mother angrily whispered.

"He's just a foolish young man. He doesn't realize what he's giving up," my father replied.

"He and Rebecca are flaunting themselves in front of everybody. It's not proper."

"Please, let's sit down," I interrupted.

On our way to our usual pew, we passed the Brothers. I looked for Agnes but figured she was talking to some of our other friends.

My parents stopped to talk to Mr. and Mrs. Brothers. I tried not to look awkward, standing by myself in a room full of people who were happily socializing.

"Good morning, Ann," Todd greeted, his hands in his pockets.

"Good morning, Todd," I politely replied. Usually, that was all we ever said to each other at church, so I was surprised when he didn't leave and sit down. I pulled my eyes away from Kent and Rebecca. "Is there something you want to discuss?"

"Are you ready to finish school?"

"We still have a month to go," I absently reminded him. Rebecca's laughter echoed through the building. Out of the corner of my eye, I saw Kent smile at her. *He used to reserve those special smiles for me.*

"Have you thought about what you're going to do after graduation?"

I turned back to him. Why was he still talking to me? Not wishing to be rude, I answered him. "No. I don't know what to do." I had planned to be Kent's wife. Now my future was a blank slate, and I didn't know what to put on it. Noting that he was still standing by me, I cleared my throat. "What about you? Are you going to work at the bank?"

He glanced at his father who was talking to my father. "We'll see."

I wondered what he meant but didn't ask for clarification. I wanted him to leave me alone, so I tried to discourage any further conversation by looking around the church. I knew it was rude and my mother would not approve, but I just wanted to sit down, get through the service and hide in my house so I could get away from Kent and Rebecca.

"What a wonderful idea!" my mother proclaimed.

"Fine. Then we'll see you next Sunday for dinner," Mr. Brothers replied.

I inwardly groaned. Another dinner with them? I didn't feel like eating ever again.

"We will see you next week," my father added.

Thank you, Father! I gladly walked away from Todd and sat in our usual place.

During the sermon, my eyes kept darting to Kent and Rebecca. Once the sermon was over, Agnes ran over to me while my parents talked to other people. Relieved to talk to Agnes, I walked outside with her. The spring air was warm. I loved the feel of the sunlight on my face and shoulders but had to open my parasol to protect my "delicate, white skin".

"Tell me what happened between you and Kent," Agnes insisted.

"Kent's going to marry Rebecca."

"No!"

I nodded. "He informed me of their engagement yesterday."

"I don't believe it. He loved you. Anyone could see that."

I shrugged. "I thought so too. But we were wrong."

"What a shame. I was looking forward to being your maid of honor."

I sighed sadly as the plans we had made for my wedding evaporated right before my eyes. Now I would be destined to be an old maid. I wondered how many cats I would collect by the time I was sixty.

"I know you don't like me to bring this up," Agnes warned.

My eyes narrowed. What could she be talking about?

"If you married Todd, we would be sisters!"

I quickly hushed her. "That's impossible. Don't start trying to fix me up with him again. I will never be interested in him that way and you know it."

"Even if it means we would be sisters?"

"Yes."

She groaned. "Oh, it's just as well. We would get bored of each other because we'd see each other all the time."

I chuckled. "Yes, that would be devastating."

"I hear you're coming to dinner next week. I'll bring out the new game Father bought. It's a mind bender, so you have to think on your feet."

"Sounds fun. At least, it will get me through the dinner."

"Old people talking about how their kids are doing. I don't like it either. I always feel put on the spot."

"At least you get to share the spotlight with six other siblings."

"Yes, I just love being compared to Todd's intelligence, Abigail's dancing, Lucy's drawing, Miranda's spelling, Colleen's cooking, and Judy's writing. What have I got? I'm Agnes the big talker. A talker. That's my special talent."

"Talking is good. You tell wonderful stories."

"And what good is that?"

"Well, you've made me feel much better. You're a great source of encouragement."

"Thank you, Ann."

I smiled. "You're a wonderful friend. Thank you for listening and caring."

"Any time." She looked at the church door and saw that her family was ready to leave. "I'll see you at school tomorrow."

I nodded and strolled to my parents.

***

The week passed. I hardly ate anything. I spent my free time locked in my room so I could cry. I didn't even want Ginny to comfort me. I wanted to be left alone. At school, I went through the necessary motions. I couldn't concentrate much on what the teacher said. What would it matter anyway? In one month, I would never have to learn anything new again. I would attend many social functions in hopes of finding a husband. That was what my whole life was about to become. The quest to find the man who would care for me and the children we'd have together. Though I greatly desired those things, I didn't see how anyone but Kent would adequately fill that position.

Rebecca let as many students as possible know of her engagement. One time, I thought she gave me a cold look but decided I imagined it. After all, she didn't have any reason to dislike me. She had Kent.

During lunch on Wednesday, Creepy Alex put a frog on Rebecca's chair. She bolted from her seat and screamed so loud the entire school could hear her. Agnes and I giggled from across the cafeteria.

"What do you think you're doing?" Kent yelled at Alex, his face red with anger.

"Don't get upset," Todd defended his friend. "He was joking around."

Kent stood in front of the two boys. Todd and Alex weren't as tall as he was, so they looked small compared to him. By now everyone was quiet.

"It was a small frog," Alex said. "We meant no harm by it."

I rolled my eyes. It was obvious that Alex did it himself, but once again, he was pulling Todd into his pranks with him.

"I ought to teach you a lesson about playing pranks. Nobody likes a joker." Kent looked directly at Alex. Apparently, Kent knew Todd had nothing to do with the prank too.

"Come on, Alex. Let's go," Todd said. "He's not worth your time."

"Is that an insult?" Kent demanded.

Todd shrugged. "Depends on how you take it. I just don't want to see anyone get into a fight, that's all."

"I'll let this one go. But don't play anymore pranks on Rebecca."

"I won't," Alex promised, his face glum.

Kent sat back down as Todd and Alex sauntered away. The students slowly turned back to their conversations.

"Creepy Alex strikes again," I commented under my breath.

"Oh Ann, it was just a harmless prank," Agnes replied.

"He's extremely annoying."

"I don't know. I actually think he's good looking. I'd let him call on me if he wanted."

I gave her a disgusted look. "It's a good thing I'm not going to marry Todd because I'd have to kill Alex if he ever became my brother-in-law."

"I doubt Alex would find me interesting anyway. He's going to go to a college and make something of himself."

"Something like a fool." I chuckled at my joke.

"When are you going to get over that pebble incident? He hasn't bothered you since that day."

"That is true. Hmm... Maybe if he had, Kent would have stood up for me."

"You don't need anyone to stand up for you. You're so strong-willed and independent, you can handle people on your own. Rebecca's weaker. She needs support."

I frowned. "Do you think that's why Kent is marrying her instead of me?"

"No. He's just stupid."

I stared at the half-eaten food on my plate. It would be nice if a man felt the need to protect me. Someone who'd treat me as if I were the most important person in the world.

Someone like Todd.

Chapter Three
Todd's Point of View

I contemplated telling Ann about my love for her. I didn't think she would be pleased, which was the only reason I hesitated to do so. It was apparent to anyone who cared to notice that she loved Kent. I knew there was no way she would go to North Dakota with me, and even if I stayed in Virginia and worked at my father's bank, she would either continue to mourn over Kent or find someone else. The realization depressed me, but it did help me realize which path I should pursue. I would go to North Dakota without her. Perhaps I could find someone else out there. I wondered if anyone could ever take her place.

It was Thursday after school when I had another confrontation with my father. I was sitting at my usual desk at the bank and wishing for the five o'clock hour so I could go home. I worked there every day after school. Though I was still a newcomer to banking, my father insisted I take a position as the loan officer. He had dreams of me owning the bank someday and was eager to start me at a higher pay scale than a teller. I saved aside all the money I made into my moving account. I had already purchased two horses to replace the two I would take with me. I had been with Lightning and Thunder since I was fifteen and couldn't bear to part with them. I also had a covered wagon. I had even packed aside my belongings that I planned to take. I was just waiting for Alex's relatives to confirm that Mr. Martin was indeed selling his house and farm.

"Todd, please come into my office," my father said as he walked by my desk.

Since I didn't have any customers, I followed him and sat in the chair across from him.

He sat down in his chair and placed his elbows on the table, his hands neatly folded. It suddenly felt like I was at an inquisition. "What do you think of your position here at the bank?"

I sighed. This wasn't going to be a good discussion. "I don't like it."

He frowned. "Perhaps I should give you another position."

"That won't work either. I keep telling you that I don't enjoy this."

"How can you be sure? You haven't given your job a chance. I'm offering you a legacy. Surely, you will want something to leave your children."

I inwardly groaned.

"Someday you will get married and have children. What better gift can you leave them than this bank?"

"There's no guarantee I will get married or that I will have sons. I would have to have a son to leave the name 'Brothers' on the bank."

"Miss Statesman is no longer seeing that Kent Ashton fellow. Perhaps you can court her. I could arrange something with her parents if you'd like."

"No. She's not interested." The last thing I wanted was my father to arrange my love life for me. "What made you think of her anyway?"

"It's obvious to everyone that you love her. My advice is to be there for her and let her cry on your shoulder. It may be the very thing that will get her to finally notice you. It worked for your mother."

My head was spinning. It was obvious to everyone that I loved her? Did that mean she knew too?

"Well, don't let any of that trouble you," my father continued. "There are plenty of other young ladies you can choose from. You have years to explore your options. What matters now is your job."

I tuned him out as he ran through a long list of reasons why banking was the perfect job for someone in my economic status. I had heard this many times, but today it was especially irritating. Perhaps the realization that everyone knew what I felt for Ann was the final straw.

"Father, please stop." I tried to be kind while being firm. "I have no intention of working here after I graduate. I've been thinking about this for a long time, and I really feel led to farm."

"Farmers don't make as much money as we do. It's a necessary profession since we all need to eat, but it is beneath you. You were born into a wealthy family. Your name means something. Don't waste it."

"Life is more than money."

"Money helps you provide for your wife and children. The Bible makes it clear that a righteous man leaves an inheritance to his children's children. It also says to honor your parents. The best way to honor me is to work here."

"Is there anything else?" I finally asked when I realized he wasn't going to listen to me no matter how many times I told him that his dream wasn't my path in life.

"I'll open up the mortgage officer's position for you next Monday. You might find that more to your liking."

I couldn't believe it.

"One more thing before you leave," he added. "If you pursue this farming thing, you can consider yourself dead to the family. You may go."

I quietly stood up and left his office. I returned to my desk and willed myself to calm down. *If I ever have children, I will let them do what they want with their lives.*

***

The next day before school began, I stopped by Alex's desk and sat in the seat next to his before Debbie needed it. "Have you heard anything about the Martin farm?" I whispered my question so no one overheard us.

"It's available. Do you want me to get my aunt and uncle to get a loan set up for you? I can send them your down payment."

I glanced at Ann. She looked like she was trying to ignore Kent and Rebecca who were sitting close together and talking.

"When are you going to give up on Scary Annie?" Alex asked.

I laughed. "She's not scary."

"Any girl who dumps sand on me and hits me with a broom is scary." He shook his head. "I can only imagine what she'll do when her future husband upsets her. If it were me, I'd sleep with one hand on a gun for protection."

"You're exaggerating."

"Maybe. But I wouldn't take my chances. I don't know why, but you like to live dangerously."

"What you interpret as scary is what I call passion. If you grew up with a house full of sisters who never fought back, you'd understand."

"I still wouldn't sleep with the light off." He momentarily shuddered.

If I was in bed with Ann, the last thing I'd be doing was sleeping. I doubted she'd let me sleep either. When she got involved with something, she gave it everything she had. But I didn't dare voice that opinion.

"As much as she scares me, I do feel bad for her," he admitted. "I also feel bad for Rebecca. Kent's not the person he appears to be."

I turned back to him in interest. "What do you mean?"

"I don't wish to go into detail. Let's just say that Ann is much better off without him. It may not seem like it, but she's the lucky one between her and Rebecca."

My eyes widened in surprise. I knew Alex didn't like to spread gossip, even when it was true. He would only warn someone that something or someone else wasn't a good idea to pursue. As much as I wanted to know what he saw Kent doing, I decided to keep quiet.

"Should I tell my aunt and uncle to get the loan for you?" Alex pressed.

"Yes. It's not like Ann will ever want me. I have nothing to stay here for."

"You're better off."

I saw Debbie enter the classroom. "See you at lunch," I said as I left her seat.

***

That Sunday night I chose my best suit. I knew it would be the last time I would see Ann at a dinner party before I left for Jamestown, North Dakota. I fixed my tie as I went over the words I would tell her. There was nothing to lose at this point. I would simply tell her how I felt and tell her that I knew she didn't return my feelings but I wanted to let her know before I left. At least, she would know someone loved her even if Kent no longer did. Perhaps, it would give her courage to find someone else.

I glanced at the picture I had of her on my dresser. I hesitated to take it with me to North Dakota. What was the point in holding onto the past? I picked it up and stared at it for a long moment. If she loved me, I could marry her and take her with me. But even if she did love me, would she really be content to go without the luxuries we were used to? From what Alex said, the farmer didn't enjoy servants who did their every bidding. Ann wouldn't be able to afford her jewelry and fancy dresses. She would have to learn to cook, clean, and do whatever it was farmer's wives did. No. She wouldn't want to deal with the hardships out West. I walked over to the trashcan and held her picture over it. Alex was right. It was time to let go of the past and move on.

"Sir, the Statesman family has arrived," one of my parents' servants said.

"I'll be right there," I replied. I dropped the picture in the trashcan. After tonight, I wouldn't have anything else to do with Ann.

I joined my sisters who were giggling around Ann who seemed overwhelmed by the attention. I stood to the side while Agnes and Abigail discussed corsets. I closed my eyes. I knew more about female clothing items and other feminine details than I cared to admit. Maybe being alone on a farm would be a blessing. Then I wouldn't have to concern myself with such things ever again.

"Todd," my mother greeted as she walked over to me. "I think it would be nice if you offered to escort Ann to the dance this Wednesday."

"I'm the last person she wants to go with," I replied.

"Oh, she just doesn't know what a fine young man you are. She probably needs a nudge in the right direction."

"Please don't. I appreciate what you're trying to do, but it's not meant to be."

"Well, from what I heard, there are no other available bachelors to take her. It might be God bringing you two together. You never know."

"She doesn't love me. Besides, she might like to stay home for a change. She doesn't look like she's up to dancing."

In fact, during the meal, she looked like all she wanted to do was go home and stay locked up in her bedroom. Despite Alex's insinuation that Kent wasn't good for her, it was still rough to watch her. She seemed sad and trapped at the same time.

Our parents made their usual rounds of updates on what their children were up to. I cringed as my father discussed his plans for me at the bank. I hated to disappoint him. I knew he would be upset when he woke up one morning and I was gone. I would leave a note explaining what I did and that I was still thankful to him and my mother for all their care, but I knew it wouldn't help. I was about to get disowned.

At one point, my mother asked Ann if she planned to go to the dance, but Ann stared at her plate, absentmindedly fiddling with her peas.

"Ann?" Her mother lightly tapped her on the arm.

She immediately turned her attention to her mother.

"Mrs. Brothers asked you a question, dear."

"I'm sorry. What did you ask, Mrs. Brothers?" she politely asked.

My mother smiled at her. "Are you going to the dance this Wednesday?"

"Yes, I will be going," she softly answered.

I realized that she didn't feel like going but would go to please her parents. I sympathized with her predicament. Only, I was getting out of my prison.

"Todd, would you be so kind as to escort Ann to the dance?" my mother blurted out.

My face grew red from a mixture of embarrassment and anger. Hadn't we already discussed this? "She may not wish to go with me, Mother," I kindly, but firmly, replied. I couldn't look at Ann since I was too humiliated.

"Of course, I would be honored to go with you, Todd," Ann replied.

I couldn't say no with everyone staring at me. I knew she only agreed because everyone expected her to. And now I would take her because everyone expected me to. I forced myself to look at her and smile. "Then I will take you."

I pretended to be intensely interested in the roast beef dinner after that. If the dinner could have gotten worse, I didn't know how. In three weeks, this would all be a memory. It was the only consolation I had.

Once dinner was over, I decided it was time to tell her what was on my mind. I didn't want her to spend the next couple of days worried about whether or not I would ask to court her after the dance. The situation was awkward enough as it was. Since she was ready to run off with Agnes, I had to yell her name across the room in order to get her attention.

She and Agnes stopped. Turning around, she politely asked, "Yes?"

I hated being put on the spot. Everyone was staring at us, and it irritated me. I would have to speak with her in private. I walked up to her before I spoke. "Could I speak with you on the veranda?"

I knew our parents would be fine with this since they could see us from the window.

She nodded and followed me out.

Now that she was in front of me, I forgot my well-rehearsed speech. She sat on the bench and patiently waited for me to talk. I shifted uneasily from one foot to the other. I was going to tell her and that would be it. "What I have to say isn't easy for me," I slowly began, staring at the ground. I couldn't make eye contact with her. I feared she would laugh at me. Taking a deep breath, I quickly said, "I love you."

It wasn't the way I had envisioned telling her a year ago. Back then, I planned to hold her in my arms and tell her before I kissed her. This wasn't anything like that. I felt like a fool who was out of place. Hoping to avoid any further awkwardness, I continued to talk.

"I know you don't love me," I admitted.

Before she could interrupt, I requested that she let me continue. She simply nodded and waited.

I sat next to her, making sure there was adequate distance between us so I didn't spook her. "I wanted you to know how I felt about you before I left. I don't want to work at my father's bank. I know it's what my family expects of me, but I'm not going to do it. I want to be a farmer. I know it sounds silly but I believe it's God's purpose for my life. I have a friend who knows a man out West who wants to sell his farm and house so he can be close to his grown children. I'm going to purchase his property."

"You're leaving? When?" She was obviously stunned. No one but Alex knew my plans up to this point, so I wasn't surprised by her reaction.

"I'll leave the day after we graduate."

"Where are you going?"

"North Dakota."

"That far? But what about your parents and sisters?"

"My sisters will get used to it. I think it might even show them that they need to pursue their dreams so they can live the lives they want. My parents will most likely disown me."

"Oh, they wouldn't do something so drastic. Sure, they will be upset but they'll accept it."

"No, they won't. Trust me, Ann. I know them better than you do."

She closed her mouth and nodded.

"I know how you feel about Kent and I've accepted that," I went on. "It's not my intention to make you uncomfortable. Now you don't have to dread going to the dance with me."

Her mother tapped on the window. "We need to go," she yelled.

Ann turned back to me and smiled. "I'll miss you when you leave. I won't tell anyone what you plan to do. And I'm sorry I never gave you a chance. You are very nice."

"Thank you." I stood up with her. "I hope this will make going to the dance with me easier for you."

"I don't want to go to the dance because Kent and Rebecca will be there, but it will be less of a burden since you'll be with me."

That was the first time she seemed glad to be in my presence. I took her picture out of the trashcan when I returned to my room. I stared at it again. If nothing else, she was a friend. I packed it in my suitcase. I could always throw it out after I made it to North Dakota.

Chapter Four
Ann's Point of View

Wednesday after school, I started getting ready for the dance. I wanted to wear the nice emerald dress, but my mother insisted I wear the pink one.

"But it's so tight," I argued. "I can hardly breathe in it."

"I know it's uncomfortable, but it is your best dress. Discomfort is a small price to pay for beauty, my dear. Besides, you don't want Rebecca showing up in a more expensive dress."

I sighed as Ginny pulled on the strings of my corset. I almost passed out when she was done.

"You will be nice to Todd tonight, won't you dear?" My mother handed the dress to Ginny who put it on me.

"Yes, I promise." I winced as Ginny fastened the many buttons up the back of the dress. "I might faint though."

"Once you are married, you may relax your dress code. I want to be sure you find a suitable bachelor."

I nodded. I already knew who would make a good husband. Someone who wanted what was best for me. Someone who loved me and not my family's money. Someone dependable. Someone I could trust. Someone like Todd. My parents were right, and it was time I listened to them.

I looked up at the mirror. This was it. I'd come too far to back out now. I slipped on the pink gloves and hat to complete the outfit.

I left my bedroom when the doorbell chimed. Todd was here. In the hallway, I glanced at my reflection in the mirror one last time. No one would guess my sudden plan. I would ask Todd to take me with him when he went to North Dakota.

"Here's your fan, for when you feel hot at the dance." My mother handed the white lace fan to me. "Now, our servants are taking the rest of the night off, and your father and I will be visiting with Mr. and Mrs. Brothers at the Clemmens' house. We should be back shortly before midnight. Mr. and Mrs. Carson will be chaperoning the dance. If you should need anything, go to them."

"Does that include smelling salts?"

"Yes, it does. A lot of ladies feel faint after dancing."

"Very well. Thank you, Mother."

George opened the door and let Todd into the parlor where he waited for me. I wanted to take a deep breath, but my dress prohibited the simple action. My mother wished me well and left me alone. Well, I was as alone as possible with George standing to the side of the parlor room.

Todd held a bouquet of red roses. His blond hair was neatly combed back under his gray hat. It was a strange contrast to his black suit and gray tie. He was not bad looking. In fact, one might consider him to be handsome. I wondered how his appearance would change once he started farming.

"Good evening, Ann," he said, smiling at the sight of me.

"Good evening."

He motioned to the roses. "These are for you."

I nodded and took them. "Thank you. They're lovely."

After I put them in a vase, we left for the dance. Once he sat next to me in the double buggy, I asked, "Aren't you going to miss all of the comforts we're used to?"

He shrugged. "I'm not sure. Perhaps I will. Perhaps I won't. I won't know until I'm gone."

I fanned myself. This dress was already making me feel unbearably hot. The material was too thick for the warm spring weather.

We arrived at the dance, and he helped me out of the buggy. The horse neighed but I barely noticed it. Instead, I heard Rebecca's familiar cackle. I groaned. Must she let the entire town know she won?

I braced myself for seeing Kent and Rebecca as Todd escorted me into the building. Thankfully, he led me to the opposite side of the room from the two lovebirds. We danced to two songs. We discussed our classes, how warm the air was getting and what Agnes was up to that night since she wasn't allowed to go to dances until next year. At the end of the second song, I thought I was going to pass out.

I waved my fan furiously back and forth, but the building was so hot that it did little to cool me off. "I need to sit down."

"Would you like to go outside?"

His concern surprised me. It wasn't something I was used to.

"Yes," I admitted.

"Can I get you something to drink?"

"That would be nice. Thank you." I walked outside, walking numbly past Kent and Rebecca who were dancing. *Don't look at them. Just keep going.* Once I was outside, I exhaled as much as I could, considering the tight dress, and sat down. The cool evening breeze felt good against my flushed face.

When Todd handed me a cup of punch, I glanced around us. No one was near us on the veranda, so it would be easy to have a private conversation.

"Will you please sit?"

He sat by me and looked at me. "What is it? Are you feeling ill?"

"I feel fine." Well, that was partly true. I was about to take a giant leap that would change my life forever. How could a person remain calm during that? I cleared my throat. "I have a request."

"I would do anything for you," he softly replied, looking down at the ground.

I hesitated. He meant those words. I almost decided against my plan, but another round of laughter from Rebecca strengthened my resolve. "Will you marry me and take me with you to North Dakota?" I blurted the words out so fast my head was spinning. I anxiously waved the fan as I waited for his response. I couldn't bring myself to drink the punch, so I just held it, hoping I wouldn't spill it since my hand was beginning to shake.

His head shot up and he looked at me, shocked. "I must be dreaming," he whispered.

I sat still, not daring to speak another word. I figured since he loved me, he would agree to my request. However, his response surprised me.

"I don't think it's a good idea. As much as I would love to take you with me, you would be doing it for the wrong reason."

"You love me. You will treat me well."

"But you will be doing this to get away from Kent and Rebecca. It wouldn't be right."

Panic flashed through me. "Why couldn't I learn to love you? Just because you've loved me first, it doesn't mean I won't come around to loving you."

"You love Kent."

"Now. But that can change." Couldn't it? Was I destined to love Kent for the rest of my life?

He shook his head. "I'm sorry, Ann. It wouldn't be appropriate."

I set the cup down before I smashed it on the ground in frustration. "It wouldn't be appropriate. It wouldn't be proper. God forbid I should do anything that defies the standards we are to live by. I'm sick and tired of doing what everyone else wants me to do. No one bothers to ask me what my opinion is, except for you." I waved the fan faster. My face was heating up as my anger surfaced. I managed to keep my voice down, but my agitation was apparent. Hopefully, people would assume it was because of Kent and Rebecca. "I hate being stuck. I hate having to watch those two." I nodded to the lovebirds. Again, Rebecca laughed. Ugg! "And if I hear her laugh one more time, I'm going to pour this cup of punch on her head."

"Ann, calm down. It will get easier."

I grunted. "You have no idea what it's like for me, Todd. There are things I want to do, things I want to pursue. But I can't because I'm a lady. I have to attend every social function and learn to be a proper hostess. I have to walk, talk and act delicately. I can't go outside unless I have a parasol or hat. I have to go to dinners I don't want to go to. I have to spend hours shopping for new clothes." I paused. "Well, that part isn't so bad."

He chuckled.

I tried not to give into my own urge to laugh. "Seriously though. My parents are more lenient than other parents, but I do have a set of rules I have to obey. You're getting out of here. You can do that because you're a man. A woman going out West by herself is impossible."

"I have a plan," he gently reminded me.

"And I have a strong desire to be somewhere else, to do something other than what I've been doing all my life."

"I wish I could help you but I can't."

I jumped up and waved the fan as fast as I could. "You have the ability to take me out of here but you refuse.

What good is your love if you won't help me?" I set my jaw in firm determination as I stared at the trees in the moonlight. "I will get out of here. You're not the only one who can do it. I'll run away if I have to."

He stood up and walked over to me. He took the fan out of my hand. "Before you break it," he explained when I started to protest. He stared at me for a long moment. "Yes, I will take you. I planned to leave the day after we graduate."

"Do we have to wait?" I was afraid if we waited, he wouldn't take me with him. As it was, I was having trouble talking him into it now.

"Graduation is in a couple weeks."

"Do you need to graduate to be a farmer?"

"No."

"Then what's stopping us? You've been planning this for a long time. Surely, you have all the stuff you need in place."

"Yes, I do."

"Then let's leave tonight."

"It's best to be patient. We should think about it."

I groaned. "I've already thought about it, Todd. I don't want to wait another minute." He seemed to be searching for another excuse, so I touched his arm. "Please."

He closed his mouth and studied the sky for a moment. Finally, he sighed. "I can't deny you anything. Alright. We'll leave tonight."

"Good!"

"After you tell your parents. They need to know you're safe."

"I'll leave a note." Thankfully, the house was empty so no one would stop me.

"It might be better if you tell them in person."

"If I do that, they'll talk me out of it." They would never let me leave Virginia, even if it was with Todd. "I need to get out of here, and I want to go with you."

He reluctantly complied, so we managed to leave the dance while no one noticed.

Chapter Five
Ann's Point of View

Our departure was rushed, so I left many things behind. There wasn't much room in the horse-drawn covered wagon he had purchased. He already had his supplies loaded into the back, so all he had to do was hook up his two horses. Since he didn't have to go into his house, he had an easier time avoiding unwanted eyes than I did.

I was relieved my house was empty and quickly packed my carpetbag. I tried to take sensible clothing. At least, the dresses would fit better so I could breathe adequately. I didn't dare change my dress, though I desperately wanted to. I was afraid if I hesitated, then Todd would change his mind and leave me here. I wrote my parents a note to let them know I was marrying Todd and going with him to North Dakota. I decided not to tell them where I was going to be in North Dakota. I took a moment to look around the parlor and wiped the tears from my eyes. I uttered a prayer for my parents and left the house.

He stood outside the front door. "It's not too late to turn back."

My stomach tensed. "Do you want me to come with you?"

"Of course I do, but it's not about what I want."

I handed him the carpetbag. "I'm going with you."

He nodded.

I followed him to the wagon and waited for him to load my carpetbag in with his other belongings before he assisted me onto the wagon seat.

Some people marry for love, some for money, and some are forced into it. I married Todd because I was afraid if I didn't, then I would have to settle for someone who wouldn't treat me as well as he did. I was wrong about Kent. I had thought he was the right one for me. My parents had warned me about him. They also recommended Todd. So, in the end, I decided to trust their judgment. Maybe it was a selfish reason, but I was afraid I'd give up the best husband I could have.

We stopped by our minister's house, and fortunately he was there so we didn't have to go find another one. We did want the minister we grew up with to marry us. During the simple ceremony, I thought about my parents' dream for me to have an elaborate wedding with lots of guests, food and music. The only person to witness the event was his wife. There was no food or music. The minister did question us about our decision, but since we had reached the age of accountability, he agreed to marry us.

Once we were married, we thanked the minister and headed out of Virginia. Todd's cautious nature made me anxious, for I feared our parents would find us and make us return. I kept looking behind us, only reassured that we were safe when I didn't see any lanterns in the distance.

"I've been mapping out a trail to North Dakota for months," he assured me when he noticed my distress. "Someone who hasn't studied the trails will get lost."

Still, I couldn't relax, especially when he stopped to let the horses take a break.

"Do we have to stop now?" I wondered, fiddling with the white lace on the sleeve of my dress.

"They need to rest for a few moments. They have a long journey ahead of them. We don't want to wear them out." He hopped off the wagon, untied his horses and led them to the stream so they could drink the water. Afterwards, he fed them some carrots.

I wondered what time it was as I stared at the full moon. It really was a beautiful sight. Why hadn't I noticed it before?

When he hooked the horses up and sat next to me, I asked, "What if our parents do find us?"

He paused for a moment. "Then we were meant to stay in Virginia."

I frowned. Why did we have to rely on horses for transportation when trains were much more practical?

"Are you cold?" he asked.

"Actually, I am."

He grabbed a blanket from behind the seat and wrapped it around my shoulders.

"Thank you," I whispered, pleased by his concern.

He stared at me, as if he wished to say or do something. Suddenly, I felt strange. We were married now. How would things change between us?

The moment passed, for he must have decided against whatever thought raced through his head. I chose not to ask what he wanted. Instead I closed my eyes. We didn't say much that night as we traveled. It seemed that words weren't necessary. I was actually comfortable in the silence we shared. Eventually, I went back into the wagon and fell asleep.

***

Todd didn't sleep that night. He made frequent stops so the horses could rest. I slept through most of the night, which proved my mother correct when she once commented that I could sleep through anything. By the time dawn arrived, I woke up. My back and neck were stiff. I never experienced such discomfort before and asked Todd if it was normal. He assured me it was and stopped the horses so I could stretch and walk around in order to loosen my tight muscles.

When we were ready to ride again, he handed me food called jerky. "It won't last us all the way to North Dakota but it's suitable for now."

That was the first cold and tough meal I ever ate, but I was so hungry that it tasted better than the meals I was used to.

By mid-day, my dress became unbearable. I asked him to stop so I could change into one of my more comfortable dresses. He stopped so I could do so. I took one of my other dresses out of my carpetbag and went behind some bushes to change. In all my years of wearing dresses, I had never dressed myself. Ginny had done that for me. I stood, surrounded by bushes, wondering how I was going to get my pink dress off. There were so many buttons in the back and most of them were out of my reach. I hated to ask Todd for help but seemed to have no other choice.

I peeked through the bushes. He wasn't at the wagon. When I saw the horses weren't there either, I knew I would have to wait until he returned with them. I sighed. I wasn't used to waiting. I paced back and forth, anxious for the horses to be done drinking and eating.

I really needed to learn patience. At home, the servants met my every desire immediately. How did someone learn to wait and like it? As I turned to pace in the other direction, something moved on the ground. A snake! I tried to scream but couldn't find my voice. I stumbled backwards and fell on my rear end. My hat flew off my head and I heard my dress tear in the side. The snake, more frightened of me than I was of him, slithered out of the bushes. I took a deep breath, relieved it hadn't been poisonous.

I stood up to examine the tear in my dress. This was the only pretty dress I had taken with me, and I had no idea how I could repair the damage. I wiped the tear that fell on my cheek and frowned when I realized I had dirt on my hands. I didn't have to look down at my dress to know it was dirty as well. I quickly wiped my hands and cheek on the clean part of my dress.

I decided I wouldn't tell Todd how hard and confusing this new life was for me in case he decided I couldn't handle it and took me back to my parents. I would rather roll around in the mud than face Kent and Rebecca. I forced back my tears and ripped the dress and six out of eight petticoats off of me. I was tired of being hot and sweaty. I could handle two petticoats much better than the mountain of eight of them. Besides, no one could tell how many I wore anyway.

My sudden determination prompted me to put on my other dress. I couldn't button some of the top buttons, so I decided it was time to get Todd's help. I peered out of the bushes and breathed a sigh of relief when I saw him hitching up the horses. As soon as he was done, I called out his name. Even though no one was around us for miles, I couldn't go out into the open without all of the buttons fastened.

He walked to me, careful to keep his eyes on my face. I blushed, grateful for his consideration.

"I can't button my top buttons in the back of this dress. Can you help me?"

He nodded shyly. I smiled to myself as I felt his hands tremble as he fastened the rest of the buttons. It was a relief to know I wasn't the only one who was nervous. When he was done, he spotted the torn and dirty dress and petticoats on the ground next to my hat.

"Have some problems?" he grinned good-naturedly.

My face flushed hot from embarrassment. "I didn't like that dress anyway," I lied as I picked them up.

"I could carry those for you, if you'd like," he offered, probably trying not to laugh.

"I can handle this myself," I stiffly responded.

I hastened past him and threw the clothes into the back of the wagon. I hopped up into the front, glad to be able to move around freely. Unable to make eye contact, I stared at the ground as Todd got in beside me and urged the horses to start moving. We rode in silence for a while. The sun was hot but it suddenly occurred to me that I wasn't wearing a hat or carrying my parasol. I closed my eyes and enjoyed the freedom of letting the sunlight hit my face.

Later that afternoon, he said, "We should be entering the next town soon. I think we should stop there for the night. What do you think?"

"You're asking me if I want to stay in the next town tonight?" I couldn't remember ever being asked if I wanted to do something.

"Yes."

I found that I liked to have a choice to make. "I would like to sleep in a soft bed tonight."

We reached the next town by sunset. By this time, I was hungry and tired. We ate first, but as the meal continued, I grew nervous. I knew how a married couple consummated their marriage. I just couldn't imagine myself making love to him. I made my vows before him and God. I would fulfill my wifely duty if I had to, though it was difficult for me to make the leap from friendship to romance.

When we checked into our room for the night, he took my hands in his and asked, "Do you need more time before we consummate our marriage?"

Once again, he was asking for my opinion. He had no idea how much I appreciated it. "I don't feel ready yet," I slowly admitted.

"Thank you for being honest. Will you tell me when you're ready?"

"Yes. I will tell you." I tilted my head curiously. "What about you?"

He smiled. “I won’t be ready until you are.”

I knew he meant it too. He would never force himself on me.

I hugged him and thanked him for being understanding.

He set his pillow and blanket on the floor. He insisted that I use the bed. And so, our sleeping arrangements were established.

Chapter Six
Todd's Point of View

Though the journey was arduous, I enjoyed every minute of it because I was learning more about Ann and she seemed to enjoy learning about me. The more time I spent with her, the more I wanted to be with her. She did mention missing her parents and Agnes, but she didn't express a desire to go back to Virginia. Instead, she confessed that she was beginning to look forward to our new life.

"It's an adventure," she said.

I was secretly pleased that she still wanted to stay with me.

"Do you remember that time you brought my homework to me when I was sick?" she asked. "I believe it was in October."

"Yes, I remember."

"Do you also remember one of the days you came over, I said I wanted to go out in the sun with my hair down and not have a hat or parasol with me? You said you wanted to be there when it happened. Well, here we are and I'm out in the sun!"

"I didn't think you remembered any of the conversations we had."

"Of course I do. It may not have seemed like it, but I did consider you a friend." She frowned. "I suppose my manner toward you was rude. I'm sorry for that."

I shrugged. "Since you didn't love me, you probably worried that if you showed more interest, I would have taken it the wrong way, and then you would have had to tell me that I misunderstood your actions. I understand."

"Yes, I did worry about that." She looked down at her hands.

"If I were in your position, I probably would have done the same thing. I didn't realize my feelings were obvious until my father told me. I tried to hide them."

"I'm glad you weren't able to." She looked up at me and smiled. "It gave me the courage to ask you to take me with you."

"Let's just put the past behind us and start our new life getting to know each other? You know, as friends first."

"Yes, I would like to start at friendship. It would make me feel less uneasy. I'm going to do everything I can to be a good wife for you. I will love you the way a wife is to love her husband. You treat me so well. Please, be patient with me."

"We have our whole lives ahead of us. Patience is not a problem." I smiled as I took in her long wavy hair falling gently over her shoulders. "You're beautiful. I am happy that I got to see you with your hair down in the sunlight. It's too bad you weren't able to do that in Virginia. You look lovely no matter what you do with your hair, but I always liked it best when it was down."

She touched her shiny brown hair. "I'll have to wear it down more often then."

I was surprised that she would do such a thing because I liked it.

We spent the next few weeks talking about things we would and would not miss about Virginia, her experiences with Agnes, and the fun times we had while growing up. I didn't realize she had a sense of humor, for she seemed serious most of the time.

"I do have to admit there was one prank that Alex pulled that was funny," she admitted. "I don't think he intended for it to end up the way it did though. It was the Christmas show we were forced to participate in when we were fifteen. Alex brought that bag of nuts along so when Mr. Clemmens came on the stage to introduce the play, he'd step on the nuts. I don't know how that squirrel found its way into the bag, but I'll never forget how loud Alex screamed when he opened it and the squirrel jumped on him."

"He suspected you had something to do with it," I informed her.

Her eyes widened. "Me? Why in the world would I put a squirrel in his bag? I wouldn't touch one of those disgusting things."

"That's what I told him. Ever since that day we threw pebbles in your hair, he suspected you were going to do something else to get even with him."

"I was just glad he left me alone. I didn't want to do anything to get even." She placed her blue hat on her head. "Why did you join him in throwing pebbles at me anyway?"

"To be honest, it was a bet we had. I told him that you wouldn't put up with his pranks like the other girls did. I told him you stood up to me plenty of times whenever your parents brought you over to my house. He wouldn't believe me, so I told him that if he was right, I would do his homework for a month. But if I was right, he had to give me his bicycle. He threw a couple of pebbles but I threw most of them. I was beginning to fear you weren't going to retaliate. You almost made me look bad. I had such confidence that you weren't like the other girls. I was relieved when you dumped the sand on us."

She laughed. "Why Todd, that is sneaky. Here I thought Alex insisted you join him in his pranks. I had no idea you were capable of such deceit."

"I knew you weren't weak. You could hold your own."

"I can't believe you did that."

"You made me proud."

She shook her head, amused. "It did get him to leave me alone, so I suppose it worked out well enough. But I am surprised it was your idea. Apparently, there's a lot I don't know about you."

"To put your mind at rest, I won't throw pebbles in your hair."

"Good. Because if you did anything sneaky like that again, I'd have to dump sand on you."

I raised an eyebrow. "What if I put a squirrel in your bag?"

Her jaw dropped. "That was you?"

"Guilty."

"You're rotten!" The twinkle in her eye revealed that she was enjoying it. "Why didn't you confess?"

"And miss him panicking over what you might do next?"

"I'm going to have to keep a close eye on you."

I chuckled.

***

On the first of August, we were due to reach Jamestown. I got up early and quietly grabbed my good suit and bathing supplies while Ann slept in the bed. I glanced at her for a moment. She had bathed the night before, and she smelled and looked wonderful. I liked to watch her sleep. She seemed peaceful and content. I hoped it wouldn't be too long before I could sleep next to her. I would like to see her first thing every morning. I already knew that we would start out sleeping in separate bedrooms at our new home.

I left our room and went to the lavatory. Fortunately, it was vacant. After bathing, I took out my shaving kit and rubbed the lather on my face. I couldn't help but smile as I recalled the previous afternoon while we were on the wagon. She was curious about my facial hair.

"Do you plan to keep the beard?" she had asked.

"No. I just haven't shaved because we've been traveling. Why? Would you like me to keep it?"

"Honestly, no. I can't see much of your face. Does it feel strange?"

I hadn't thought about it, so I shrugged. "I don't really know it's there."

She looked like she wanted to ask me something.

"What is it?" I prompted.

"You'll think it's silly."

Curious, I urged her to continue.

After a moment's hesitation, she asked, "Can I feel it?"

I thought it was an odd request but agreed she could. I stopped the horses so she could move closer to touch my face.

This time it was her fingers that trembled, which I found a relief since she was just as human as I was. My breathing quickened with her sitting close enough to me that I could almost feel her body against mine. Her fingers lightly brushed my cheek.

She grinned. "It tickles. And it's a little rough."

I smiled at the memory as I shaved. I didn't care for the look or feel of it myself, but apparently, some men liked it. I got dressed in my dark gray suit and returned to the room.

She was already dressed, and she was putting her brush into the carpetbag. She had her hair pulled back into a braid. When she finished packing, she put her hat on. As much as she liked to go without it, she realized that wearing the hat protected her skin from the heat of the summer sun.

"Good morning," I greeted. I packed my things away and picked up my blue tie.

She smiled at me. "Did you sleep well?"

"Yes. Spending all day on a wagon wears a person out. How did you sleep?"

"Wonderfully. It's good to be clean for a change. I didn't realize how much I missed baths until I took one last night."

"It does make a person feel better." I slipped the tie around my neck and began to tie the knot. I stopped when I noticed she was staring at me. "Is it the wrong color?"

"No. I...I was just thinking that you are a handsome man."

I blushed at her compliment. I didn't know who felt more awkward. Finally, I said, "Thank you" and finished working on my tie. I was glad she liked looking at me. I wanted to be as desirable to her as she was to me.

"Can I feel your face now that you shaved? I'm curious to know what the difference is like."

You can touch me anywhere you want to. "I'm all yours." I tried to sound nonchalant about it, but I suspected she picked up on my excitement.

I stood still as she walked over to me and gently stroked my face. She had wonderful hands. I wondered how they would feel on other parts of my body. My face tingled at her touch. I longed to take her hand and kiss it but forced myself to remain still. Her fingers lingered on my cheek.

"I like it," she whispered. Was she as excited as I was? "It's smooth but masculine." She blushed and quickly put her hand down. Then she turned to put on her shoes.

I pushed aside my disappointment and picked up our luggage. I missed her touch.

Chapter Seven
Ann's Point of View

When we reached Jamestown, a sense of peace washed over me. I gazed upon the flat farmlands further out of town.

He pointed north. "The way to our house is in that direction."

"It's beautiful," I whispered. A strong wind tossed my braid around so that it flapped against my back. It wasn't this windy in Virginia.

He urged the horses forward. "I saw pictures of this place, but it didn't prepare me for it. I'm glad we came here."

I turned my attention to the town. It was smaller than the one we grew up in. Even the houses were smaller than what I was used to, and it didn't appear that any of them had servants. The people dressed in a different material and style than I was accustomed to. I felt sorely out of place here but was determined not to show it.

Todd stopped in front of the mercantile. I had heard of a mercantile but never entered one before. Servants did that kind of shopping, but we didn't have servants anymore.

"I'm going to apply for a job at the bank." He pointed to the building down the street. "I plan to work there until I have enough money saved up to buy farming supplies. Since my father insisted that I work at his bank, I know I can do that job. Afterwards, I can help you through the mercantile if you'd like."

I eyed the store warily. It would be comforting to have him with me, but I didn't want him to think I was incompetent.

Besides, I had to learn to take care of these things on my own. "I'm sure I can figure it out. How hard can it be to buy food?"

"You're right. We eat it every day." He dug into his pocket and handed me some money. "Do you think this will be enough? I know it's not much but it's all I can afford right now."

Since the issue of cost never crossed my mind before, I was sure it was enough. "This will do fine."

After Todd helped me down from the wagon, I entered the store, trying to act as if I did this all the time. I frowned as I walked around, examining the contents on the shelves. I recognized fruits, vegetables and eggs, but everything else seemed to be in jars or paper sacks. Why didn't anything look like food? I read labels for flour, yeast, broth and baking soda. My eyes scanned the labels. I felt as if I were reading a foreign language. Where were the breads, mashed potatoes, and steaks? Very little of this resembled actual food.

I sighed in despair. First, I had ripped my pink dress, stunk for weeks because I hadn't bathed, and now this? Was living without servants going to change everything? As I began to feel sorry for myself, I imagined Kent and Rebecca together. My jaw clenched. So my life would be different. I could handle it. I began to pick things at random. I would make sense of it later. Luck was on my side, for I saw a recipe book. Of course, I grabbed it.

"Hello," a warm voice greeted me.

I looked up from the recipe book that I had just placed in the basket. The woman who stood before me was dressed in simpler clothing that looked like it had seen better days. She looked like she was my mother's age. I noticed her rough hands. Would my smooth hands be that rough one day? Was I staring at an image of who I would become living out West?

I shoved the thoughts away. "Hello," I replied, nervously smiling. I wasn't sure what the proper method of greeting someone was in this town.

"I haven't seen you before," she kindly said. "Are you passing through or are you moving here?"

"My husband bought a farm out here." I cleared my throat. I wasn't used to referring to Todd that way. "It's north of here actually."

"That's wonderful! My name is Beth Coley. My husband and I own this store. We have a son who owns his own farm west of here and a daughter who sews clothes down the street. Where did you move from?"

"Virginia. My name is Ann, and my husband is Todd Brothers. We just arrived here. We haven't even checked out the farm yet."

"My, that's a long way to travel. You must be exhausted."

I nodded.

"Do you have pots and pans to cook your food in?"

My eyes widened. I hadn't thought of any of those things. "I don't think so." What exactly did cooking entail? "Could you recommend some things I might need? I'm not familiar with cooking. I had servants who did that for me." I blushed.

She didn't judge me as I feared she would. Instead, she told me the basics of cooking. She examined the items in my basket and placed some unnecessary things back on the shelves. She put the things I would need into my basket.

Unfortunately, the total amount for all I had collected was more than what Todd had given me. It was embarrassing, but she smiled.

"You can put the difference on credit and pay it off later," she offered. "Many people do that. Payment doesn't necessarily have to be money. It can be items you make, such as potholders. It could be jewelry. I have a couple of merchants who like to purchase jewelry from me. Payment can also be in the form of fruits, vegetables or eggs. I even accept it when people help me maintain this store."

"I'm not sure. I better put some things back for now." I wasn't sure what skill or item I had that would be useful for her store.

"Whatever makes you comfortable. The offer will always stand in the future."

"Thank you."

A man entered the store with a box full of eggs. "I have a couple more boxes in the wagon. Mr. Johnson's hens are really pushing them out today." He smiled when he saw me. "Hello. My name is Mark Coley."

"I'm Ann Brothers."

"She and her husband are the new owners of the Martin farm." She looked at me. "It's the only farm vacant at the moment. That's how I know. Mr. Martin left most of his supplies there, so you should be in good shape. I know he took good care of his things."

He nodded. "We look forward to seeing you more often then."

"And please, take this recipe book as our gift to you."

"Thank you," I replied. I was overcome by their kindness.

I glanced out the window and saw Todd leaving the bank. "I have to go. My husband is waiting for me."

"Let me help you with those bags," Mr. Coley offered.

"Thank you, again."

I joined Todd and introduced him to Mr. Coley. After Todd and Mr. Coley put the bags in the wagon, they shook hands. Mr. Coley gave him directions on a quicker and easier way to get to the farm. Todd thanked him and then we left.

"The people here are nice," Todd commented.

I nodded. Turning my attention to other matters, I asked, "Did they hire you at the bank?"

"My interview with the boss is the day after tomorrow. I'll know then."

After the months we traveled for what seemed like endless miles, I thought the trip to the farm would be quick, but it seemed longer than our trek across the states.

An hour passed by the time we arrived at the empty white two-story house. Mr. Martin had left modest furnishings, which were still in good shape except for the kitchen table that had a wobbly leg.

"I had to take out a loan to pay for it," Todd explained as I looked around.

I tried not to get discouraged as I looked at the dust and cobwebs covering everything. My parents would never accept such living conditions. *You're not in Virginia anymore. This is a different world.*

"The water from the well should work," he said. He left to check it.

I went to investigate the small house. The parlor was spacious and led to the front door. The dining room led to the kitchen. The kitchen led to the back door. There were two closets and a small room with things in it that I didn't recognize. The wooden stairs led to three bedrooms. I stepped out of the last bedroom and walked down the stairs. The kitchen had a pump at the sink.

"We're in luck," Todd said when he came back into the house through the front door. "The water is good."

I hesitated to ask the question that pressed on my mind but had to because sooner or later, I'd have to use the privy. "Where is the toilet?"

"The outhouse is in the back. I'll show you where."

I followed him to the kitchen window, which overlooked the fields and the barn. He pointed to a small wooden building the size of a closet that had a door. It was between the house and the barn.

"The well's out front, so the water won't get contaminated from…" He shrugged. "You know."

The idea of going to the bathroom outside made me cringe. It didn't seem sanitary. Just what other unpleasant things would I face out here?

He sighed. "I'll help you clean this place. Once we get rid of the dust, it will look better. Why don't you sit down and rest? I'll bring our things in."

I shook my head. "I'd rather help. I want to do something other than sit." I had done enough sitting over the past couple of months. It felt good to move.

We didn't have much, but after the tiring trip, it seemed that we would never finish putting things away where they now belonged. I was glad that Mrs. Coley recommended that I get pots and pans, because the kitchen cupboards were bare. Once we finished our task, we were so tired that we fell asleep. I slept on the couch and he slept on the chair.

***

Early the next morning, I woke up refreshed and in a good mood. I wasn't a morning person by nature, so it was unusual for me to wake up with a smile on my face. In the daylight, the house didn't look as bad as it had last night. We could make it work.

Since Todd was still asleep, I decided to surprise him by making breakfast. I took out the recipe book that Mrs. Coley had given me.

I decided to make scrambled eggs. It looked like a meal that was difficult to ruin. I stared at the cast iron stove and the wood on the floor in the corner. A box of matches sat on the counter. I hadn't been allowed in the kitchen while I was growing up, so I did as Mrs. Coley instructed in starting a fire under the range. The oven door was right next to the compartment where the fire burned. Neither the oven nor the range looked easy. How would I know when the range was too hot? Or what if it didn't get hot enough?

I turned back to the task of making scrambled eggs. I threw the eggs into the pan and used the wooden spoon to stir them around. I stopped when I realized the eggs didn't mix well. I read the recipe again and groaned. I wasn't supposed to keep the shells. I tossed the eggs into the sink. This time I tried breaking the eggs, but I either used too much force to crack them open or not enough. In the end, I was stuck with egg white and bits of the shells splattered all over the table. After five attempts at it, I didn't dare use any more eggs. I quickly put out the fire and cleaned up the table. I threw the bad food into the pail in the corner of the room.

I angrily sat in the kitchen chair. Cooking was not as easy as Mrs. Coley made it sound. What made me think I could live out here? None of the classes I took prepared me for any of this. Everyone just assumed I'd spend my life surrounded by servants who did the "trivial work", as my father once put it.

My eyes fell on the fruits on the counter. At least I knew how to cut fruit. I took some apples and strawberries and cut them up. Then I ate my portion and waited for Todd to wake up so he could eat his.

"Good morning," Todd greeted as he entered the kitchen.

I waited for him to sit across from me so he could eat. It still felt strange to think of Todd as my husband. I knew he was the right choice for me, though I didn't feel the romantic feelings toward him that I had felt for Kent. I hoped the feelings would come in time. I meant what I told him. That I would do my best to be a good wife. I had messed up with

Kent, and my parents warned me about him. Since they liked Todd, then Todd had to be the right choice. I hope I didn't make a bad decision. The last thing I wanted to do was to hurt Todd because of my selfishness.

Todd smiled. "It sure is a beautiful day. It's too bad we have to spend it cleaning."

"Do we have any cleaning supplies?" I hadn't thought to purchase those at the store.

"Mr. Martin left some in the closet by the stairs."

"Oh." I watched as he ate. "Do you think you'll get the banking job?"

"I think so. I know enough about it. If, for some reason, I don't get it, I'll apply for another job." He must have noticed my apprehension because he stopped eating and smiled at me. "We'll be alright."

My spirits lifted and a new comfort came over me. I smiled back and nodded. I was glad to have him with me, and I could tell he was glad to have me with him. That was the first time I was thankful that he loved me.

***

We spent the entire morning cleaning the downstairs. By the time we were done, I noticed the blisters forming on my thumbs from sweeping the broom. I wanted to please Todd, so I didn't complain.

To my surprise, he offered to help me cook lunch.

"What do you want to eat?" he asked.

"I don't know. I hadn't thought of what to make," I slowly replied as I glanced at the recipe book. I had no idea what to make without burning it. "What do you want?"

"What did you buy?"

I motioned to the cupboards that held some vegetables, fruits, eggs, and bags of flour, yeast, and other items that I was still trying to figure out how to cook with.

"Hmm... This isn't what I expected," he replied. "Is this all the mercantile had?"

"For the most part, yes. Mrs. Coley gave me a recipe book and some cooking tips."

"This is all we could afford?"

Embarrassed because I didn't know what to buy and knew we didn't have much, I turned away from him. I was a failure as a wife. I didn't know the first thing about taking care of a house or how to cook food. I wondered if I could get anything right out here. It was such a different world than Virginia.

Todd put his arms around me. "Forgive me, Ann. I wasn't criticizing you. I just didn't realize food cost so much."

Relieved, I hugged him back. "I felt lost in there. Thankfully, Mrs. Coley was very nice and helped me."

"I should have gone in with you, though I don't know if I could have been much help. I don't understand what we're supposed to do with flour or yeast."

"Apparently, you can make bread with it." How, I didn't know.

"I thought I was prepared to be out here, but I didn't consider cooking food."

"I'm going to learn to cook. I know I can do it."

"One thing I do know about you is that when you set your mind to something, you succeed."

He had no idea how much I appreciated those words. "Do you know how to start the fire for the stove?"

"Yes."

I watched in amazement as he got the fire burning. He obviously practiced this. I should have expected it, but it made me feel inferior as a wife.

"I had to buy some pans, pots and utensils too," I added. "I'm sure I can get more food next time."

"You did good, Ann. You've always been good about the choices you make."

I frowned. "I suppose if you don't count Kent, then I do make good decisions." I turned to the recipe book and opened it.

He didn't respond, and I wasn't sure what else to say either. After we decided to make soup, I took on the task of cutting up potatoes, carrots, and celery, which I added to the broth and water in the new pot so I wouldn't have to mess with the stove again. I stirred the pot.

"Are you ready to put it on the range?" he asked.

I nodded and carried the pot to the stove. My hands got too close to the range. I almost dropped the pot as I pulled my hand away from the stove.

Todd quickly grabbed the pot and put it in place for me. "Are you alright?"

"I'm fine," I replied but my hand was already showing signs of being lightly burnt. I made a mental note to never get too close to the range again.

"Maybe cool water will help."

I followed him to the sink. He picked up a clean washcloth and pumped the handle until water came out. He washed the cloth under it before he turned to me and wrapped the cool cloth around my hand.

"That's much better," I assured him.

After a few minutes, he uncovered my hand so he could inspect the wound. "It looks superficial." He sighed. "I didn't think to bring any bandages."

I took a deep breath. Somehow, the way he carefully held my hand seemed more intimate than any kiss Kent and I shared.

"I'm fine. It doesn't even hurt." Uncomfortable, I asked, "Do you know how to work everything in this house?"

He nodded. "It helped that I talked with the servants back home. My father thought I was crazy for following the servants all over the place, but I wanted to make sure I could make it out here."

"So, you know how to do laundry?"

"Yes. Would you like me to give you a quick tour of the scullery room?"

Was that the name of the small room I saw with the unfamiliar objects in it? "Yes, I would like to learn what you know."

He stirred the pot before he showed me the wringer washer machine and washtub. It all seemed confusing, but he demonstrated how to use them.

"It took me a couple of times of helping the servants before I got the hang of doing laundry," he said.

I didn't look forward to doing laundry. It looked like a lot of work. But I was determined to press on and learn the tasks I needed to.

We finished cooking the meal and had a good lunch. Then we headed upstairs to clean the bedrooms. Todd let me have my choice of the bedroom I wanted. He would sleep in another room until I was ready to be intimate. I was grateful for his patience because I doubted that other men would have been as understanding.

Chapter Eight
Ann's Point of View

When I woke up the next morning, my entire body ached. I glanced at my hands, which were red and sore. The burn was going to leave a scar but was healing nicely. I didn't want to get out of bed, but I wanted to make Todd breakfast and wish him luck on his interview.

I attempted to cook scrambled eggs again. Again, I had difficulty getting the egg yolk and white out of the shell. Bits of shells kept finding their way into the small bowl. After trying to successfully crack four eggs, I finally got two eggs perfectly cracked. I stirred them together with butter and poured the mixture into the pan. I turned to clean up the mess from my failed attempts. When I returned to the pan, I realized the eggs were badly burnt. My aggravation surfaced and I angrily threw the pan across the room. Would I ever get the hang of cooking?

"Ann, are you alright?" Todd yelled from upstairs.

I gasped and quickly ran to pick the pan and burnt eggs off the floor. "I'm fine! I...I accidently dropped something. Everything's fine."

I hastily cleaned the pan and cracked the remaining eggs I had into it. I hoped I would succeed this time or else Todd would have to eat fruit again, which I knew wasn't very filling. I stayed with the pan and carefully stirred the eggs. Fortunately, they turned out correctly this time.

Todd's eyes lit up when he saw me. "Thank you for making breakfast. I hope you didn't go through too much trouble."

Surprised, I realized that I would go through the horrid ordeal all over again because it made him happy.

"Aren't you going to eat anything?" he asked as he sat at the table.

I placed the plate of eggs in front of him and handed him a cup of water. "I'll eat when I feel hungry." My stomach growled but I ignored it.

After he ate, he left for the interview and I decided to eat. It was easier to make mistakes without someone nearby who might witness them. I threw the slices of potato in the pan without wiping oil on the bottom of the pan first. I knew the recipe book said to do that, but how important could oil possibly be? Since potatoes didn't require stirring like the eggs did, I left the kitchen and collected the laundry.

I didn't notice the smoke right away. At first, I assumed the sudden odor was coming from the laundry. Perhaps, this soap smelled bad. As the smell grew stronger, I lifted the wet laundry to my nose. It smelled good and clean, not smoky.

That was when I remembered the potatoes. I ran to the kitchen, my hands still wet and soapy, and inspected the potatoes. I grabbed a flour sack towel and grabbed the handle of the pan. I tried to scrape the potatoes off with a spoon, but they stuck to the bottom. Once again, I had botched up cooking a simple meal.

That's when I started crying. What was I doing here? I was used to servants who waited on me and served me food. I had no idea how I'd manage to survive out here. I couldn't live on fruits for the rest of my life. What made me think I could do this? I shoved the pan into the sink and threw the towel on the table.

Many thoughts raced through my mind. I could go back to Virginia. No, I was married now and I must stick to that decision. But what about an annulment? We hadn't consummated the marriage. No, I made a vow to God. I could persuade Todd to go back. No, he'd be miserable and I'd still have to face Kent and Rebecca.

Then my anger surfaced. This was all Kent's fault! He was the one who approached me. He asked my father for permission to call on me. Why did he initiate a romantic relationship with me if he was going to choose someone else?

I broke into a fresh wave of tears. I made the choice to come out here, and Todd was being kind to me. I didn't deserve him. Not only did I not deserve him, but I couldn't take care of the household tasks that farm wives did.

"What made me think I could do this?" I asked myself as I stared at the burnt pan.

***

The next day, I experienced a bitterness toward Kent and Rebecca that took me by surprise. While Todd was at his new job at the bank, I paced back and forth in the parlor, unable to concentrate on the household chores I needed to accomplish. The bitterness turned into anger, which burned brighter and hotter as I recalled all the lies that Kent once told me. How foolish I was!

Hoping to burn off my anger, I took a long walk through the fields. The sunlight brought out the brilliant yellows and light greens of the land, but I was too caught up in my memories to notice. At one point, my anger reached a point where I had to run. I ran as fast and as hard as I could, hoping to drive all traces of Kent from my mind. But he haunted me without reprieve. "She actually believed I loved her," I imagined him telling Rebecca. I squeezed my eyes shut, as if that would stop the pictures of Kent and Rebecca laughing at me.

At some point, I collapsed on the ground, exhausted. My mind rushed through memories of my relationship with Kent, the end of it, my hasty marriage to Todd, and the long trek to North Dakota until they all became one big mix. My rapid breathing and aching muscles prompted me to lay still. The images in my mind finally began to fade as I became aware of my hunger. I had forgotten to eat anything that morning.

After a few minutes passed, I grew tired. Relieved, I gave myself up to the darkness that enveloped me. By the time I woke up, the sun was low in the sky. I gasped. Todd! He would be worried. I jumped up and ran in the direction of the house. I hadn't realized I had gone so far into the field. I ran until my side hurt and then I had to walk, and the walk back seemed to take forever. I saw Todd riding his favorite horse in the field, calling out my name.

I stopped and waited to catch my breath. When I could manage it, I called out to him and waved my arms. I grinned. I looked as silly as my mother.

He turned his horse, which galloped to me. He jumped off the horse and hugged me tightly. "Thank goodness you're alright. I feared the worst."

Overwhelmed by his reaction, I returned his hug. Did he think I left him? Did he think someone took me away? "I went for a walk and I fell asleep in the field. I didn't expect to be gone for long."

"There are coyotes out here. You could have been harmed."

Coyotes? I shivered.

He released me. "I'll need to buy a gun, just in case one tries to attack either of us. But we can worry about that later. You must be hungry. Would you like to take a break from cooking and get something to eat in town?"

I felt empty as soon as he pulled away from me. My growling stomach reminded me of more pressing matters I needed to attend to than wondering about his hug. I readily agreed, excited to eat a good meal for a change.

***

The anger did not leave as I hoped it would. If anything, it seemed to intensify. Sunday came and we went to church. Unlike the church we went to in Virginia, this one was filled with farmers who wore old clothes. I shouldn't have been surprised but I felt out of place in my extravagant dress.

Todd seemed as nervous as I was. A momentary flicker of homesickness washed over me. If I could see my parents again... If I could talk to Agnes... I quickly brushed the tears from my eyes and followed Todd to the pew.

After we sung the hymns, the middle-aged preacher talked about anger and how we needed to forgive those who upset us. The lesson wasn't lost to me. I knew that this was something I had to deal with. I reflected on my anger at Kent and Rebecca. Did Kent care for me, even a little, during our courtship? Could he help loving Rebecca?

I sighed. I was angry, and I needed to forgive them. When it came time for everyone to silently pray, I prayed for the ability to let the past go.

The service ended. Todd and I stood up, ready to leave, when John and Barbara Russell approached us. They were ten years older than us, and they had two sons and a daughter. Calvin was eight, Bruce was five, and Molly was two. I was thrilled to discover that they owned the farm next to ours. They invited us to dinner at their house, and I was happy to get out of cooking again.

By the time Todd and I arrived at their house, we were famished. Barbara's food tasted so good that I ate until my stomach ached in protest. I wondered if I could ever learn to cook as well as her. I hesitated to question her cooking methods, but I was sick and tired of eating overcooked and bland food.

After the men left for the barn, I offered to help Barbara clean the table and dishes, which was one of the few things I was good at. As we worked, I tried to think of how to ask for cooking advice without sounding incompetent.

"So, what brings you and Todd to North Dakota?" she asked as she washed a plate.

I dried a cup. "We moved here because Todd knew someone who knew Mr. Martin. Todd's currently working at the bank in town in order to save up enough money to buy farming equipment."

She smiled as she washed a dish. "I'm sure John will love teaching Todd all he knows about farming. Calvin and Bruce are learning, but they are still too young to do the bigger tasks. Did you grow up on the farm?"

"No. I lived in a city. Actually, Todd and I grew up in wealthy households, so we're new to everything out here." Something about Barbara told me I could trust her. "Todd's father refused to offer him assistance if Todd left banking. I think it's hard on Todd to be alienated from his family. I hope they come around to accepting his decision."

"What about your parents?"

"They like Todd, but I'm not sure they will approve of how I married him. We eloped without telling anyone. I left a note telling them about it before we left Virginia."

She handed me the dish. "Well, you'll find there are more important things than wealth. What John and I don't have in riches, we make up for in other areas."

"Is it hard to make money as a farmer?"

"We live modestly. Sometimes I sell quilts in order to buy nice things."

Making quilts? "I have a lot to learn."

"So did I when I married John ten years ago. I grew up in town. My mother taught me to cook and sew, but I didn't know what I had to do to be a farmer's wife until I came out here."

I set the plate in the cupboard. "How did you meet him?"

"When I was seventeen, I went to a barn dance, and he asked me to dance. The rest is history. I didn't believe I could live on the farm and like it, and the first year was tough. But I wouldn't give up this life for anything. Getting through the first year is the secret."

I hesitated before asking, "Did you always cook as well as you do now?"

She grinned at my compliment. "Good cooking comes with practice."

"I never learned how to cook." I hoped she wouldn't laugh at me.

Thankfully, she didn't. "I suppose a wealthy mother figures her daughter wouldn't have to cook. You had servants cook for you?"

I nodded.

"Would you like me to teach you what I know?"

"Yes. I was going to ask for your help."

"Then we'll start tomorrow. I can go to your house, if you don't mind Molly tagging along."

"It'll be good to have a child around."

"I'm sure you'll have your own soon."

I chose to keep quiet.

For the rest of the visit, she continued to tell me about her childhood, courtship with John and marriage.

***

During the rest of the month, I gained an incredible amount of knowledge in cooking. At first, my meals were poor in quality but I soon improved. Todd had complimented my poor cooking, but I thought he was glad to eat better meals. I know I was glad to eat them.

Todd didn't like his job, so many times he came home depressed. He couldn't fully enjoy his days off because he kept thinking of Monday when he'd have to go back. I didn't realize that working at the bank would make him moody. Barbara assured me that most men got that way if they didn't like their work. Upon hearing this, I decided that leaving Virginia so he could farm was the best thing for him.

In addition to our meeting with John and Barbara on a regular basis, I enjoyed their children. I hadn't realized how much I loved children. In Virginia, I was surrounded by people my own age. I did look forward to the day I would have my own, but I also enjoyed the time Todd and I had to ourselves to get to know each other. I was sorry I didn't give him a chance in Virginia. He was actually very fun, to be around, when he wasn't upset about his job.

One warm evening in late August, I sat next to Todd on the porch swing. I had set a nice blanket on it with a large pillow because it looked comfortable. I enjoyed the fact that it was the one place we could sit together and be close. I found that I looked forward to the evenings for this reason. Since he hadn't initiated any physical contact since he hugged me in the field on the day I went for a walk, I wasn't sure if he wanted to be close to me. But he was probably waiting for me to be ready, and I didn't want to rush things. Not when Kent and Rebecca were still on my mind. Though I'd come around to accepting what happened, it was taking time to heal from it. In the midst of these emotions, I did find comfort in being with Todd. I had thought I was close to Agnes, but my friendship with Todd seemed to run deeper than it had with her.

We'd spend most of our time on the swing reading a book together. Though he held a book in his hands, he didn't open it on this particular evening.

"Dinner was terrific," he said, fingering the pages.

Pleased, I smiled. "At least I didn't burn the bread."

"You haven't burned anything in a week."

I raised my eyebrow at him. "Oh? Did you forget the potato slices from last night?"

He chuckled. "Those weren't burnt. They were nicely browned."

I laughed, not understanding how he could overlook that mishap. I thought I had enough time to hang up clothes on the clothes' line. I'd been wrong. After a moment of silence passed, I asked, "How are things going at the bank?"

"As good as it can be. At least Mr. Richard is a good boss."

"That is good news. It should make working there more bearable."

"It does."

I sighed. He seemed preoccupied. I wasn't sure of what to say.

I glanced at the front yard. Usually, our conversations were easy, but this evening it seemed forced. I focused on the way the strong wind shook the leaves on the trees that formed a shelter belt around the house.

"Do you ever regret leaving Virginia?" he asked.

Turning my attention back to him, I shook my head. "No. But I do miss my parents and Agnes."

"I could get some time off of work around Thanksgiving. Would you like to visit them?"

"Do we have enough money?"

"With all the overtime I work, we do."

"Will you come with me?"

He grinned. "Of course. I couldn't bear to be away from you. I can hardly stand to be gone while I'm at work."

I was pleased by this. I also looked forward to being with him. Maybe that's what happened when people got married. They became a part of each other.

"We'd take the train," he continued.

I nodded, returning my thoughts to the idea of going back East. "Good because that wagon ride was long. Don't get me wrong. It wasn't boring because I was with you, but I was exhausted when we finally got here. I wouldn't have survived another day."

"You would have made it. You have great strength. I'm impressed with you. I don't think many women could handle the trip or getting used to living here."

"It is an adventure. I wouldn't trade this life for Virginia or anywhere else. I'm happy here."

"I like hearing that. I want you to be happy." He handed me the book. "I better take care of the horses for the night." He stood up. "I was going to stop working overtime at the bank, but it would be nice to see your parents in November. After that, I can work less and be around here more. Is that alright?"

"Yes, but you don't want to read tonight?"

"No. I'm not in the mood. Why don't you read a couple of chapters and tell me what happens?"

I nodded and opened the book to the marked page.

He went down the porch steps and walked around the house so he could go to the barn.

Chapter Nine
Todd's Point of View

Ann and I didn't progress as fast toward intimacy as I would have liked, but I was continually reminding myself to be patient. I knew that until she put Kent behind her, she wasn't going to be able to open her heart to me, and I wanted her to see me as a man, not as the boy she grew up with or the friend who shared a house with her. Waiting for her to reach this point wasn't always easy. There were times when I got upset and unintentionally snapped at her. She assumed it was my work that was irritating me. That was partly true, but my increased awareness of her physical beauty wore on my nerves because I couldn't do anything about it. I was married to her, yet I wasn't free to explore the physical side of our relationship.

I wouldn't tell her the truth of my irritations because I didn't want her to consummate our marriage because she felt guilty or obligated to. I wanted her to want me as much as I wanted her. I actually looked forward to going to work at times because at least when I was at work, I was just bored. Being bored was easier than being aroused without relief. I focused on my goal toward farming while I worked. I kept a calendar in my desk where I was marking down the days to when I could quit.

I did enjoy giving Ann money so she could buy new foods to cook. She seemed to enjoy trying new foods, and I liked eating them. She was quickly turning into an expert cook. Coming home to one of her meals was the highlight of my day. It wasn't just her cooking I looked forward to though. I mostly enjoyed coming home to her sweet smiles. This was one of those situations where I wanted to be with her and away from her at the same time.

On the third Saturday in September, I went into town so I could do some additional bookkeeping for Mr. Richard. Afterwards, I took out enough money I had saved aside for a gift to buy Ann. She didn't complain about a lack of anything, but I knew she liked to wear pretty dresses. She wasn't able to buy any new dresses, and the ones from Virginia were wearing out. They weren't made for housework. I found the pink dress she had worn at the dance. She had thrown it away, but I found it and set it aside for when I could afford to buy her a dress that was pretty but also durable.

Since Mrs. Coley's daughter, Daphne Rhodes, sewed dresses and other clothing for a living, I handed her Ann's old pink dress and informed her that it was a little tight on Ann because Ann did complain about it at the dance. Daphne had a new blue and green dress ready on that Saturday, so after work, I went by to pay her and collect the dress. Daphne knew I wanted to keep the dress a secret, so she never mentioned it to anyone. I wanted Ann to be surprised by it since it was her birthday gift.

Daphne wrapped it up in a pink cloth with a pink ribbon. I couldn't wait to show it to Ann. Though I didn't see the dress, Daphne had shown me the design and I thought it would look terrific on Ann. Of course, Ann could wear a potato sack and still be beautiful.

"I hope you don't mind that I included a bonnet to match the dress," Daphne said as she handed me the present.

"Thank you, Mrs. Rhodes," I replied. I paid her for the dress and included a tip for her thoughtfulness.

"Thank you, Mr. Brothers. You are very generous. If you need any more dresses, I will be happy to make them for you. Your wife is a very nice woman. I know my mother enjoys her conversations with her."

I was pleased to hear this so I thanked her again and left. Ann didn't seem to have any problems making friends. She naturally drew people to her with her sunny personality.

As soon as I got home, I was anxious to surprise Ann. She wasn't in the kitchen, parlor, dining room or any of the bedrooms. I hesitated to go to the scullery room because that's where we took baths in the metal tub, but my excitement overcame my awkwardness. I noticed the scullery room door was shut so I tapped on the door.

"Ann? Are you in there?"

"Oh, Todd! I didn't expect you back so early."

The sound of water splashing in the tub brought images of her taking a bath. I hadn't seen a woman naked so I really couldn't visualize anything specific. I was enjoying the imagery that did come to mind, however. I pushed the thoughts aside.

"I didn't have to work the entire day. I have a surprise for you."

"Really?"

"You didn't think I forgot your birthday, did you?"

"Well... I didn't even know you knew when my birthday was."

"Of course, I do. I've been to enough birthday dinner parties to remember."

"I need to finish washing my hair. I'll be out in a few minutes. Can you put the surprise in my room? I'll be there soon."

Can I help? I can wash your back. I wanted to say this but I didn't. Instead, I went to her bedroom and set the gift on her dresser. Her room was simple in its decoration since she didn't bring many of her things in our hurried trek to North Dakota. Still, there was no denying it was a woman's bedroom. Dresses hung in the wardrobe, the blanket she laid out on the bed was embroidered with pink and white carnations, and her comb, hairbrush, and two hats were neatly set out on the dresser. I liked the smell of the room. It reminded me of her.

To my surprise, she walked into the room in nothing but her robe. Her hair was still wet from her bath, and for some reason, this was even more arousing than I figured it should have been. I shifted, hoping she wouldn't notice my erection.

She blinked, as if surprised. "Oh. I didn't know you were going to wait in here."

"Should I leave?" *Please say no.*

She seemed to consider my question. "We are married," she softly replied. "I suppose sooner or later, this was bound to happen." Then her eyes fell on the gift. "Is that for me?" In her excitement, she forgot the awkwardness of the situation.

I was secretly relieved. I wanted to look at her. It was as if I was a starving man and there was a banquet right in front of me.

She smiled widely at me. "You got me a present?"

I could only nod.

"How thoughtful of you! What is it?"

I cleared my throat and willed my breathing to go back to normal. "Open it and find out." I sat on her bed, not trusting myself to stand. I was ready to run over to her and kiss her. I didn't trust myself to get too close to her. As it was, I almost felt guilty for staring at her, but I remembered that we were married and looking at her was acceptable.

She gently removed the ribbon. Why did women feel the need to take their time opening gifts? I didn't bother to ask. In fact, she could take all day if she wanted. I suddenly caught sight of her reflection in the mirror and saw the skin below her collarbone. She wasn't aware of my response to her. It didn't even occur to her that I was thinking about sex.

She removed the cloth and squealed with delight. "It's gorgeous!" She picked up the dress and put it up to her neck so she could inspect it in the mirror. "Oh, and there's a bonnet to match! This will be more comfortable than the hats."

I wanted to tell her to put the dress back down so I could continue to look at her skin, but she was happy with the dress so I didn't. I was glad she liked my gift.

"How did you know my measurements?" she wondered.

I blinked and looked at her eyes. They were such a pretty brown color. I always liked her eyes.

Her eyebrows furrowed. "Are you feeling alright? You look flushed." She forgot to hold her dress up to her neck and walked over to me. She leaned over and touched my forehead.

I couldn't move. Her sudden movement loosened her robe enough for me to catch a glimpse of her breasts. Perfectly formed white mounds with pink tips. They were much better than I imagined.

"You feel warm. Maybe you should lie down," she said, concerned.

"No, I'm fine," I quickly argued. The beating of my heart sounded loud in my ears. She was, without a doubt, the most exquisite woman in the world.

"I don't know. You look like you're going to faint." She stood back up and studied me, as if determining whether I was sick or not.

I shook my head to clear it. "I'm fine. It's just a little hot in here, that's all."

"I feel cold. Maybe that's because I just got out of the bath. Would you like to take a bath? Maybe it would cool you off."

"That's a good idea."

"I can boil some water for you."

"No. I'll just take cold water."

"Are you sure? That can't be comfortable."

"I'll survive it." It was either that or throw her on the bed and act on the thoughts that were racing wildly through my mind.

She stood there and stared at me.

I looked back at her. "What is it?"

"Aren't you going to take the bath?"

"I was hoping to see how you look in the dress first." There was no way I was going to stand up with her looking at me. I didn't want her to see how aroused I was. I cleared my throat. "You can put it on in the third bedroom." *Or you can put it on right here.*

She blushed. "Oh." She quickly tightened the top of her robe.

I sighed. I was hoping she wouldn't remember to do that.

"I'll be right back," she said before she left the room.

I jumped off the bed and opened the window so that the fresh, cool air would calm me down. There was no way that the dress would look better than her wearing nothing. She was incredible.

When she returned, she wore the dress. I breathed a sigh of relief. I didn't think I could handle watching her in her robe anymore.

She ran to the mirror and examined her reflection. "This is a wonderful dress. How did you know my measurements?"

Now that she was fully dressed, I could concentrate again. "That was easy. I took that pink dress you wore at the dance to Mrs. Rhodes."

"It fits better than that dress."

"I told her the pink dress was a little tight because you felt faint in it."

She went to the mirror and combed her hair, which was drying nicely. She placed the bonnet on her head and turned to me. "What do you think?"

"You're the best looking woman I've ever seen," I whispered.

She beamed. "That is very thoughtful of you to say." She walked over to me and hugged me. "Thank you. This is the best gift anyone's ever given me."

"You had better dresses back in Virginia." It felt so good to hold her.

"But this took some thought."

"I know how much you like dresses."

"Todd, you're the best husband a woman could ask for. I'm very thankful you love me so well." She kissed me on the cheek.

I turned my head in hopes she would kiss me on the mouth, but she had already pulled away from me and was admiring the dress in the mirror.

"I think I'll take that bath now," I weakly said before I left the room.

Chapter Ten
Ann's Point of View

I was thankful for the fall season. It was good to feel the cool breezes drift in through the open windows. Early in October, I woke up and realized I had finally forgiven Kent and Rebecca. I was relieved and happy to be able to move on with my life.

Since Todd and I slept in separate bedrooms, I wasn't aware he had trouble sleeping. How many sleepless nights had he spent pacing in his bedroom or downstairs in the parlor?

I wouldn't have even known he was having trouble sleeping if I hadn't gotten cold in the middle of the night and had to close my window. I realized I was thirsty, so I decided to go to the kitchen to get some water. On my way down the steps, I heard the sound of footsteps in the parlor. I gasped and stood still, afraid to move. I held my breath and considered what to do. Suddenly, it occurred to me that an intruder wouldn't spend so much time in one place.

I slowly walked down the stairs and tiptoed to the sound, curious as to what Todd would be doing up at such a late hour. I was ready to let my presence be known when I saw him, slouched over the desk in the parlor. The candlelight by his side showed his worried expression. I stayed out of sight in the shadows.

He never told me anything was bothering him, so I had no idea what it could be. He sighed loudly, stood up and paced in front of the desk, sat back down in front of a pile of papers, wrote something down, threw his pen down in aggravation and paced the floor again. Obviously, whatever he was writing wasn't working. Finally, he blew out the candle and walked back up the stairs. I quietly hid in the shadows.

Once he shut his bedroom door, I crept over to the desk and pulled open the drawer that contained the papers he had been scribbling on. I pushed aside my guilty feelings and walked to the window so I could study what was on the papers by the light of the moon. It didn't take me long to realize that I was holding the household budget. I frowned. We needed more money. I put the papers back where I found them. I didn't know if I felt better or worse now that I knew what kept him up at night. He wanted to protect me from financial worries, but I was partly responsible since I bought extra food that I wanted to cook. Some of the food was expensive. Plus, he originally planned on coming out by himself, so I was an extra person to care for.

Winter was coming soon, and Barbara recommended that I get warmer clothes, coats and boots. Now I was worried. How could we afford those things? I wanted to help him but didn't feel comfortable approaching him since he was determined to handle this on his own. That night, I stayed awake, tossing and turning in my bed as I thought of ways I could ease our financial burden. As I cooked breakfast, I found the answer. I would take Mrs. Coley up on her offer to give me food in exchange for my services.

Barbara came by to pick me up later that morning. We went to town once a week so she could visit her mother. Molly usually joined us while Calvin and Bruce helped John. While Barbara and Molly visited her mother, I went to the store.

Mr. Coley was stocking the shelves. "Hello, Mrs. Brothers. How are you and Todd doing this morning?"

"We are doing well, thank you," I replied.

Mrs. Coley walked out from the backroom. "You're early. You don't usually come for another hour."

I took a deep breath. "Yes. I had something I wanted to ask you."

Mr. Coley stopped and looked at me.

"Is your offer to help you with the store still open? I would like to work for free food."

Mrs. Coley thought for a moment. "We could use someone to clean the store, update our books, and keep an inventory list of the supplies we have. Are you willing to do those things?"

I nodded. "I know how to do all of that." For once, I was grateful for my schooling. "I'm not sure my husband would appreciate it if I worked here. He might not like the fact that I'm helping with the finances."

"You don't need to explain," Mr. Coley replied. "We won't say a word about this."

I sighed, relieved. "Thank you." I didn't want Todd to feel like he couldn't make it out here on his own.

So we agreed that I would come in twice a week to do these chores in return for food and cooking supplies. Since Todd didn't go shopping, he didn't know the cost of food, so I was able to fib on the cost of different items. I simply explained that I had found ways to cut back on the grocery bill. He accepted my reason for the sudden decrease in food expenses.

After two weeks, I took a midnight peek at the budget and smiled when I saw we were back in good financial shape.

As it turned out, Mrs. Coley and I became good friends. She would fill me in on her past memories, especially funny stories of her children's childhood. She loved to tell her stories, and I enjoyed listening to them. She also gave me advice on staying warm during the winter. It was funny how I got used to doing the chores at home and in the store. I didn't even notice how exhausting they were anymore.

***

That Sunday evening, Todd and I sat on the porch, watching the sunset as the wind tossed orange and red leaves on the ground.

"I wish time would stand still at this moment," he commented. "If only things could always be this peaceful."

"It is beautiful," I agreed.

He closed his eyes and leaned his head against the chair. It had been a couple of weeks since he sat next to me on the porch swing. I worried that he no longer loved me like he used to, but I didn't ask him about it in case I was right.

"I wish tomorrow wasn't Monday."

I sighed. It seemed that he hated his job more with each passing day. "Try not to think about the bank."

"I try, really I do. I tell myself once winter is over, I can afford to quit. John's going to help me purchase farm equipment. He'll know what I need to get started. He recommends I start planting-"

I bit my lower lip so I wouldn't scream. Instead, I said, "Todd, I've heard this a dozen times already. Can we talk about something else? Maybe you should quit your job at the bank and get another job until spring." When he didn't respond, I continued, "There's an opening at the post office."

"Do you think I can't handle the job I already have?" He sat up straight, his eyes wide.

Why did he have to be so touchy? "You're a great banker. It's just hard to watch you spend all your waking hours in misery. You might enjoy life more if you did something else for the next few months."

He frowned. "I don't know."

"What do you have to lose?"

"I'll think about it."

I hesitated but decided to speak. "There's not only a job at the post office but the stable is hiring as well." When I saw him clench his jaw, I realized he wasn't listening to me. "I've had it! I'm tired of hearing you complain about your job. I don't understand why you don't quit." It hadn't been my intention to raise my voice but the more I spoke, the louder I got.

He glared at me. "Unlike some people, I don't run away from my problems."

I bolted to my feet. "That's the last time I'll try to help you!" I quickly ran into the house before I said something I would regret.

I locked myself in my bedroom. So what if I left Virginia in order to get away from Kent and Rebecca? Todd didn't refuse to take me with him! I crossed my arms and sat on my bed. Perhaps leaving Virginia the way I did wasn't the smartest thing I ever did, but I liked it here. I didn't regret coming out here, even though I missed my parents and Agnes.

I spent most of the night fuming at his words. Did he think I was staying here because I was still mourning over Kent? Did he think that was the only reason I stayed married to him?

By the time morning came, I was tempted to make Todd fix his own breakfast. I stared at the cook stove. I wondered how long it would take him to figure out how to make pancakes and biscuits.

"I'm sorry, Ann. I didn't mean to say that about you running away from your problems," Todd softly stated.

I hadn't heard him enter the kitchen. I turned around, my heart melting. "I'm sorry too. You know how to handle the situation at work better than I do."

He seemed as relieved as I was to have things go back to normal. Unlike the other times we apologized, he hugged me. The action startled me for a moment, but then I returned his hug. I found that I enjoyed hugging him. Maybe fighting wasn't so bad after all.

"You don't run away from your problems," he said when our hug ended. "If you did, you wouldn't be here. I know it wasn't easy for you to learn to cook and clean. It's hard work, and I want you to know that I appreciate it. Thank you for taking care of me."

My eyes lit up at his compliment. I kissed his cheek to show my appreciation. "Of course, you take care of me too." Again, I was thankful that he loved me and treated me so well. I gladly turned to the stove and made his breakfast.

***

The next afternoon when he came home, he rushed into the house and said he had a surprise for me. Interested, I followed him out to the barn and paused when I saw my gift. He bought me a horse?

"Do you think this is a good idea?"

"Of course it is," he replied, smiling proudly at the brown animal that was eating hay in her stall. "Do you want to name her?"

"Why do we need another horse?"

"I noticed you've been going into town more and thought if I was at work and you needed to go to town, you can hook up Thunder and this horse to the buggy."

I considered my words carefully. I didn't work at the Coley's so he could buy things we didn't need. "I appreciate the thought. You are very kind to think of me."

He frowned. "But…?"

I shrugged. "I don't know. I just think that it may be unnecessary. Barbara takes me into town whenever she goes."

"I thought you would be pleased."

I noted his disappointment. "I am but isn't a horse expensive?"

"Are you saying I can't afford it?"

"Can you?"

"Yes."

I rubbed my forehead. I saw the budget that night. I knew he couldn't. Not really. Not without sacrificing something important, like food or clothes or blankets for the winter.

He sighed and looked at Thunder and Lightning who rested in their stalls, munching on their portion of the hay. He turned back to me. "I work all the time to give you what you want and no matter how hard I try, I can't please you. I really thought you'd appreciate this horse. I bought her for you."

"I don't need a horse."

"You want more clothes?"

"No. I'm content with what I have." Why was he getting upset? I was trying to ease his financial burden, not increase it. "You don't have to buy me things. I don't need things to be happy. I just want to be a blessing to you."

He looked as if he was about to say something but decided against it.

I shook my head. "Forget about the Thanksgiving trip and the horse. You don't have to work overtime at the bank. Do you think I want you to suffer over there just so I can have more things? I already told you I wasn't going to buy as many clothes anymore and I have managed to cut back on the food expenses. I did all of that for you, but you take the money I have saved you and you run off and buy an animal I don't need. Then you're going to run back to the bank and overwork yourself again."

"I keep telling you we can afford things. Why don't you ever listen to me?"

He was too proud to admit that he needed help. I couldn't make him tell me the truth, and I didn't want to have another fight about his job. I turned to the mare. He did show a great deal of thoughtfulness in buying her for me. I should graciously accept it and just hope it didn't create a hole in our finances. "Thank you for the horse. I'm sorry I wasn't appreciative of it before. I do like it when you buy things for me."

He looked uncertain. "You do?"

I nodded. "It lets me know you think about me."

He smiled back. "That's good information to have."

Relieved, I returned his smile. "Why don't we name her Storm? I think it goes well with Thunder and Lightning."

"I like it. Storm it is."

Chapter Eleven
Todd's Point of View

One night, I couldn't sleep at all. Thoughts of Ann continually replayed themselves in my mind. I recalled the day I brought home her dress for her birthday and how beautiful she looked in her robe. I recalled her perky white breasts when she leaned over to touch my forehead. I wanted to see everything that was under that robe. I managed to drift off into a fitful sleep halfway through the night, and my dreams were filled with images of Ann coming to me. My hands caressed her breasts. I recalled the feel of her silky hair, the way her lips felt on mine, and how her body felt when I hugged her. I reluctantly willed these thoughts away as I woke up. I was too aroused to go back to sleep. I jumped off my bed and opened the window.

I shivered as my body finally cooled. I didn't dare close the window. Instead, I decided to go downstairs. I didn't feel like taking care of my sexual needs that night. I'd just wait it out. I quietly walked down the stairs and lit a candle in the parlor. I went over to the desk by the window and opened the top drawer where I put the papers I wrote on to plan our spending and savings. I took out my pencil and began working on a new idea on ways I could cut spending. I had already cut back as far as I could on my clothing. I had enough warm clothes. I did odd jobs for John for some hay to feed the horses, so I managed to save aside some extra money there.

I looked at Ann's clothing and the food budget. I sighed loudly and stood up and paced in front of the desk. I hated to cut back on the things she enjoyed. She had bought some warmer and prettier dresses, which I liked. She not only looked good in them but she had fun buying them. It was one of the things she did enjoy back in Virginia. I sat back down in front of a pile of papers and considered cutting back the food budget. I wrote some amounts down to the few foods I knew. I did enjoy her cooking, and she had fun trying new recipes. Some of them were fancy but it tasted just as good as the other stuff she made. If I cut back on the food and clothing, it would save more, but I didn't want to do that to her.

I stared out the window and recalled the last time she brought a new dress home. Her face glowed with pleasure. I wished she liked me as much as she liked those dresses. I threw the pencil down in aggravation and paced the floor again. I didn't like thinking such thoughts. I had to be important to her in some way. She wouldn't even tell me she loved me, but she had no trouble expressing her pleasure for cooking and buying clothes. I groaned. So I wasn't going to sleep tonight. I blew out the candle and crept up the stairs. Despite my frustration, I quietly shut the bedroom door. I wanted slam it so she would wake up and come running out of her bedroom to ask me what was wrong.

Then what? I would get to look at her in her nightgown, which didn't hide as much as the dresses did, but she'd be oblivious to the fact that I was in pajamas which didn't hide much either. She'd be relieved that I was alright and go back to her room. She wouldn't invite me to her room or come into mine. Then the next day, I'd be just as miserable but with the reminder that she didn't care to do anything interesting with me the night before when she had the perfect chance. I laid on my bed and resigned myself to another sleepless night. Again, the thought crept into my mind that I should have left her back in Virginia.

***

That Sunday evening, we sat on the porch again. I sat in one of the chairs. I was finding it harder and harder to sit next to her. Instead, I put as much distance between us as possible. I was afraid if I got close, I wouldn't be able to control myself. There were too many intimate thoughts running through my mind. If she had any idea, she would probably think there was something wrong with me.

I wanted to ask Ann what she thought about sex but knew it wouldn't be appropriate since we weren't actually having it. Or would it? Could it be something that would open the door to consummating our marriage? I could talk to her about anything else. So why not this?

"It was nice that we spent the day together," Ann said. "We always have fun with John and Barbara, but sometimes it's nice to spend some time alone."

Breaking out of my thoughts, I turned to her in interest. Did she enjoy being with me?

She shifted on the porch swing and cleared her throat. "It's just that sometimes I feel like I don't get to see you very much. You work so many hours at the bank. Not that I'm complaining," she quickly added. "I know you're doing everything you can to provide for us."

"You like having me around?"

She blushed. "Of course I do."

I appreciated her comment more than she realized. "I like being with you too."

I closed my eyes and leaned my head against the chair. It had been a good day. She sat closer to me than usual in church. Usually, there was some space between us, but now that I thought about it, our arms were touching. I had assumed she sat close to me because Molly wanted to sit right by her and she didn't have enough room to leave some space between us. Was it possible that she intentionally sat close to me? There was enough room on Molly's side. Then I recalled the way she sat next to me at dinner and touched my arm a couple of times. I had assumed it was innocent Ann behavior. Was there more to it than that? A spark of hope went through me.

"If you want, I could stay home more." Suddenly, I wanted to be with her. Perhaps I should stop working overtime and see if more would come from her actions.

"I understand that you need to be at work as much as you are," she argued. "I don't want you to stop doing what you need to do."

I frowned. "What do I need to do?" Be away from her? Did she want me around or not?

She looked startled. "I didn't mean anything rude. I... Well, you know what you need to do. That's why you work overtime."

I blinked, confused. "What are you talking about?"

"Nothing. Forget I said anything. It doesn't matter anyway. We're having a lovely day. Let's not ruin it with another argument."

"I don't want to forget it. I want to know what you're talking about." I sat up in the chair, aware that I was getting upset. Something in her comment bothered me and I didn't know why.

"I'm not saying you're inadequate. You do a great job."

"Why should I feel inadequate?" Was that why she didn't want to have sex with me? Because I didn't measure up to her standards?

"You shouldn't feel inadequate." She looked alarmed. "Really, I meant nothing wrong."

"Fine. Then you can tell me what you meant." I didn't mean to sound as harsh as I did, so I forced myself to take a deep breath to calm down.

"You do a great job at the bank. You're a hard worker."

What did that have to do with sex? "Are you trying to avoid the topic?"

"No. I've been talking about your job. That is what you're talking about too, isn't it?"

Her words broke through my confusion. She was talking about my role as the provider. "Why should I feel inadequate about work?"

"No reason. Can we just forget it and talk about something else? What did you think of the preacher's sermon today?"

I narrowed my eyes. I couldn't let go of her insinuation that I wasn't a good provider. "Are you saying you don't get enough money?" How many dresses or food could a woman possibly buy? I thought I was already being generous on those accounts.

"No! I'm not saying that at all."

"I don't believe you." Now I was fuming. "This may not be Virginia where you had tons of money to throw around, but I work hard and I do make a good living at what I do."

She looked like she was ready to panic. "Of course you do."

"I'm sorry I don't meet up to your standards, Ann. Perhaps you'd like to go back."

She angrily stood up. "I'm not going anywhere. I like it here and you can't make me leave. It's my house too!"

"You sure do enjoy living here. It's almost like I'm living with one of my sisters."

She gasped. "Is that what you see me as? A sister?"

"You treat me like I'm your brother."

"I can't believe you said that. I've just been giving you time alone. You're so upset with your job that it's hard to be around you."

"Or are you upset because you can't buy everything you want?" What was going on? Were we really having this conversation? I wasn't even sure what we were talking about. Were we talking about money, sex or my job?

"That's it! I can't take this anymore. You go ahead and stay at your job all you want, and we'll spend all of our Sundays with the Russell family. I told Barbara that I wanted to spend the day alone with you since I do enjoy being with you. But all we do lately is argue and I don't understand how your job can affect your mood so poorly. Really Todd, if it's that much of a pain, then quit and do something else."

Again, she was insisting that I quit my job. "In case you haven't noticed, I'm a man. I can handle my job. I don't need you to tell me what to do."

"Fine. And in case you haven't noticed, I am a woman. I am not one of your sisters, nor do I consider you to be my brother. Apparently, I was the only one who listened to the preacher today. I am sorry that I offend you, but I refuse to leave. It's too bad you're stuck with me." She ran into the house and slammed the door behind her.

I sat on the chair, unable to process what had just happened. I knew it wouldn't do any good to follow her. She usually ran up to her room and locked the door. I didn't understand her. She was too complicated. One minute she was telling me how much she enjoyed being with me, then she told me to work more, and then she acted as if I had insulted her. What did I say that was wrong? Irritated, I closed my eyes and rocked back and forth in the chair. She was right about one thing. Whenever we spent time together, we did fight. I couldn't remember the last time we had a pleasant day.

I didn't imagine that marriage could be so hard. I loved Ann for years. I thought we were having fun being together up until the beginning of this month. What changed in that time? True, I did complain about my job and dreaded going to it, but I didn't think it was as bad as she said. Was she afraid I was going to stop working so she couldn't afford her precious dresses?

I took a deep breath to calm my nerves. I understood that we would have our fights when I married her. I didn't expect things to always go perfectly. I even anticipated female mood swings that were common with my sisters. But Ann was a lot more complex. Why couldn't we get along anymore?

***

The next morning, I went to the kitchen. Ann stood at the sink and stared out the window. She liked to look outside while she cooked. She said it gave her a feeling of peace to look at the flat landscape.

I took a deep breath as I drank in her beauty. She wore her hair down so that it reached the middle of her back. Her waist and hips were incredibly feminine. How could she think I saw her as one of my sisters? I never looked at them the way I looked at her. She knew I loved her. I had told her I did. Granted, I hadn't told her recently, but did she really need to hear it all the time? If she would give me some indication she was the slightest bit interested in me as her husband, then I could show her exactly what I thought of her.

One thing I did know was that I didn't want to fight with her. Neither one of us enjoyed that very much. "I'm sorry, Ann," I said.

She jumped around. "Why don't I ever hear you enter the kitchen?"

I smiled, glad the tension was broken. "Apparently, I have quiet shoes."

She returned my smile. "I'm sorry too. Will you eat some French toast?"

"Aren't you going to eat anything?"

"I'm not hungry this morning. I'll make a snack later."

She usually didn't eat much when something was bothering her. I sighed. I didn't know what else to say so I sat down and ate my breakfast while she cleaned the dishes. I couldn't take my eyes off of her. Wasn't she aware of how attractive she was? Just as I finished the French toast, she sat next to me.

"Please don't think I intended to criticize you yesterday evening," she began. She considered her words carefully. "You are a good husband. I know how hard you work for me, and I appreciate it. I may not seem grateful for you but I am. And I don't look at you as a brother. You're very handsome."

I was pleased by her words. "Thank you, Ann. We can afford the dresses you like to buy. Do you need more money?"

"No. I'm doing fine. I'm even getting good deals on some food from Mrs. Coley's store. I've learned how to economize. I don't want to be a burden to you."

Where did she get the idea that we didn't have enough money for the things she wanted? I never told her we were having financial problems. "You don't have to do that. We have plenty of money."

"I want to learn to watch what I spend." She paused for a moment. "I don't miss the things I had back in Virginia. They were just things. What matters is you." She put her hand on my arm. My body tingled in response. "You are a wonderful man. I admire and respect you."

"I don't think of you as one of my sisters. You're too beautiful for that. Don't you know that I love you?"

"It's nice to hear it once in awhile." She smiled and peered at me through her thick lashes. "You really think I'm beautiful?"

Did the sun light the day and the moon light the night? "You look in the mirror. Surely, you can see how desirable you are."

"I know I'm not the most beautiful woman in the world. I just want to look good for you."

"I disagree. You are the most beautiful woman in the world."

She blushed. "You are very kind. I am glad we're married."

"Me too."

"I hope you have a good day at work."

She leaned over and kissed me. Right on the lips. It wasn't one of those pristine kisses on the cheek. Before I could respond, she stood up. I wanted to bolt out of the chair and grab her so I could kiss her. I wanted to kiss her the way I'd been wanting to kiss her ever since we were sixteen and she showed me how to play Solitaire.

She took the empty plate and put it in the sink. She left the room. Curious, I followed her. She brought me my coat and hat.

"I thought I would get your things for you today," she explained. "I know you have to get going."

I glanced out the window on the kitchen door. The sunrise graced the barn. It would be a nice day, even if it would be chilly. I looked at her. She was smiling, and her eyes twinkled in a way that I'd come to learn was a clue that she was happy.

I didn't know what to do. Was she giving me permission to touch and kiss her? Or was she trying to make amends? I wanted to kiss her, to see how she'd respond. I wanted to touch her soft hair. I wanted to hold her so I could feel her body against mine. But I did none of these things. Instead, I put my coat and hat on and thanked her before I left.

Chapter Twelve
Ann's Point of View

In the beginning of November, Barbara picked me up to take me into town.

"These blankets will keep us warm," she said as I hopped into the carryall carriage.

"Where is Molly?"

"John decided to keep her home so they can discuss what gift to make for me this Christmas." She urged the horses forward. "John didn't say that's what he's doing, but I know it. I think he likes to make gifts with them. Children can be a handful but they are worth it."

"They are adorable, except when they're fighting. As I grew up, I wanted a brother or sister that I could argue with over things like candy. Todd was the oldest of seven children and since they were girls, he didn't argue with them very much. Despite all the fights his sisters did have amongst themselves, they were close." I sighed. I missed Agnes and her funny stories.

I decided to tell Barbara my two favorite Agnes stories, and she couldn't stop laughing as I told them. We reached town by the end of the second story.

She yielded to a couple who crossed the street. "You're wonderful with Calvin, Bruce and Molly. They look forward to when they can see you."

"I have a lot of fun with them. They know how to brighten my day."

She smiled at me before she urged the horses forward. "You're a natural mother. I bet you and Todd can't wait to have children. Who knows? Maybe you're expecting and don't even know it yet. That would be a good Christmas gift, wouldn't it?"

I didn't know how to respond so I stayed quiet. I breathed a sigh of relief as we pulled up to the post office. We usually checked the mail when we got to town.

To my surprise and delight, my parents sent me a letter. I had only told them I was going to North Dakota. I did not mention where in North Dakota. My mother wrote three pages alone on how hard it was to find me. "Oh, your father worried about you," she continued in the letter. "We know Todd is taking good care of you, but we do worry when we don't know what's happening out West."

I wiped the tears from my eyes, thankful that my parents had forgiven me for leaving like I did.

"Are you alright?" Barbara asked as we left the post office.

I nodded and laughed. "Yes, I'm fine. I didn't mean to upset you. My mother wrote me. I miss my parents."

She smiled. "Maybe you could visit them."

"Todd and I already discussed it. He said we could go later this month. He's even been working extra hours at the bank so we can afford the trip. I am fortunate to have him. I know he's sacrificing a lot so I can see my parents."

"He can also visit his parents while you're there."

"I'm not sure. He doesn't think they will have anything to do with him."

"I know I couldn't turn my children away. Perhaps they will change their minds once they see him."

I hoped so. Since she had to get to her mother's, I waved to her as she left. On this particular day, I remained outside the post office for a few minutes despite the chill in the air. I wouldn't be able to focus on my work until I finished reading the letter. To my delight, my mother announced that she and my father would come to visit for Christmas.

"It is vital we stay in touch, my dear," she wrote. "We look forward to seeing you again."

I quickly checked the clock in front of the bank. I went to the mercantile and cheerfully did my work. As usual, I finished my tasks several minutes before Barbara was due to pick me up, so I had a few minutes to spare. I wanted to be sure Todd was alright with their visit. If he wasn't, I would have to tell them we'd go visit them instead. According to the letter, they planned to stay at a motel in town, but I didn't want them to do that. I wanted to see as much of them as possible.

I ran to the bank. In my excitement, I ran into someone by mistake. "Excuse me."

The man grumbled something but I was too happy to care what it was.

I hurried up to one of the tellers since I didn't see Todd anywhere.

"May I help you?" a balding man with glasses asked in a whiny voice.

"Yes. I'm looking for my husband. His name is Todd Brothers. Has he gone to lunch?"

"Mr. Brothers is talking to the owner of this bank." He nodded in the direction of the owner's office. "To be honest, it doesn't look good."

I blinked. "What do you mean?"

"I don't know what's going on except that the owner didn't look happy when he asked your husband to join him in his office. Oh, I need to help the next person in line."

I numbly moved out of the way. A sense of dread washed over me. What could Todd have done to upset his boss? I waited for Todd to come out, but after ten minutes, I realized I had to wait. I put the letter in my coat pocket. I hated leaving Todd when he was facing difficulty but didn't see that I had a choice.

Barbara was still at her mother's, so I decided to do some extra cleaning in the backroom of the store in order to alleviate my anxiety. What could the owner want to discuss with Todd that was so serious? I didn't have to wait long to find out. Mrs. Carson, the town gossip, came in to tell Mrs. Coley what occurred between Todd and his boss.

As soon as I heard Todd's name, I froze and listened. I was still in the backroom so she didn't see me.

"You won't believe what happened at the bank between Todd Brothers and Samuel Richard," Mrs. Carson began.

"Is this all you are buying today?" Mrs. Coley interrupted her. She hated it when people gossiped in her store.

However, Mrs. Carson wasn't to be deterred. "Who would have thought Todd Brothers was capable of stealing money from his own employer? That's what we get for welcoming people who grew up with lots of money. He just couldn't handle the fact that he wasn't rich anymore. You'd better watch Mrs. Brothers closely next time she shops here. You know what they say: two birds of a feather flock together."

"Mrs. Carson, I would greatly appreciate it if you'd leave now," Mrs. Coley coolly stated.

"Well! Never say I didn't warn you," she huffed before she left the store.

I stood still, my hand frozen as I held a jar of peaches. *My* Todd was accused of stealing money? That explained the 'unhappy' look on his employer's face. I knew Todd would never steal anything. So who did? I suspected that even Mrs. Carson didn't know the answer to that question.

Mrs. Coley appeared around the door. When she saw my stunned expression, she sighed and shook her head. "Mrs. Carson doesn't know when to keep her big mouth shut."

"It's a lie. He didn't do it."

She took the jar of peaches out of my hand and gently put it on the shelf. "I know. Mrs. Carson has spread false rumors before. She's not someone who can be trusted, and most of the people in town know that. Maybe it's best if you went to comfort him. Men may not realize it, but sometimes they need our support."

I smiled and hugged her, grateful for her friendship. Then I shrugged into my coat and ran to see Todd at the bank. But he was already gone. I figured he was on his way home to tell me what happened.

Barbara appeared with her horse and carryall. Her cheeks were red with anger. "Some people have too much time on their hands," she commented. "Have you heard about Todd?"

"Yes." I climbed in next to her. Word had already reached Barbara? Was there anyone in town who didn't know? I pulled my coat tightly around me, suddenly feeling exposed.

"That Mrs. Carson makes me so mad! Apparently, she was there at the bank when Todd came out of the owner's office, and someone at the bank told her what happened."

My jaw dropped. No one told me anything but Mrs. Carson got the whole story? "Do you know who told her?"

"She won't say. Isn't that funny? Mrs. Busybody blabs everyone else's business but she never reveals her source. Well, John and I will stick up for Todd. We'll set them straight."

As she continued to talk, I wondered how Todd was taking this. Was he angry, sad or relieved to be rid of his job? How could I comfort him when I had never comforted him before? Did I ever try to comfort anyone?

As soon as she paused in her monologue, I asked her for tips on being supportive. I breathed a sigh of relief when she didn't laugh at me.

"Listen to him and let him know you are there for him," she replied. "Really, that's all you can do."

I hugged her. "Thank you."

I suppressed my anxiety. Could I help him through this? I was surprised at how fast my heart was pounding. I knew Todd all of my life, so why was I nervous? Saying good-bye to Barbara, I walked around the house and to the barn. Patches of snow decorated the grass. I hardly noticed the beautiful landscape. I took a deep breath then entered the barn.

Todd was chopping wood. The axe slammed through the wood with so much force, I jumped. Todd wasn't just mad. He was furious. Maybe this wasn't a good time to approach him. I quickly turned to leave.

He stopped chopping. "You heard." It was a simple statement but I could hear him fighting back his anger.

I took a deep breath as I walked to him. "I think the whole town's heard, but I know you're innocent."

He dropped his axe and held me close to him. "As long as you believe me, I don't care what the rest of the town thinks."

"Do you have any idea who started this whole thing?"

"I have a suspicion but I can't prove it. I can't believe my boss thought I'd steal money, especially after all the overtime I put in." He shook his head in exasperation.

I rested my head against his shoulder, wondering if he took as much comfort in my embrace as I took in his. "What happened at the bank?"

"I was counting money at my desk when my boss told me to go to his office. Mr. Richard is usually a mild-mannered man, but he nearly lost his temper when he told me he discovered my bookkeeping was totaled incorrectly. I was short by five dollars. I told him I didn't know how that was possible but he didn't believe me. Since the other employees have worked there for at least two years, he decided that I had to be the one who took the money. Then, to top it all off, he had me search my desk. There was fifty cents in a place where it shouldn't have been. As if that wasn't bad enough, there was a piece of paper with the combination to the safe written on it."

"Someone must have made you look guilty," I said.

"I agree. That's the only explanation for it. It doesn't matter now though. Mr. Richard said he hated to let me go but didn't know what else to do. I don't know what to do. Who's going to hire me? And we can't afford to take that trip to see your parents."

"We'll make it through. And speaking of my parents, they sent me a letter. They plan to visit for Christmas."

"Your parents wrote you? How did they find out where we are?"

I took the letter out of my pocket and handed it to him. "I told them I was going to North Dakota, and they narrowed it down from there."

After he read the letter, he gave it back to me. "They're wonderful people."

I grinned. "Did you notice that they asked how their new son is doing?"

He smiled and nodded.

I sighed. "Your parents will come around. When we save up the money, we can go visit them. We don't need to go to Virginia as soon as I wanted. I can wait. But we can go when you want to."

He didn't respond. Instead, he picked up the axe and said he needed to be alone. I nodded and went back to the house.

I picked up the Bible and began to read it. I fell asleep on the couch and woke up as the sun was setting. I blinked a few times as I recalled the day's events. Todd's chopping wood assured me it hadn't been a dream.

I quickly put on my coat, gloves and hat. Why had he stayed outside for so long? I entered the barn and frowned when I saw he didn't have on his gloves or coat.

I shivered in the cold weather. "Todd, you're going to get sick if you keep this up. Will you please come into the house?"

He wiped the sweat from his forehead. "I need to chop more wood."

I shook my head in disbelief at the piles of wood he had already chopped. "If you keep this up, there won't be any more trees on our land. We have enough wood to last us the entire winter."

He sighed heavily and sat on the ground. "I keep wondering how Mr. Richard could believe I stole that money. I thought he knew me better than that."

I didn't know what to say, so I sat beside him and put my head on his shoulder. I reached for his hands, which were red from being cold, and rubbed my gloved hands over them. He knew better than to stay outside for so long when he was underdressed. Didn't he know I worried about him?

"You're wonderful, Ann."

"It will work out, Todd. I know you'll find another job. Maybe you'll find something you enjoy."

He remained silent while I continued to rub his cold hands.

"Is it alright if my parents stay in the guest bedroom? They mentioned wanting to stay in a motel, but I would like to have them here."

"That is fine."

"Thank you." I gulped the nervous lump in my throat as I considered how to make my confession. I wasn't sure when the feelings developed but going through this ordeal with him made me aware of them. It was time I told him what was in my heart. "I do appreciate you. I know I don't say it much, if at all. The feelings I have for you are still new. I didn't feel this way with Kent. It's better with you."

I stared at our hands, and despite the frigid air, my cheeks flushed with warmth. I could tell he was looking at me, which made me even more nervous.

"Sometimes," I continued in a whisper, "I get cold at night. I..." I paused, wondering how I could be bold while being discrete. I was ready to consummate the marriage but wasn't sure how to come out and say it. "It would be nice to feel warm."

"Do you need more firewood?"

I cleared my throat. "Well, I was hoping you'd come by my room." My heartbeat pounded loudly in my ears. This was harder than I thought it would be.

"I'll tell you what. I'll start a fire in your room in the afternoon so by the time you're ready for bed, it'll be warm. I'll even add more wood before you go to sleep."

"Oh." I was surprised by how disappointed I felt.

"Is there something else?"

I shrugged. I didn't have the courage to come out and say it. "No. I suppose not." I let go of his hands and looked at him. "Will you please come into the warm house before you get sick?"

I thought he was going to argue again, but he stood up and grabbed his gloves and coat. I took the lantern. We walked side by side into the house.

"You're so cold," I commented when I noticed how red his face was. I set the lantern on the desk in the parlor. "I want you to lie down on the couch in front of the fireplace. I'll get some blankets and a pillow so you can warm up while I make dinner."

I took his coat and gloves and went upstairs before he could argue. By the time I returned, he was lying down. I put the blankets over him and placed the pillow under his head. The fire felt nice and warm.

"There. Now I order you to relax. If you need someone to talk to, just say my name," I said.

As I began walking away, he reached for my hand.

Surprised, I turned to him.

"You're my strength," he softly remarked.

I knelt in front of him. Despite my beating heart, I allowed myself to follow my instinct. I leaned over and kissed him. It was a simple kiss but it filled my heart with a new sense of joy I hadn't experienced before.

We smiled at each other for a moment.

"Everything will work out," I whispered.

Then I went to cook dinner.

After I finished dinner, Barbara, John and their children came over with an apple pie. We spent the rest of the evening just talking as the children played games. From the look on Todd's face, I knew he was grateful for our support.

Chapter Thirteen
Todd's Point of View

To my surprise, I didn't get sick. I fully expected to after staying out in the cold for so long, but it was Ann who got sick. It reminded me of the time when I visited her when she was seventeen. Unlike that time, we didn't have Ginny watching everything we did. I didn't miss the presence of servants, and I found it refreshing to do something for Ann for a change. I never appreciated all her work around the house until I had to do it myself. I didn't mind doing it since it meant she could get her much needed rest. She was still sick on Sunday, so I went to church without her. The seat beside me felt empty even though Calvin sat next to me. I missed her.

After the service, I waited for Barbara, Bruce and Molly to leave to talk to one of her friends. Usually, Ann would run off with her too. Calvin liked to hang around his father and me. I think it made him feel like a grown up. I grinned as Calvin followed John and me out of the church. The air was cool but still refreshing enough to enjoy.

I waited until we were out of earshot of anyone else and said, "I need your advice on women." It was the first time I ever came to him with such a concern.

"I'm still figuring them out myself, but I'll do what I can. What's the problem?" John asked.

"It's not actually a problem. I was wondering what you do when you want to show Barbara you love her?"

"I have a box that I keep things in for Barbara. Whenever we have a fight or if I forget an important date or if it's just the kind of day when a little surprise gift is in order, I take an item out and give it to her. I don't know what she wants, to be honest, so I have Calvin go along with her to town."

"I buy things that Mother says she likes when I'm in town with her," Calvin explained. "That way we know she'll like it."

"He's my eyes and ears when I'm not around." John grinned at him. "This way I don't have to wonder what she likes. I already know."

"Very clever."

"Mrs. Brothers likes a gold ring in the mercantile," Calvin said. "She told Mother that she didn't want to spend the money on it since she needed food more."

"It would make a nice wedding ring," John added. "I think every woman wants a wedding ring. It's a symbol of your love for her."

"She also said she liked the kitchen towels with snowmen sewed on them," Calvin continued, obviously enjoying his role as a spy.

I chuckled. Who knew kids could be so resourceful?

"Thank you, John. And thank you, Calvin."

***

The next day, I went to the Coley mercantile and walked to the counter.

Mrs. Coley glanced up from her jewelry display.

At least I found the ring.

"May I help you, Mr. Brothers?" she warmly asked.

"I would like to purchase a couple of items for my wife. Calvin Russell told me she mentioned liking them, so I want them to be a surprise."

Her eyes twinkled. "Oh how delightful! She will be pleased. What did the boy tell you she liked?"

"He mentioned a gold ring."

She nodded and took out her rings. "You're in luck. The merchant who usually comes to buy the jewelry was delayed, so it's still here." She took the ring out that Calvin mentioned and handed it to me. "What do you think?"

"I think it would be nice to give her a wedding ring. I wasn't able to buy her one when we got married."

"What a wonderful Christmas gift."

"Does it fit her finger?" I looked at the price tag and decided I could afford it if I took some money out of my savings account.

"Yes. Ann couldn't resist trying it on. It's very pretty."

"Calvin also mentioned some kitchen towels decorated with snowmen."

She nodded. "One of the women in town made them. She just brought in a matching washcloth this morning. Would you like to see them?"

"Yes."

She led me to an aisle filled with various kitchen cloths and decorations. I didn't know a woman could do so much for a kitchen. She held up the complete set of items. "They look like friendly snowmen. Mrs. Grant always does a lovely job."

Again, I checked the price tags.

"You can get the entire set for half price," she said.

I blinked in surprise.

"Your wife does more than her share to help me whenever I need someone to fill in for me. I tried to give her this set at the discounted price, but she wouldn't take it. I hope you will."

"Is there anything else you think I should give her?" It seemed that Calvin and Mrs. Coley knew Ann better than I did.

"There is something a woman always likes but never tells a man she wants. I'm not saying that Ann has ever told me this. It's just something I know a woman likes since I am a woman." She handed me a card that had a red rose painted on it. The edge of the card was covered with dark pink lace. "My suggestion, and you don't have to take it if you don't want to, is to write one thing you appreciate about her and set this card with the snowmen cloth set on the kitchen table after she goes to bed tonight. I always like surprises, and Ann seems to like them too."

"Thank you, Mrs. Coley. I'll take them."

She nodded. "Barbara told me that Ann is sick. When do you think Ann will be able to come back to help me?"

I wondered what she meant by 'helping' her but decided I would ask Ann later. "She's almost better now. I'll let you know what she tells me."

After I purchased the items, I walked down the main street. It felt odd carrying a bag full of items that only a woman would want, but John had mentioned that Mr. Fields was looking for help with fixing some tractors. "He's only looking for someone to work until spring, and I mentioned your name to him. He said he would be interested in talking to you," he had told me.

Mr. Fields' Tractor store wasn't too far from the mercantile, so I didn't have far to walk. I ignored the looks several people threw my way. I knew it would take time for the gossip to die down. It didn't bother me since the people I cared about knew I was innocent. I entered Mr. Fields' store.

One of his grown sons came out from the backroom as soon as he heard the front bell ring on the door. "Good morning, Mr. Brothers. Mr. Russell said we should expect you to come by today." He shook my hand.

"Good morning," I returned, surprised by his warm welcome.

I had expected there to be some hesitation on his part, given my sudden reputation in town.

"I'll tell my father you're here." He motioned to the room on my right. "Have a seat in his office."

"You trust me?" I tried not to sound guilty as I said it.

"You're a friend of John Russell. That's good enough for us."

I nodded and went to the office. No one was in it. It was small but comfortable. There were two wooden chairs in front of a small wooden desk. A wooden chair behind the desk had been pushed back, so apparently, Mr. Fields had been sitting there earlier and had to leave in a hurry. There were stacks of orders for tractor parts neatly piled on the desk next to a cup holding pencils. Mr. Fields was a neater person than Mr. Richard was. I set the bag down next to me and sat in one of the chairs. I adjusted my tie so it didn't feel so tight around my neck. On the wall was a calendar with appointments written on it.

"Sorry to keep you waiting," Mr. Fields said as he entered the office.

I quickly stood up and shook his hand. I liked him right away. He was in his 50s but seemed younger. "Hello, Mr. Fields. I wasn't here long."

"So, John tells me you are looking for work and would prefer something that involves farming," he stated. He sat on the edge of his desk.

I sat back down in the chair. "Yes, that's right. I plan to start farming next spring."

"You bought Mr. Martin's old place?"

I nodded. "He left it in excellent condition."

"He was a good man. He still is, I suppose. He moved to Fargo to be near his grown children. I believe he was good friends with Robert and Patricia Dawson. He mentioned that you were a good friend of their nephew. Alex. Isn't that his name?"

"Yes. We grew up together in Virginia."

"What made you decide to leave?"

"Alex's relatives used to visit and I would listen to them tell stories about farming out West. They brought books that I looked forward to reading, and I used to bother Alex to get pictures for me. It just felt like something I was meant to do."

He smiled. "When can you start?"

I blinked. "Aren't you going to ask me if I have any experience?"

"Do you have a desire to farm?"

"Yes."

"Do you think you'll need a tractor?"

"Yes."

"Do you want to learn how to build and repair a tractor?"

"Yes."

"Then that's all you need. Desire is more important than experience. My sons and I will teach you everything you need to know. According to John, you can't get enough of hearing him discuss farming."

"Yes. I must be a pest with all my questions."

"Nonsense. You're passionate about what you want to do. Passion is what makes a good employee. You'll have to lose the suit though. Working with machines is dirty work. Can you start today?"

I had told Ann I was going to an interview with Mr. Fields and would be back as soon as it was done, but I didn't think she would mind if I stayed longer than I had planned, especially when I told her I got the job. "I can," I replied.

"Great. We have a huge order due by Friday. You came at the right time. You can borrow a pair of my work clothes today and then wear suitable clothes tomorrow."

I nodded, excited and grateful.

***

The next morning before Ann woke up, I set the snowmen kitchen gift set on the table. I hesitated when it came time for me to write something in the card Mrs. Coley gave me. Finally, I wrote, "I greatly appreciate your support and care for me. Your worth is above rubies. Yours, Todd."

I didn't usually leave before she woke up, but I wished to surprise her with the present. I didn't realize how good it would feel to give her something. I enjoyed giving her dresses, but this was different. It was something she would never have guessed I thought to give her. Thanks to Calvin, of course. I would have to give him a piece of candy next time I saw him. I was looking forward to Christmas so I could give Ann her wedding ring. I really wanted to get her something to mark the beginning of our life together.

I washed up as well as I could before I returned home. I wasn't sure what to expect. I walked through the back door and hung my coat and hat on the hook. I took my boots off. The house smelled of freshly baked cake. I grinned. She only made cake when she was in a good mood.

I turned to face the kitchen and saw that she was waiting for me. She was only a few steps away, and she was smiling.

"I got your message and the gift," she quietly said. "Thank you."

"You're welcome."

She walked up to me and hugged me.

I hugged her back, enjoying the feel of her in my arms. I kissed the top of her head. She smelled like lavender. I reached up and lightly touched her silky strands which she let fall down her shoulders in gentle waves. Did she wear her hair down for me? I liked thinking she did. My hand descended to the side of her face. Would she mind if I touched her? I hesitated to do so but since she hadn't backed away, I let my fingers brush her cheek.

"Your skin is soft," I whispered.

She stepped back and ran her hands up my arms. "You have gotten stronger out here. It must be all that time you chop wood." She reached up and caressed my cheek. "I'm glad you shave. I like the feel of your face."

My heart pounded as I looked into her eyes. I didn't know what to do so I stood still and waited for her to make the next move. I promised her I would wait for her to be ready, and she said she would let me know when she was. I was shocked and pleased when she kissed me. It was longer than the kiss she gave me before.

When the kiss ended, she cleared her throat. "I made steak and potatoes for dinner and cake for dessert. They're ready."

I was so happy that she kissed me that it didn't bother me that she didn't want to do more. It occurred to me that she was opening up to me and that knowledge was enough to satisfy me.

Chapter Fourteen
Ann's Point of View

When I returned to working for the Coleys the next day, some additional gossip regarding Todd had spread through the town. No one came to me directly, but they talked freely in the mercantile as I checked the inventory in the back. I heard various comments such as, "Mr. Fields better watch his money," and "That Todd Brothers should be forced to leave town," and "If Mr. Richard wasn't such a forgiving Christian, he would have had Todd arrested". As many people as there were to discredit Todd, there were those who stood up for him. They said that if the Russells and Coleys said he was innocent, then that was all the proof they needed.

That night, I sat on the couch in front of the warm, cozy fire as Todd got out a book to read. When he sat next to me, I couldn't help but notice he sat close enough to me so that our shoulders touched. My heart pounded with an unexpected excitement. I didn't know when things had changed between us, but I found that I looked forward to being with him. It wasn't that I didn't enjoy being with him since we married, because I did. But something was different. I wanted to explore the physical side of out relationship.

After he finished reading, he put his arm around my shoulders, and in response, I snuggled up to him.

"Ann?" he whispered, as if afraid to break the silence.

"Yes?"

He hesitated.

Curious, I sat up so I could look at him. Part of me was relieved to see that he was as nervous as I was about consummating our marriage, but another part of me found his blushing very flattering. Hoping to encourage him, I smiled and reached for his hand. "What is it?" I gently pressed.

His eyes held mine and I could feel his love flow into me. "I love you."

Before I could respond, someone knocked on the front door.

Startled, I jerked away from him.

"Who would be coming here this late?" he grumbled as he stood up.

I was just as disappointed as he was but worried someone might be in trouble. Was one of our friends sick? I jumped up and followed him.

I laughed when he opened the door. "Agnes! What are you doing here? How did you find us? How did you get here? Is anyone else with you? Why didn't you write? Oh, it's so good to see you!" I hugged her.

Todd chuckled as he waved her inside. "Give her a chance to come in before barging at her with all those questions. This is a pleasant surprise."

Once he brought her carpetbag in, she sat in front of the fireplace. I insisted that she tell us everything.

Todd, who realized how much I missed Agnes, took the bag up to the third bedroom and started a fire in the box stove.

Meanwhile, Agnes told me all about her journey. "I signed up for a three week retreat to New England, but I came here instead. I can figure out how to be a proper lady in social situations any old time, but I don't get a chance to see my closest friend anymore. As soon as several of my lady classmates left for New England, I hopped a train and headed out West. Your parents were gracious enough to give me your address, though they assumed I wanted to write you a letter."

"Do your parents know where you are?" I whispered so Todd wouldn't hear me.

Agnes understood my reason for the secrecy. "They don't approve of what he did at all. We can't even talk about him."

"Surely, they will come around. He is their only son."

She shook her head. "My father feels betrayed. Family loyalty is everything to him. Todd was supposed to work at the bank, but he's out here farming. My father is very strict about duty and obligation. My mother, however, is in tears most of the time. She misses Todd but can't do anything about it. My father makes the decisions for the family."

"That's awful." How was Todd going to take this news?

Agnes proceeded to tell me all the details of her train trip, especially regarding the people she sat next to. One elderly couple was also going to North Dakota, so she joined them for the most of the trip.

"Weren't you scared to travel alone?" I asked.

"I was but I figured if I stayed around other people the entire time, I would be safe. And it worked!"

As she rambled on about her journey, my thoughts drifted to Todd. Was he giving us time alone to talk? I marveled that I should wish for him to be near me after trying to avoid him all the other times Agnes and I talked.

"This woman had so many feathers on her hat, I wondered if she was imitating a peacock," Agnes continued. "Oh, that hat was gorgeous, just like the male of the species. I told her so. I think she was offended at first, but when I assured her that I meant her no ridicule but considered the hat to be one of the most beautifully decorated I had ever seen, she became amiable toward me."

Todd brought us a cup of hot cocoa. He sat across from us. I hid my disappointment. I had some room next to me on the couch even though I sat next to Agnes. There was a time I dreaded his closeness, but I couldn't seem to recall why.

"Agnes, are you going to let anyone else talk?" Todd asked. "Yours is the only voice I've heard since you got here."

"For your information, she wants to know all about my trip, right Ann?" Without waiting for me to respond, she described her strange encounter with an old lady who confused her cat with her dog. "She was the best part of the trip though. She was so funny."

"You should have told us you were coming. We would have gone to town to meet you."

"Oh, the stage coach driver didn't mind when I offered him extra money to bring me here. Besides, the looks on your faces were worth it. I wish I had a picture of that moment." She giggled and then sighed. "It is beautiful out here. I can see why you wanted to come here. Alex's pictures didn't do this land justice."

After a moment of silence, I turned to her. "I missed talking to you. So much has happened. It seems like it was only yesterday when we arrived, but I have a year's worth of stories to tell you. I'm sure Todd has a lot he wants to tell you too."

He stood up and collected our empty cups. "What I have to say can wait. I'd better get some sleep so I can wake up for work."

We thanked him.

"Don't bother getting up early for me tomorrow. I'll get breakfast in town," he told me.

I smiled at him. "Thank you. I appreciate it." He was so good to me.

He returned my smile. To Agnes, he said, "I'll talk to you when I get home from work."

She grinned. "I can't wait."

Once he was upstairs, she squealed with delight. "He adores you more now than before you got married! I knew you were perfect for each other. To be honest, I was thrilled when my parents discovered his letter announcing his marriage to you and your quick departure to the West. It was so romantic."

I blushed. Maybe it had been romantic. "Have you found a beau yet?" I wondered.

"Oh, there's no one worthwhile. I don't want to settle for second best."

"You shouldn't have to," I agreed. "You don't want to be with someone who doesn't treat you well."

"I won't." She hesitated for a moment before giving me a sly smile. "So... When am I going to be an aunt?"

I had a funny feeling that my parents would be asking me when they would be grandparents. I bit my lower lip. She had been my friend since childhood, and if there was anyone I could confide in, it was her. I explained how I wasn't ready to engage in marital relations on my wedding night since I was still in love with Kent at the time, and I added that Todd was waiting until I was ready.

She shook her head. "My brother has an abundance of patience." Then she looked at me with a question in her eyes. "What about Kent?"

"I haven't thought of him for at least a month."

"Maybe I should rephrase my inquiry. If Kent were to show up and ask you to annul your marriage to Todd so you could run off with him, would you?"

"Annul my marriage?"

"You haven't consummated it yet so it permissible, not that I'm recommending that."

Feeling uneasy, I shifted on the couch and asked, "Is there something you're not telling me?"

She sighed heavily, as if the weight of the world rested on her shoulders. "You might as well know. Kent broke off his engagement to Rebecca. I don't know why he asked her to marry him in the first place. And I don't care why they're not together. You and Todd are what I care about. Kent kept asking me about you, especially where you are living. I refused to tell him anything, but I think he found out from someone else. That's why I wanted to know how you feel about him. He could arrive any day now. I just wanted to warn you."

I stared at the fire.

"Ann, what are you thinking?" She tugged the sleeve on my dress. "Ann, please speak to me."

"I have to be alone to sort things out," I calmly replied. The truth was, I didn't know want to think. Kent still wanted me? He didn't want Rebecca after all? I stood up. "I'll show you to your bedroom."

"Promise me you won't do anything rash!" she anxiously whispered.

I purposely ignored her because I was afraid of what I might say.

She mutely followed me, her head hung low. I knew that she figured she had said enough already.

I didn't get undressed when I closed my bedroom door. I sat on my bed and stared at the box stove. Todd faithfully started a fire in it every evening so my room would be warm by the time I went to bed.

Agnes' words haunted me.

"Kent kept asking about you..."

But Todd takes good care of you. He would never hurt you the way Kent did.

Kent was coming for me. What would I do?

I blindly stared into the box stove, willing my feelings away.

Do you love Todd?

Kent's image blocked any rational response to that simple question.

Oh God, I don't want to feel this way. Why am I pleased that Kent is coming?

***

By morning, I couldn't bring myself to face Todd, even though I was wide awake and could make him breakfast. I heard him moving around in the next bedroom. He was getting dressed for work. I wondered what he looked like as he got dressed in his cotton shirts and denim pants. I turned over in my bed and caught sight of my dresses hanging in the wardrobe. They weren't as fancy as the ones my parents bought me, but he worked hard for them. He wanted to give me nice things. I sighed heavily and squeezed my eyes shut to force the tears away.

When he left for work, I got out of bed. I needed to put Todd and Kent far from my mind. That meant I had to keep myself busy. I finished some light housework by the time a yawning and sleepy Agnes came down the stairs in a pink dress. My body relaxed at her familiar face.

"What would you like to eat for breakfast?" I asked as I took out a skillet.

"You cook? I mean, you know how?" She shook her head as she walked over to me. "Is it hard?"

I laughed, recalling my uneasiness when I started cooking. "It's a lot easier than it looks. I'll teach you. What would you like to eat?"

"Can you make French toast?"

"Sure. Todd eats that all the time." I paused for a moment as I realized I had mentioned him. I hoped she wouldn't ask me about Kent. Fortunately, she didn't. I breathed a sigh of relief. "First, we need some bread," I began and turned my attention to the meal.

After breakfast, I introduced her to Barbara and the children. "We didn't even know she was coming, but we're glad she did," I said. "Barbara has been my friend and mentor. She's the one who taught me to cook and take care of children."

It was exciting for me to be with both of them at the same time. I did most of the talking on the way to town in Barbara's carryall.

After Barbara dropped us off at the mercantile, Agnes looked around the town. "This place is small. Don't you miss the entertainment in Virginia? There doesn't seem to be anything to do around here."

"At first, I was dismayed at the small population, but now I'm familiar with most of the people here. It's cozy."

"Hmm... I don't know. I feel trapped."

"Yes, I suppose you aren't meant for the small town life." That's when I realized that we were different. I had assumed we shared all the same interests while we were growing up.

We entered the mercantile and I introduced her to the Coleys who were as friendly and generous to her as they had been to me when I first met them. I smiled at her startled expression. She wasn't used to such welcoming introductions, but she quickly began talking to them as if she had known them her entire life. I happily did my work while they shared stories.

Everyone I introduced her to seemed to enjoy her. Everyone, that is, except for Barbara. I didn't notice Barbara's discomfort right away. On our way back home, Agnes did most of the talking.

"And little Becky got so mad at Sam for putting a bug in her hair that she punched him out. He was unconscious for five minutes." Agnes giggled. "I'm sorry, Ann, but this makes the time Todd and Alex threw pebbles in your hair look like child's play. But anyway, I don't think Mrs. Bore appreciated Becky's action. Not that Mrs. Bore's ever had a sense of humor about anything, although I do believe she smiled once during a Shakespearean comedy."

"Mrs. *Byron* has a sense of humor," I argued. "You were too busy acting up to notice."

"Oh, I was a perfect eight year old. Mrs. *Bore* never appreciated my enthusiasm."

The children giggled as they played a word game. Barbara remained silent. I wondered why.

"I couldn't believe it when Rhoda decided to let Jeff court her. He's completely dull," Agnes continued. "Why he can't even-"

I stopped her. "Agnes, it's wrong to gossip." I used to enjoy these conversations but now I found gossip irritating. Who knew how many people got hurt because of careless talk?

She pouted. "You sound like Todd." Then her eyes lit up. "That's wonderful! You must be getting close to him after all!"

I sent her a "be quiet" look.

Agnes understood and started talking about the latest book she read. Agnes was always good about reading my signals. But even as we said good-bye to Barbara and her children, I couldn't figure out what was wrong with Barbara.

Chapter Fifteen
Ann's Point of View

The next day, I decided Agnes and I should spend some time with Barbara and her children. I knocked on Barbara's front door. Calvin answered it, Bruce and Molly in tow.

I smiled at them. "Hello!" I surprised them with some chocolate candy that Mrs. Coley gave me.

They squealed in delight and thanked me.

"Ann, is that you?" Barbara called out from her kitchen.

The smell of freshly baked cookies filled the air.

"Yes, it's me," I called out. "Do you need a hand?"

"Actually, I could use some help. Calvin and Bruce, I want you to clean your room. Molly, come into the kitchen."

Agnes and I followed Molly to the kitchen, amused at the way Molly's blond curls bounced as she ran.

Barbara's smile seemed forced as soon as she saw Agnes and me. I assumed she was worried about trying to get her children to clean their room while trying to cook.

"Ma, Mrs. Brothers gave me candy!" Molly exclaimed, jumping up and down.

"That's nice. Did you thank her and Agnes?" Barbara asked.

"They all did," I replied. "So, what can I do to help?"

"And what can I do? Give me an easy task though. I'm not used to this," Agnes added.

"Well," Barbara began as she looked around the kitchen, "I could use some help putting the cookie dough on the tray. I also need to decorate the ones that are done."

I stared at her, suddenly wondering if something was wrong.

Agnes asked me how to bake cookies. I spent most of my time teaching her, so I didn't have a chance to ask Barbara if something was bothering her. As the afternoon progressed, we sat in the parlor. The children played a game of hide and seek around the house. Agnes did most of the talking. Whenever I attempted to bring Barbara into the conversation, she usually gave one answered replies like, "yes," "no," or just shrugged.

I became irritated at her lack of participation, and after awhile, I ignored her. I figured if she was going to be cold, I could be cold too. At one point, the silence grew so thick that Agnes recommended she and I leave so she could send a telegram to her parents. It was a lie, but I appreciated the excuse to leave. Barbara seemed happy to let us go, which I sourly noted. I said a cool good-bye and left.

***

That night, I was in a bad mood. The good thing about being angry at your friend is that you didn't have time to feel guilty for remembering the good times with your past beau. I tried not to show my anger to Todd or Agnes, but they knew me well enough to know that something was wrong.

They decided not to irritate me further by asking me questions, which was good because I didn't feel like talking to anyone. I made dinner in silence. I ate dinner in silence. I cleaned the dishes in silence. I didn't care about the tension in the house. Todd and Agnes briefly made idle conversation at the dinner table. They glanced at me, uncertain if I would get more upset by a comment they made. I just chewed the food mechanically, lost in my thoughts. Soon, they gave up their efforts and finished their meal in silence.

Agnes decided to go to bed early, and Todd decided to get some firewood. Meanwhile, I cleaned the dishes. What was Barbara's problem anyway? I tried to be nice to her and introduce her to my childhood friend. And how did she repay me? She rejected me. It was if she resented what I was trying to do.

"We'll see if I ever do anything nice for her again," I muttered sourly.

"Did you say something?" Todd asked as he set some firewood by the stove.

I jumped. I didn't hear him enter the kitchen. Some of my anger subsided. "I was just talking to myself," I replied.

He put his hands on his hips and studied me, as if debating whether or not to say anything.

I finished the last plate and set it on a towel to dry.

"Do you want to talk about it?" he asked.

I stood still for a moment. Was he referring to Kent? Did Agnes tell him? Or was he referring to my bad mood today? Realizing that Agnes wouldn't tell him about Kent, I relaxed. Taking a deep breath, I explained the events that had transpired at Barbara's house.

Once I finished, Todd nodded. "That is upsetting."

"And it hurts too," I quietly admitted. I sighed, my anger drained. "The afternoon started out perfectly. Agnes and I wanted to help her make cookies. I thought she might like to speak with Agnes and get to know her. If I had known that wasn't the case, I wouldn't have gone over there."

"Maybe she needs time to think things through. There's got to be a reason for what happened."

"I don't care what the reason is. She had no excuse for treating me that way. It was as if I was inconveniencing her." I shook my head. "I'm just going to forget it. She's not worth the effort if she's going to be childish."

I didn't wait for him to respond. I wanted to be alone, so I went to my bedroom. Thoughts of her, Todd, and North Dakota swirled through my mind. Did I make a mistake in coming here? Maybe I should have stayed in Virginia. If I had stayed, I'd probably be with Kent. I stared out the window. It was a clear night. The kind of night that should have brought peace instead of inner turmoil.

I knew I needed to pray. I also knew I shouldn't be wanting Kent when I was married to Todd. I made a vow before God to love, honor and obey Todd for the rest of my life. My thoughts sobered. I had been so concerned about what I wanted that I hadn't bothered to think of what God wanted me to do.

Startled at the revelation, I got down on my knees beside my bed and prayed. As I prayed, I held nothing back. I confessed all my thoughts about Kent and how I was hurt when he ended our courtship. I also admitted that I married Todd to get out of a situation that I didn't want to be in. I had used Todd. He didn't deserve it, even if he knew what my feelings toward him were. I wasn't being faithful to him when I considered the possibility of leaving with Kent.

In that instant, I realized that love wasn't a feeling. It was a choice. I didn't have to be at the mercy of my whims. I had freewill. I could choose to love Todd. There was certainly nothing repulsive about him. In fact, he was absolutely wonderful. He treated me much better than Kent ever had. And he was handsome. So there wasn't any reason I shouldn't desire him. There was no reason why I couldn't love him.

I also prayed about the situation with Barbara and what to do about it. I prayed for Agnes and what she might encounter when she faced her parents who were bound to find out she came to visit me and Todd rather than go on a class trip to New England. I prayed that Todd's parents would bring him back into their hearts. Then I recalled all the good things Todd had done for me and how much he loved me. My last thought was that I loved him before I fell asleep on the floor.

***

When I woke up, my body felt stiff but my heart was light. I eagerly got dressed and hopped down the stairs. I couldn't wait to see Todd. I was ready to finally put Kent behind me and start my life as Todd's wife.

To my surprise, I saw Agnes making French toast.

"Good morning," I greeted.

She grinned at me. "Look who's cooking! I didn't want to wake you so I dared to explore the great unknown."

"That's very brave."

"Do you want some?"

I pretended to think about it. "Will I have to be brave to eat it?"

She rolled her eyes at my joke. "Who knows? It may be better than what you make."

"Then I better have some. Did Todd go to work?"

"Yes."

I sat down. He didn't usually leave this early. I thanked her as she handed me the plate of food. After taking a bite, I said, "This is good!"

"Thanks. Are you feeling better?"

I nodded. "Much better. I'm sorry I was inhospitable yesterday. My parents would faint if they knew how I behaved."

"You had a lot on your mind."

I knew she meant Kent. "Agnes, I have something to tell you. I did a lot of thinking last night, and I recalled how good Todd has been to me. I'm not going to leave him."

She looked relieved. "I was scared for awhile there."

"You really wanted us to be together for a long time, didn't you?"

"I just thought you two made a good couple. Besides, it's nice to have you as a sister."

She set the plate down and we ate in a comfortable silence.

***

Since the weather was nice, Agnes and I decided to go into town so she could do some shopping. It felt good to go shopping with the small amount of money I had saved up for Todd's Christmas gift. Agnes had her allowance to spend, and she insisted on buying things from North Dakota.

"I miss shopping with you," I said as we entered the barn.

"I do too. It just isn't the same without you."

I wiped a tear from my eye and focused on getting the buggy ready. When we got everything set up, I realized I also missed my trips to town with Barbara. I pushed aside the ache in my heart and urged the horses forward. The air was brisk but felt good. The ride into town seemed longer that day for some reason.

"Who's that?" Agnes interrupted my thoughts by pointing to the side of the road.

I glanced at the direction she indicated. I didn't hide my surprise. What was Mrs. Carson doing out here without her horse? She was all by herself and an abandoned buggy.

An instant surge of gratification swept over me. It served her right to have to walk to town after all the gossiping she did about Todd. I was ready to ride past her when a question popped into my head. *What if it was you?*

I sighed. It took all of my energy to stop and call her name.

She turned around. I saw that a wheel on her buggy had fallen off.

"What happened?" Agnes asked for me.

Mrs. Carson choked back her sobs as she spoke. "The wheel came off and the horse ran off. I don't know how he got away but he did. And I-I…can't believe it. He just ran off."

I glanced in the direction she motioned to. He went south. Suddenly, I felt compassion for her. She was cold and afraid out here all by herself.

"Can we take you to town?" I offered. "I know where your husband works."

She agreed and we helped her into the buggy. It was meant for two people so we squeezed in together. We gave her some blankets so she could warm up.

"Thank you," she softly replied, still fighting back her tears.

"We're heading into town anyway," I replied.

The rest of the ride was quiet. I supposed Mrs. Carson was as uncomfortable around me as I was around her. I didn't know what to say to her, and even Agnes was at loss for words. We all breathed a sigh of relief when we arrived in town. The trip had been difficult for all of us.

"Is your husband at lunch?" I asked.

She took note of the time on the clock in front of the bank. "No. He will still be at work."

I nodded and urged the horses to trot until we stopped in front of the small building between the library and the church.

"Thank you, Mrs. Brothers," she quietly replied.

Her humbled expression softened my hard heart. "You're welcome."

She got out of the buggy and ran into the post office.

I lightly clicked the reins on the horses so that they took Agnes and me to the mercantile. Before I set the brake, Agnes put her hand on my arm.

"What's wrong?" I asked.

"I've been doing a lot of thinking, and I think I know why Barbara has been reserved with you."

Curious, I waited for her to continue.

"She was acting fine until I showed up. I am guessing you two are close friends?"

I nodded.

"I think she's afraid that since I'm here, there's no place for her in your life."

My eyes widened. Could it be true? "Oh, that's silly! I can have both of you for my friends."

She smiled. "Of course, you can. But you and I shared our childhood together. I'm now your sister-in-law, and we have so much in common. She probably feels like she doesn't belong with us when we're together."

I hadn't considered that possibly.

"Anyway, I notice she's in town today. Why don't I do your job at the Coleys while you talk to her?" She pointed to the doctor's office across the street. "I'm sure you two will work things out."

I knew the Coleys would be fine if Agnes took my place for the day. I agreed and we parted. I took a deep breath as I walked to the doctor's office. I didn't want to lose Barbara's friendship. Though she was dramatically different from my childhood friend, I valued her just as much. I slowly opened the door.

"Mrs. Brothers!"

I immediately grinned as three little children came running over to hug me. Calvin, Bruce and Molly were excited to see me. I hugged them back, delighted by their warm welcome. I glanced up and saw Barbara say good-bye to the doctor who returned to the backroom in the small building. I hesitated for a moment but decided our friendship was too important to worry about rejection.

"How are you today, Barbara?" I asked. I stood up and walked over to her, her children on my heels.

She smiled. "Actually, I'm great. I just found out I'm in the family way."

"That's wonderful!" I hugged her. "Is that why you're here?"

She nodded. "I kept thinking I had the flu, but John insisted I come here to see if it was something else. It turns out he was right."

I frowned. "Why did you think you had the flu?"

"I feel sick all the time and I don't have my usual energy."

"Is that common when a woman's expecting?"

"With most women, it is. Didn't your mother discuss such things with you?"

I shook my head. "I don't know my real mother. My parents adopted me. They weren't able to have children."

"Oh. I'm sorry."

"You didn't know. I didn't have anyone to tell me about expecting. The teachers were too busy making sure we knew how to act at a dinner party or decorate a house. I learned how to read and write and do math though, so it wasn't a total waste of my time."

She considered my words. "If you were in the family way, would you know?"

I blushed. I knew how babies were conceived. At least, I wasn't that ignorant! Even young ladies discussed those details when no adults were listening. "I know I'm not in the family way. I still menstruate."

"Would you like me to tell you what the common symptoms are? Perhaps soon you will feel ill and figure out it's not an illness."

Her kind grin brought relief to me. It was as if nothing was wrong. Still, I knew I had to smooth things out. "Yes, I do need to know that," I admitted. "First though, I would like to discuss a matter that has been troubling me. Could we sit down?"

She seemed uncertain but followed me to a seat in the office.

"Agnes said you might be feeling ignored since she's come to visit," I finally ventured. "Is that true?"

She glanced at the floor and sighed. "It's childish. I know you had friends back in Virginia."

So Agnes had been right. I was glad that was all that was bothering her. "Barbara, I am thankful that we are friends. You are like a sister to me. It's true that Agnes and I grew up together, but she can't take your place. You are both important to me."

Her eyes met mine and she smiled widely. "I was foolish. I wanted to say something but didn't when she was around, and the longer I waited to say anything, the harder it became. I'm sorry, Ann. I should have told you right away."

"I didn't give you much of a chance. I'm sorry too."

We hugged.

I was glad things were back to normal.

"You must bring Agnes by again. I'll have to treat her better this time," she promised.

"Oh no. You are with child. You don't need to go to any trouble for us. Why don't you and your family come over for dinner tonight? That is, if you feel up to eating."

She laughed. "I may not eat much, but we would love to come over."

"I'm excited for you. Another baby! John will be thrilled."

"Yes. He wants at least seven children. You're good with children. Wouldn't it be wonderful if you were expecting soon so our children will be close in age?"

I didn't know what to say, so I nodded. My goodness! What would Todd think of this conversation? Ignoring my pounding heart, I said good-bye and left. I went to the mercantile and helped Agnes with the rest of my usual chores. After we were done, we went home so I could get dinner started.

Agnes insisted on helping me. "I want to learn more about cooking. Who knows if I'll ever need to know this? I might end up marrying a man whose grand dream is farming."

I laughed. "The chances of that happening where you live are slim." I stopped peeling a potato and looked at her. "Do you wish to stay in Virginia?"

"Yes. I do like visiting here, but my heart will always be back there."

"Then you'll probably marry someone from a wealthy family. Do you have your sights set on anyone?"

She shrugged. "Not really."

"You must be disappointing many young men. You have a way of attracting them."

"I know. Maybe that's why I don't feel rushed to make a decision. I just haven't found the right one yet."

"The important thing is how he treats you. Todd actually cares about what I want and what I think."

"I hope you remember that when Kent shows up."

"I don't understand why he would bother. He knows I'm married."

"And that doesn't matter to him. I don't know why he proposed to Rebecca in the first place, but for some reason he did."

She poured water into the pot as I added the peeled potatoes into it.

She sighed thoughtfully. "Do you love Todd?"

"Yes. But what I feel for him is different than what I feel for Kent. Well, I should say 'what I felt for Kent.' I'm over him now."

"Just when you think you're over the past, it comes back to haunt you."

"No. I won't let it. I made my decision the day I married Todd. I promised to forsake all others as long as he lived."

She still seemed uncertain but nodded and silently turned to the salad we were going to make. That was when I made my decision. I would consummate my marriage with Todd that night.

Chapter Sixteen
Todd's Point of View

After John, Barbara and their children went home, Agnes, Ann and I stood in the living room. I assumed we were going to sit and talk, but Agnes said she wanted to go to bed early.

"What a lovely day," she said. "I do confess that those children wore me out. I don't know how Barbara does it all day with them! You farmer's wives have too much work to do. I have to admit that I like to be spoiled. I would rather have the servants' help, but this certainly is a nice place to visit."

"It's really not that difficult once you get used to it," Ann assured her. "It's nice to have some privacy. When I had servants, I couldn't even sneeze without someone handing me a handkerchief."

I smiled. "I suppose there are benefits to both worlds. I'm glad you ventured out here."

Ann nodded. "I am too. Thank you for coming."

I turned to Ann after Agnes went up to her bedroom. "That's odd. I thought she'd want to stay up for two more hours. Usually, I can't get her to stop talking. Life certainly isn't boring when she's around."

"Oh?"

"You know what I mean." I grinned to show her I was joking. Life was definitely not boring with Ann. I motioned to the couch. "Would you like to stay up and talk?"

She hesitated. "Actually, I was thinking of going to bed."

"Oh." I had hoped we could sit together and talk. Perhaps, more would come of it. Even if it didn't, it would still be nice to be with her. "Are you going to wake up early tomorrow? Ever since Agnes got here, we haven't had much time alone. I guess I got used to it just being us."

She didn't reply right away, which surprised me since she didn't usually take long to answer my questions. When she did respond, I wasn't expecting her reply. "Would you like to come with me?"

I nearly bolted for her bedroom but I forced myself to stand still. "Are you saying that you're ready?" I wanted to be sure I understood her.

She nodded.

As much as I wanted to forget my nightly chore, I knew we would all be cold by morning if I didn't do it. "I'll gather enough firewood for the night and bring it to your room. I should take some to Agnes too."

"Then I'll be waiting for you."

I watched as she walked up the steps. I was so excited that I quickly slipped on my shoes and grabbed my coat. I threw open the back door and ran out to the barn to collect enough wood for the night. When I came back into the house, I hastily took off my coat. I would put it on the hook later. I didn't bother to take my shoes off. Instead I climbed the stairs and took a deep breath. I knocked on Agnes' bedroom door. I couldn't forget to give her some firewood.

Agnes opened her door. I noted that she was still in her dress.

"I brought you some firewood for the night. Would you like me to put a piece in the box stove?" I offered.

"Alright," she agreed and moved aside so I could bring in the wood.

I knelt by the box stove and inserted a piece of wood into it. I glanced over at her bed and noticed she was reading a book. "I thought you were tired."

"Oh. Not really. I just wanted to give you and Ann some time alone. I know I tend to dominate the conversation whenever I'm around. After all, my great gift in life is talking."

I smiled at her as I stood up. "That's thoughtful of you."

She gave me a quick hug. "She does love you, even though she won't come out and say it. We did a lot of talking and she likes being with you. You're a lot better than Kent ever was."

I thought her words were odd but accepted them. "I hope you enjoy the book."

She nodded and sat on her bed.

I quietly shut the door behind me and walked past my room. It felt good not to have to sleep in there tonight. By the time I reached Ann's door, I realized my hands were shaking. Now that the moment was here, I was more nervous than excited. I loved her so much. I hoped she would enjoy the night as much as I knew I would.

I tapped on her door.

"Come in," she softly replied.

I had a hard time making eye contact with her as I entered the room. I laid the stack of chopped wood beside the box stove. Since the fire was low, I added two more pieces of wood to the fire. I slowly stood up and turned around. I frowned. She had her eyes closed.

"Are you asleep?" I whispered. I really didn't want to return to my room but couldn't bring myself to wake her.

Her eyelids flew open.

"I'm sorry. I didn't mean to scare you." I smiled, relieved she was still awake. I sat next to her. "Are you sure you want to do this?"

"Yes. Do you?"

Yes! "More than you know, though I didn't think I'd be this nervous when the time came," I admitted.

She looked relieved. "Thank goodness. I thought I was the only one who was nervous."

I chuckled, glad she felt the same way I did.

I took off my shoes and slipped under the covers. She moved closer to me. I loved the feel of her in my arms. I hugged her close to me. My heart pounded with joy and anticipation. We remained silent for a long time. I wanted to enjoy the moment, but my desire to do more was steadily increasing.

I kissed the top of her head. I loved the smell of her soft hair. She lifted her head off of my chest. She was so beautiful. I gladly gave into the urge to kiss her since now I knew I could. She responded to my kiss with a passion that surprised and delighted me. She wanted me as much as I wanted her. This knowledge only increased my arousal. Our kiss deepened and I took off my shirt as she settled back into the bed. Her hands felt incredibly sensual on my bare shoulders. I had often wondered how they would feel on my body, and it was better than I expected. My hands traveled from her hair to her breasts. She was amazingly soft. She was all woman and I was aware of how my body was responding to that fact. My lips hungrily made their way down her neck. I was desperately trying to go slow but my urgency for her was starting to consume me.

"Todd, wait. Agnes is at the door."

I stopped and looked up at her, not fully comprehending what she was saying. Did she want me to stop?

"Todd, our parents are here!" Agnes yelled from behind the closed door. "They're at the front door."

My reaction to my sister's announcement was immediate. I bolted out of the bed as if it were on fire. Of all things that could kill a mood, this ranked high on the list. I quickly picked up my shirt and buttoned it. After I put my shoes on, I remembered Ann. I turned to her. I didn't want to leave her, but I didn't feel like I had a choice. "I have to see them. I'm sorry."

"No, don't be sorry. I understand." Her eyes were wide with the same shock I was experiencing.

"It's probably best if you stay here, just in case things don't go well."

She nodded.

I sighed and left her room. I faced a startled Agnes. "You didn't open the front door?"

"Of course not. I don't wish to confront them on my own. They're bound to be furious with me. I came here against their will."

"You're not the only one," I grumbled as she followed me down the stairs. I didn't feel like seeing them. I wanted to be with Ann in her bedroom.

I opened the door and my parents rushed into the parlor.

My father's face was red with rage, but my mother was softly crying into a handkerchief. I braced myself for what he would say.

"Agnes, go out to the carriage," he ordered. "I need to talk to your brother."

"Let's not be hasty," our mother sobbed. "We don't need to make matters worse."

"Mother is right," Agnes quickly agreed. "Why don't we sit down and take a few moments to calm down?"

I thought this was a good idea.

My father shook his head. "I have had enough of this. I spent many days traveling here. The last thing I want to do is spend another minute in this...this…"--he looked around my house as if it were the most disgusting thing he ever saw--"place."

"May I remind you that this is my house?" I stated through gritted teeth. It took all of my willpower to not throw him out. *He is your father. Be careful what you say.*

"Such as it is." He turned to my mother. "Take Agnes out of here. What I have to say, I only have to say to him."

"I will have to pack my clothes first," Agnes angrily replied before she headed up the stairs.

"Please, go easy on him," Mother begged. "He has his reasons."

"It would be best for you stay out of this," he told her, his tone gentle. "I will not change my mind."

She gave me an "I'm sorry" look and followed Agnes to her bedroom.

I turned to him and crossed my arms. I didn't appreciate being treated like a little kid who got caught doing something wrong.

"I raised you better than this. You could have had the entire family fortune. As the only boy, it was your right. Your sisters will find men to care for them." He took a deep breath. "Look, I am willing to overlook your rebellion if you come home with me."

"I am not a boy anymore. I'm a man. This is my house. I found work I love and I plan to stay here. I don't need your money, but it would be nice if we could get along."

"You continue to reject me, your own father?"

"I am following God's leading for my life."

"And you're dragging poor Miss Statesman down with you. Do you think it's fair to make her suffer like this?"

I clenched my jaw. Why did he have to call Ann by her maiden name? It was bad enough that he refused to acknowledge my work. Couldn't he at least acknowledge my marriage? "Her name is Mrs. Brothers. We're married."

"Even so, the poor thing must suffer out here. There are no comforts."

"It is a tough life at times, but it's worth it. She chose to come with me. I didn't force her."

"She only came because of Kent and Rebecca. Do you honestly think she will stay once she finds out he wants her back?"

Time stood still for me in that moment. Kent wanted her back?

"Rumor has it he will be here any day. Save yourself the humiliation of losing her and return to Virginia. The only advantage Kent has over you is his economic status. I will hold a job for you at the bank."

It took me a couple of seconds to process his words. If he knew that Kent was coming, then Agnes knew too. And if Agnes knew...

"I'm staying here, and she will stay with me," I finally said, though my words seemed hollow to my ears. Would she really stay once she saw him again?

"We'll see about that," he snapped. "You are no longer my son. Agnes, you have no choice. You are not old enough to defy me yet. Stop eavesdropping and get down here right now."

Agnes and Mother obediently walked down the stairs. Agnes clutched the carpetbag to her chest.

As soon as Father left the house, Mother quickly hugged me. "Don't lose hope, Todd. Maybe one day he'll understand you did the right thing."

"Thank you, Mother," I softly replied, glad for her kind words.

Agnes gave me a quick hug but I didn't return it. "Be sure to tell Ann I said good-bye. I'll try to find a way to visit again."

"You should probably wait until you graduate from school. Then you will be an adult." I forced myself to stay calm despite my sudden anger at her. She knew that Kent was coming, and she told Ann but she didn't tell me.

"Of course. You warning is well-heeded."

After she left, I stood quietly in the parlor. Many emotions coursed through me. Disbelief, shock, love, doubt, fear, and finally…anger. That was why Ann had been distant from me the past couple of days. She wasn't aloof until Agnes showed up. So Agnes told her the night she arrived. I knew something was wrong.

I closed my eyes, willing my rage to die down. I hated Kent. I hated how inferior he made me feel. I could never compete with him. I was planning to ask Ann if I could court her when he stepped into the picture and took her from me, and he was about to take her away again. In that moment, my entire world caved in. Why didn't she tell me? What did she have to hide? The only reason she wouldn't tell me was because she was tempted to go back to him. The realization had a chilling effect on my heart.

I looked at her bedroom door, which was slightly open. She heard everything. I knew she did. Why wasn't she coming down to explain the situation with Kent? All she had to do was tell me, and then she could reassure me that she wouldn't go with him, that she would stay with me. After all, why would she plan to consummate our marriage if she had no intention of staying? I shook my head. I didn't know what to think.

I took a deep breath before I walked up the steps. I thought about leaving the house, but I knew I had to confront her first. I had to give her a chance to confess what had been bothering her. If she admitted it, then we could work through it. My heart raced as I softly knocked on her door.

"Come in."

I opened the door. She was standing by the bed in her robe. Did she look guilty?

"I suppose you heard all of that." It wasn't my intention to sound cold. *Give her a chance.* I crossed my arms, suddenly feeling vulnerable, and waited for her to say something.

She didn't say anything. She just pretended to be interested in the cord on her robe. Why wasn't she telling me Kent was coming?

"It actually went better than I expected," I said, wondering if beginning the conversation would help her to open up. "I knew my father wouldn't approve of what I did. My mother, however, did surprise me. I didn't anticipate her concern."

"Then that part is good news." She stood there, just looking at me and waiting for me to continue.

I couldn't believe it. After how close we'd gotten, she wasn't going to say it.

"You're going to make you ask it, aren't you?" I finally stated.

"If I had any idea of what you are referring to, it would help."

"Agnes keeps nothing from you, but she does have her share of secrets from me." My anger was quickly surfacing.

She stared at me as if she had no idea what I was talking about.

"I can't believe this. You are actually going to make me ask it."

"I have done nothing wrong, but you make me feel like I did."

I noted the anger in her voice.

My jaw tensed. "Agnes told you about Kent, didn't she? Surely, if my parents knew, then she did too."

Her eyes grew wide, as if she had just heard the news. "Yes, she told me. No, I haven't seen him nor do I plan to."

"Why didn't you tell me? Do you understand how this looks to me? It's like you're trying to hide your guilt."

"But I have done nothing wrong."

"Then why didn't you tell me?"

"What was the point? I don't plan to run off with him."

"Is there anything else you're hiding from me?" Did I really know her?

She gasped. "I don't appreciate being treated like a child. I have kept my vow to be faithful to you."

I forced myself to calm down before I said anything I would regret. "I'm sorry that you feel that way. I just want the truth. I thought you were beginning to love me. But after this news about Kent..." I shook my head. "I don't know what to think. To find out that you knew and didn't tell me makes me think I can't trust you. I have to wonder what other things I don't know about you."

"I can't believe this. I have opened my heart to you in a way I never did with him. You can rest assured that I have never done anything to harm you. What I do, I do to help. And since you must know every single detail of my life, I help the Coley's out at the store in town. I noticed you were pacing downstairs one night and realized you were having trouble with the finances, so I decided to do some cleaning, bookkeeping and inventory in exchange for some free food and cooking supplies. I still do it and will keep doing it. It gives me a sense of purpose, and I have met some wonderful people while in town. Would you like a list of their names?"

My jaw dropped. "You don't have to be condescending."

"Neither do you."

Now was not the time to argue. Emotions were running too high. Just calm down. "It's been a long night. I suggest we get some sleep. We can talk more in the morning."

She stared at me as I left and went to my bedroom. I wanted to slam the door in frustration but didn't. Instead, I quietly shut it and walked to the window. It was a clear and cool night. I should ride my horse. I needed to burn off my anger somehow. I turned to the picture of Ann that I kept on my dresser. I picked it up. The solid frame felt unusually cold.

When I asked Agnes for the picture, I had no idea what was going to happen in the next two and a half years. I loved Ann for so long and she never noticed me. I spent many nights trying to think of things to say that she might find interesting. I wasn't the one she wanted. She wanted Kent. Did she want him now? How could she still want him when she was willing to give all of herself to me? I should have left her back in Virginia. I never should have brought her with me.

I lifted the picture over my head, ready to smash it on the floor. *Break it! Just break it and get it over with! Do you really want her to haunt you for the rest of your life? She's bound to leave once Kent comes for her.* I stood still for the longest time. I couldn't move. I wanted to break it. I wanted to let go of her and be free. But how free could I possibly be when she lived here? Memories of her penetrated every room in the house.

Despite my best effort, I gently placed the picture in the top drawer of my dresser and started to cry. It didn't help that I could hear her crying in the next room. Why did we have to be miserable tonight? I should go in there and hold her. I wanted to make love to her. But she might not belong to me. What if she decided to go back to Kent? I could hardly breathe now. She'd completely destroy me if I enjoyed physical intimacy with her and she ran off with Kent.

I threw on a sweater before I headed down the stairs. I picked my coat off the floor, grabbed my gloves and hat and raced to the barn. I had everything on by the time I got to the horses. I quickly set the saddle on Lightning, since I knew he ran the fastest, and hopped up on him. The other two horses barely moved as I urged the horse forward. They were probably glad I didn't pick either of them. They knew when I was angry.

I rode him through every acre of land I owned. Even out in the fields I loved so much, I couldn't escape her. I recalled the day when she went for a walk out here and fell asleep. I was scared that something bad happened to her, and now I was scared she was going to walk out of my life. A wave of intense sorrow mingled with a wave of rage. I loved her and hated her at the same time. I remember asking her why she wasn't mad at Kent when he announced his engagement to Rebecca. I couldn't understand why she could still love him even when he was part of the reason for her heartache. Now I knew. She was mad at him while she loved him. It seemed like a cruel paradox. But the hardest lesson I had to face was the knowledge I brought all of this on myself when I agreed to take her with me. I knew it was wrong but I wanted her so badly I didn't care. In the end, I had to admit I was to blame for the way things turned out. And I'd pay for that decision for the rest of my life.

I wished I could go back and do it all over again. This time, I wouldn't even tell her I was going to leave Virginia. I would simply wait until the day after graduation and slip out of sight. She wouldn't have missed me. I would've missed her, but at least she never would have gotten as close as she did. What was I going to do?

I knew the answer. I'd have to let her go if she wanted to go.

I slowed the horse to a trot and headed back to the barn. I noticed two coyotes sniffing around in the fields. I sighed as I rode the horse into the barn and shut the door. I took the rifle from the shelf above the stack of piled firewood in case the coyotes had followed me, but they didn't.

I entered the kitchen and set the gun next to the back door. I hung my coat and set the gloves and hat near it. I slowly took off my shoes and sighed as I walked up the stairs.

I picked up some firewood from the guest bedroom and started the fire in the box stove in my room. I could hear Ann crying. Was it possible that she did love me? I recalled how affectionate she had been before Agnes arrived. She seemed to genuinely care for me. She shared everything with Agnes, and Agnes told me she loved me. I shook my head. I didn't know what to do or what to think.

Should I go to her? Ask her what she wanted to do about Kent? She said she didn't plan to go with him when he came, but would she be able to resist him? I couldn't resist her.

My steps were silent as I made my way to her bedroom. My hands pressed firmly on the cool, closed door. Did she want me to come back? I hesitated to knock on it. What if she was crying because she wanted to leave me and felt obligated to stay? That would be worse than if she left with him. I didn't want to take second place in her life anymore. I wanted to be her first choice. I pressed my forehead against the door in defeat. The only way I would know what she wanted was after she saw Kent. I would have to wait and see what happened.

Please choose me, Ann. I need you.

My shoulders slumped in defeat, I slowly walked to my room, which seemed as empty and miserable as ever. I quietly sat on my bed with my head in my hands and listened to her as she cried through the night.

Chapter Seventeen
Ann's Point of View

The next morning arrived, and I was exhausted. I didn't want to get out of bed, but I knew if I didn't, then I wouldn't be able to go to town. I desperately wanted to go to the Coley's store and help them today, even though I didn't usually come in on Wednesdays. I needed to take my mind off the previous night's events. I put on my well-worn but comfortable light blue dress and brushed my hair back into a braid. I glanced at my bed and sighed. Nothing went as planned last night. Agnes was gone and Todd suddenly felt like a stranger to me. I left my bedroom and went to the kitchen.

To my surprise, Todd was drinking a cup of coffee at the table. He looked worse than I did.

"Would you like something to eat?" I asked.

I braced myself for whatever he might say, but nothing prepared me for the sad look in his eyes.

"I owe you an apology," he softly stated.

I stared at him, unsure of how to respond.

He stood up and set his cup in the sink. "I had no right to be harsh with you. I married you knowing the situation between you and Kent. I hoped that you would learn to love me." He shook his head. "I brought this on myself."

"Todd, I do love you."

He came over to me and gently placed his hands on my arms. The simple action shocked me. I dared to look at him. He really loved me. He didn't need to say it. I could tell by the way he looked at me.

"You must understand why I didn't consummate our marriage last night," he began. "You may not belong to me. I don't know what you'll want when Kent comes to see you. Maybe you'll discover that the love you have for me is not enough. I only want you to stay with me if that is what you want. Please, don't stay with me because you feel obligated to. Since we haven't been intimate, we can annul our marriage."

"I don't want that." I knew he was trying to do what was best for me, but his words were breaking my heart. "I want to be here."

"Until you see Kent, how can you or I know for sure? After all, you did love him when you married me."

I couldn't look at him anymore. I wanted to kiss him and assure him that I would stay with him, but would he believe me?

"I have to go into town today to order some seeds for next spring. Would you like to come with me? You could help out the Coley's or do whatever it is women do in town."

"So you're not mad about my working there?"

"Of course not. I don't know why you wanted to keep it a secret."

"I was afraid you would be upset. I didn't want you to give up on farming because we were having financial problems."

He gave me a light kiss. "You have no idea how wonderful you are." He cleared his throat and retrieved his hat and coat. "You should eat. I won't leave until I feed the horses."

"Yes, I suppose I should. Are you going to eat anything?"

"I ate early this morning. I will be back soon. I want to make sure the wagon is ready."

I nodded as he went out the back door. I decided on scrambled eggs because it was quick and easy. I felt much better now that we had worked things out, at least as much as we could at this point.

When he had the horses hooked up to the wagon, I came out to join him. I carried the blankets.

"You should let me bring those out," he said. He ran over and took them from me.

"I thought I would help this time."

"Don't do too much to help. I like taking care of you."

I nodded and let him help me get into the wagon. I wrapped two blankets around my shoulders. There was a light blanket of snow on the ground, so our trip into town would still be smooth.

"I usually go to town with Barbara," I told him. "It's nice to be going with you for a change."

He clicked the reins so the horses moved forward.

"Do you think Agnes will be in trouble when she gets home?" I asked.

"I'm sure she will be fine. Besides, it's not her that my father's really mad at."

We rode in silence the rest of the way. The clouds were gathering. I wondered if we were due for more snow. Our path was straight and level, so the ride was easy. I looked forward to Christmas when my parents could see the landscape. It was so different from Virginia.

By the time we reached town, I was sitting so close to Todd that our shoulders touched. I had moved by him for additional comfort but found the closeness exciting as well. I hoped we would soon get a chance to continue what we began the night before but worried how Kent's impending arrival would affect the situation. I was beginning to dread his arrival. Up to that point, I hadn't considered the reality of it. For the first time, I wished that he was still with Rebecca. Then Todd and I would be enjoying each other as a married couple should be.

I nudged Todd gently in the side as he stopped in front of the mercantile. "There's Barbara at her mother's. I didn't realize she was coming in today."

He urged the horses to trot over to Barbara's carryall.

"How are you this morning?" Barbara greeted when she saw us.

"Good." I smiled, glad to see her.

"I need to get going but I'll come by the store to pick you up around noon," Todd told me. After he helped me down from the wagon, he said, "I hope you two have a pleasant visit." He tipped his hat to Barbara. "It's good to see you."

Once he left, she took my hand in hers. "Something is wrong."

"Is your mother ill?" I asked, suddenly alarmed by her concern.

"No. She is fine. She's playing with the children. I am on my way to the mercantile to pick up some items for her. You are troubled. I can see it."

"You can?"

"There is something about your expression that doesn't seem right."

"You're right. Is there a place we can talk in private?" I didn't wish to stand out in the cold.

She nodded and led me into her mother's house in the kitchen. "My mother's entertaining the children in the parlor. What is it, Ann?"

I didn't know where to begin. I did not wish to upset Todd by revealing too much of our personal information so I tried to stick to the main points. "When Todd and I left Virginia, I was being courted by another man. His name was Kent Ashton. He decided he should court another lady instead of me, so when Todd told me he was heading out West, I insisted that he marry me and take me with him. I knew Todd loved me so I figured he wouldn't deny my request, and I was right. It was probably selfish of me. But we married and came out here. We are husband and wife in name only, though I thought that was going to change last night. Last night Todd's parents came by and demanded that Agnes go back to Virginia. Before they left, his father informed him that Kent was coming here for me."

She took a moment to absorb everything I had told her. Finally, she asked, "What will you do?"

"I love Todd. I won't leave him."

She squeezed my hand. "Then stay firm when you see Kent. Todd does love you. I can see it when he looks at you."

I nodded. "He's a good husband."

"Yes, he is. Will you come with me to the mercantile?"

"I was planning to go there," I replied.

As we walked to the store, our talk ranged from her future child to our plans for Christmas. "My mother and cousins and their families will be coming out to my house this year. Will you and Todd join us as well? I figured since you and Todd are far from Virginia, it would be nice to be around your friends."

"Oh, my parents are coming."

"They are invited too. Of course, if you'd rather have your own get together, that is fine. I just wanted to make sure you know you are welcome to our place."

"I'll ask Todd and see what he thinks."

She nodded.

We entered the mercantile. I was relieved to be back in a warm place. The walk from Barbara's mother's house seemed long in the cold weather.

"Good morning, Ann and Barbara," Mrs. Coley greeted warmly. "What brings you into town today?"

"I came for a few food items for my mother," Barbara replied. "She sprained her ankle and the doctor ordered her to stay off of it for the next month."

I removed my bonnet. "I hope you will let me help you today. I came in with Todd and he won't be leaving for three hours."

She smiled. "I can always use your help."

I went to the back of the store to work on the bookkeeping while Mrs. Coley helped Barbara gather some food. The smells and sounds of the store took my mind off of Kent and Todd. I enjoyed being here. It had become a second home to me. After some time, Mrs. Coley stuck her head in the doorway of the backroom.

I glanced up from the desk, startled. "Did Barbara leave?"

"She's been gone for fifteen minutes. I have taken care of two other customers since then."

"But I didn't hear the bell on the door."

"That's because the bell fell and broke last night. Mr. Coley is getting a new one later today."

"Oh, that explains it." I grinned. "I lose track of the time back here."

"I find it a peaceful place too. Whenever something is troubling me, I like to come back here and take inventory of the supplies."

"Mrs. Coley? Are you here?"

I grimaced. I recognized Mrs. Carson's shrill voice.

Mrs. Coley chuckled. "You won't believe this. I don't know what happened but she's actually quite pleasant now. I'll be right back." She left to take care of her customer.

She was right. I didn't believe it. It was hard to imagine that someone whose favorite past time was gossiping could be pleasant. I kept my thoughts to myself and returned to work. I finished the bookkeeping and turned to the inventory list. Good. She hadn't filled it out yet. I picked up the paper and began scanning the items on the shelves.

Mrs. Coley returned. "Mr. Randolph fell on some ice and broke his hip, and Mr. Grant's assistant isn't back from a home visit yet. Would you mind taking care of the mercantile so that I can help the doctor?"

"I would be happy to help." I followed her to the front of the store.

"I shouldn't be gone for longer than thirty minutes. Thank you, Ann."

I was familiar with what she did to help her customers since I observed her many times in the past. I stood at the counter for five minutes, waiting for someone to enter the store but no one did. I walked to the window and peered at the people who strolled by. I tapped my fingers on the table holding jars of candy. I grinned. Children naturally gravitated to this area of the store.

I looked up as a man with white hair pulled a wagon to the front of the store and stopped it. I went back to the cash register and waited for him to enter. To my surprise, he brought in a basket of eggs.

"I don't recognize you," he said.

"I'm Mrs. Brothers. I'm filling in for Mrs. Coley while she's helping the doctor."

"Oh yes. She mentioned you. Mighty proud of the work you do. You save her hours of work."

I blushed, pleased by his comment. "She has been gracious to me."

"Tell her that Mr. Whitman stopped by with the eggs. She can pay me next week."

"Yes, sir."

"Good day."

I nodded as he left. I took the basket to the backroom. I thought it was very kind of Mrs. Coley to say positive things about me to other people. I smiled, grateful she worked here. Who knew if anyone else would have offered me free food for helping in this store? I went to the shelf where Mrs. Coley usually put her eggs.

"My goodness, Ann. You're just as beautiful as I remember."

I paused. I recognized that voice. My hands trembled as I finished putting the basket down before I turned to him. Why now? Why here?

Kent's smile widened. He was dressed in his best suit. He looked as handsome and charming as I remembered. But he wasn't Todd. And in that instant, I knew that I really did love Todd more than I had ever loved Kent.

"I believe I caught you by surprise," he smoothly stated. "I admit we parted under dire circumstances. I made an error in judgment. I am no longer engaged to Rebecca. She was a mistake. I came to apologize and ask if I can court you again."

"I'm married." I glanced around the room. He was standing in the doorway. An uneasy feeling crept up my spine.

"I know why you married Todd Brothers. You were distressed over my brief encounter with Rebecca. It is understandable that you ran to the first person who offered you comfort. This is my fault."

"But that doesn't change the fact that I am married. I belong to someone else now."

He laughed. "I'm sure we can find a way to get you 'unmarried'. Really, we can work through it."

I couldn't believe my ears. "I vowed to be with him for the rest of our lives."

"Vows are made to be broken."

"I'm not leaving him."

"Hmm... I suppose you're expecting then?"

I was shaken by the fact he would ask such a personal question. I shook my head. What was I doing? What time was it? Would Todd come by earlier than expected?

"Then there's nothing to fear. This marriage can easily be dissolved."

"No."

It struck me as odd that I would say that so clearly when my hands shook. There was something in his eyes and in the way he stood that I didn't like. Why hadn't I noticed it before?

He sighed, as if with deep regret. "I hurt you more than I realized. I promise that I will never hurt you again. There is no other love in my life. You will always be the one."

He took a step toward me. His movements and words flowed so smoothly together. He was very charming and confident. He was nothing like Todd. No wonder I didn't notice Todd in Virginia. Todd was quiet and sometimes clumsy. But he was sincere. He would lay down his life for me. He would even give me up if it meant I could be happy.

"I love Todd," I finally said.

Kent laughed. "That's sweet. Todd is a good boy. I'm sure he's treated you very well out here, in the middle of nowhere. But a lady such as yourself deserves better in this life. You were meant for comfort and riches. Look at your clothes, your hair, your hands! You don't even own a single piece of jewelry. You may love Todd but he has you living like a beggar. You were born for beautiful gowns, servants to wait on you, for your every desire to be fulfilled." He stepped closer to me. "Things I can give you."

I had to get out of here! I felt like I was going to suffocate.

"Enough of playing wife," he continued as he walked closer to me. "Come with me. I can give you things that he can't."

He reached out and touched my cheek. Startled, I shrieked. His hesitation gave me the strength to move. I bolted for the doorway. His reflexes were quick, for he grabbed my arm.

"You can't be serious," he hissed. "You would give up what we had for Todd?"

"Yes. Let me go!"

"Perhaps I need to show you what you're missing." He put his free hand behind my neck and brought my mouth to his.

"What is going on here?"

Kent released me and I nearly fell to the floor. Looking up, I saw Todd, staring at us.

"Todd!" I ran to him but he backed away.

Todd shook his head, looking bewildered. "I can't believe this. I mean, it was a possibility but..."

"No. No! It's not what it looks like," I insisted.

"Don't lie to him, Ann," Kent softly stated. "It will do you no good to deny it."

Todd didn't say anything. He simply turned and left the room.

"Todd!" I screamed and ran after him.

As I passed the doorway, my eyes fell on Mrs. Carson who had her hand to her cheek, as if she couldn't believe her good fortune in overhearing a juicy piece of gossip.

I stopped when I saw her. *I'm doomed. Once she blabs the whole thing to the town, everyone will believe I'm ready to leave Todd for Kent.*

Todd was out the door before I looked away from her.

"I'll come back for you. I'm sure you'll come to your senses in time," Kent said as he left the mercantile.

I broke into tears. Obviously, Todd hadn't heard the whole conversation. He just walked in on us when Kent kissed me.

"I heard everything," Mrs. Carson said.

I groaned. Her version would be sordid. Some people still believed Todd stole money at the bank.

Mrs. Coley opened the front door and walked in. She gasped. "Ann, what's wrong?"

Relieved that she was back, I grabbed my coat. I raced out of the mercantile. But Todd was long gone.

Chapter Eighteen
Ann's Point of View

The walk to Barbara's mother's house seemed to take forever and I didn't notice the chill in the air this time. I was anxious to find Todd and explain everything to him, but would he even believe me? I knocked on the door.

Calvin opened it.

"Is your mother here?" I asked.

"Sure she is, Mrs. Brothers. Come in and I'll get her."

He ran off before I had time to enter the house. I softly shut the door behind me. Now that I was here, I began to relax. Barbara would know what to do. At least, she should have some idea of how I could make the situation better.

Barbara walked into the room, a dishtowel in her hands. She was wiping some dough off of her fingers. "What is it?"

"Kent came to the store and he wanted me to go with him but I kept telling him I was married but he wouldn't listen to me no matter how many times I told him and then I tried to leave the backroom but he wouldn't let me and he kissed me and Todd saw us and thought I wanted to kiss Kent but I didn't and I tried to explain it to Todd but he wouldn't listen and Mrs. Carson said she heard the whole thing but we all know how she interprets the truth and now she'll blab it all over town and everyone, including Todd, will believe I wanted to kiss Kent and Todd went home without me and I'm sure it's all over and I'll have to go back to Virginia now and I don't even want to be with Kent and..." I started crying. "It's all a mess and I don't know what to do."

"Calm down. You're speaking too fast. Come, sit down."

I sobbed into my handkerchief as I obeyed her.

"I need to finish making a loaf of bread," she said. "Can you wait for ten minutes?"

I nodded. "Yes, I can wait."

"Good. Now try to breathe. You can explain everything to me on the way home."

I sat in the chair and tried to slow my thoughts so they weren't all jumbled together. I suddenly realized I was exhausted. I hadn't slept the night before. I put my head in my hands and focused on slowing my breathing. The action was calming. I must have fallen asleep because the next thing I knew, Barbara was tapping me on the shoulder, asking me if I was awake. I stood up.

"Are you ready?" I asked.

"Yes. Calvin will be staying with my mother to help her around the house. Bruce and Molly, come along."

I helped her take the blankets and tuck the kids in the carryall so they would be warm during the trip home. Molly was so tired she fell asleep. Bruce was content to play with a toy train his grandmother had given him. That left plenty of time for me to explain my morning in the store to Barbara. Snow was already beginning to fall and by the time we got halfway home, it was apparent that we were going to have a storm.

When she stopped in front of my house, I heard Todd chopping wood in the barn. I sighed. He was angry.

"I saved some food for you," she said.

We got out of the carryall and she helped me bring some jars and boxes into the kitchen.

"I'll leave you now," she whispered. She put her hand on my shoulder and gave it a gentle squeeze.

"Thank you," I quietly replied.

Once she left, I put the food away. I could still hear Todd chopping wood. He'd stay out there all day if I let him. What should I say? I didn't think he'd accept anything I told him. I contemplated going up to my bedroom instead of seeing him, but I wanted to resolve the matter. If that was even possible...

I took a deep breath then headed outside. The snow was falling heavily now. I couldn't even see Todd's footprints in the snow. I pulled the hood of the coat over my head and braced myself for the blowing wind as it pressed against me. Thankfully, my gloves were thick so my hands stayed warm. I walked to the barn and pulled the door open.

Sure enough, Todd wasn't wearing his coat or gloves. He was at least wearing a sweater this time, but that hardly made me feel any better. He had a lantern lit, and, even from across the barn, I could see that his eyes were red from crying.

I looked aside for a moment, ashamed that I was the cause of his grief. But I did nothing wrong! Strengthened by the reminder, I pressed forward until I was standing several feet in front of him.

He had his axe raised to chop another piece of wood but paused when he noticed me.

My heart pounded loudly in my ears. Now that I was here, I didn't know what to say.

"Have you come to say good-bye?" he finally asked.

I blinked at his bitter tone.

He brought the axe down and sliced the wood in half.

I jumped. I wasn't guilty, so why I was acting as if I was? I took a moment to regain my composure. "I'm not going anywhere. I want to be with you, Todd. What you saw at the store was a big misunderstanding."

At first I thought he was laughing, but when he wiped his face with the sleeve of his sweater, I knew he was crying. "Even now you would lie to me?"

"I'm not lying. I do love you."

"Enough! I can't take it anymore!" he yelled. "I'm not blind. I know what I saw."

"You didn't see everything. I was trying to get away from him and he grabbed my arm. He forced himself upon me."

"Then why didn't Mrs. Carson try to stop him? She was listening to you when I walked into the store. She only said I needed to help you. Apparently, I needed to help you control yourself."

"Mrs. Carson is a busybody. She only wanted to hear all the details so she could spread her vicious rumors."

"If it was just her word, I wouldn't believe anything she said. But I saw you kissing him."

"You didn't see enough!"

He dropped his axe and walked up to me until he was a few inches from me. I instinctively backed up a couple of steps.

"Look at me, Ann. I'm a wreck."

I wanted to look away but couldn't. The anguish in his eyes and his messy hair stung my heart. There was no denying the intensity of his pain.

"God help me, Ann." His voice was so low I barely heard him. "You're a part of me now. If you leave, a part of me will die."

Tears sprung in my eyes. "I'm not leaving. I want to be here."

"Then why did you kiss him?" He turned away from me and went back to his axe. He picked it up and put another piece of wood up to chop. "The person I am mad at, more than anyone else in this whole mess, is me. I knew from the beginning you didn't love me the way you loved him. I knew it and I still married you. I never imagined he would come searching for you. As long as he stayed away, I thought you might learn to be content with me. I hoped you might even love me over time. You have no idea how happy I was last night. Then my parents showed up and I learned that Kent was coming for you. You knew he was coming but you didn't tell me, and today you're kissing him."

He used all his strength to chop the wood. Again, I jumped. His shoulders slumped in defeat.

"I never should have brought you here. You should go back." He turned his back to me and sat on the ground, his head in his hands.

I didn't know what to say. He obviously didn't believe me. He couldn't accept that I loved him. He had made up his mind. I slowly turned around and walked out of the barn. I couldn't hold back my tears as I made my way into the house and up the stairs. My feet dragged as I entered my bedroom. I couldn't bring myself to look at the bed or the memories it would give me.

Instead, I looked out the window. The wind grew stronger. I could hear it whistling against house. My forehead felt cool against the glass. I shivered. Todd hadn't started the fire in the box stove yet. The fire was roaring in the fireplace downstairs. I felt sick as I recalled the anguish in his eyes when he told me I was a part of him, for I felt the same way about him. How could he tell me to go back to Virginia? Why didn't he believe me? Why did Kent have to leave Rebecca? It would have been better if he had stayed with her.

The knocking at the door downstairs interrupted my thoughts. I stiffened. What if it was Kent? I ran down the stairs and peered out the parlor window. I gasped in surprise and delight and raced to open the door.

"Mother, Father, what are you doing here?"

They thanked Mr. Albert who brought them on his sleigh and brought their luggage into the house. I hugged them, relieved to see them.

"We're sorry we didn't warn you of our impending arrival," my mother spoke as I took her coat and hat. She kicked off her boots at the door. "When we heard that the Brothers were coming to get Agnes, we felt it best to come and be a support to you and Todd. Mr. Brothers was awfully mad. We didn't want him to say something he'd regret later on."

"I hate to disappoint you but they arrived last night. They took Agnes back late in the evening."

My mother shook her head, clearly distraught by the news. "How did Todd take it?"

I sighed. "As well as could be expected. I suppose since he's known his father would be upset when he left Virginia, it helped to soften the blow."

She put her hand over her heart. "The poor boy. What a blessing it is that he has you to get him through this difficult time."

If only she knew...

"Speaking of troubling news," my father began with an unusually serious look on his face, "Kent is coming. Apparently, he decided that you'll be his wife. This is not appropriate. He knows you are married. We came to talk him to his senses."

I groaned. "I wish you had come sooner. He cornered me today at the mercantile in town."

Their faces paled.

"I was by myself in the backroom putting eggs away and that's when Kent showed up. He wouldn't let me leave the room. I kept telling him I wasn't going to go with him, but he wouldn't listen to me. He insisted that I would be with him. As I was running out of the room, he grabbed me by the arm and kissed me. Todd walked in on us at that exact moment and now he thinks I want to leave with Kent."

I didn't realize I was crying until my mother handed me her handkerchief and hugged me. "Oh my poor dear. What you must be going through."

"Do you love Todd?" my father asked.

"Yes. I have no intention of leaving him."

"Does he know what happened?"

"I tried to explain it but he won't listen to me. The town gossip was in the store and heard the whole thing and didn't bother to stop Kent, so Todd figures I must be lying."

"Hmm..." My father narrowed his eyes as he tried to think of a suitable solution. He brought out his pipe and lit it up. It was how he handled tough situations. "Where is Todd now?"

"He's chopping wood in the barn."

"Would he mind if I went out to see him?" my father asked.

"I don't think so."

"Good. I'd like to say hello to my son-in-law."

After my father left the house, my mother took me by the arm and sat next to me on the couch in front of the fireplace. "My dear, you are very lucky to have Todd. You remember how your father and I weren't too happy about your courtship with Kent."

I nodded, curious at the hushed tone she used. There was no one else in the house, yet she spoke as if she were about to reveal a secret.

"Thank goodness Kent ended that courtship. We hardly knew anything about him. True, his parents are honorable people, and they were pressing him to marry an honorable lady, which you are sweetheart. I think a part of him may have genuinely cared for you. However, he does not act like a gentleman with certain women."

By the term *certain women*, I knew she meant *loose women.* My eyes widened. I hadn't expected this.

"Rebecca was such a woman," she confided. "Their sudden courtship was arranged privately between her parents and his parents when they found out that they were being intimate with one another. Their parents insisted that they marry to avoid unwanted gossip. As it turned out, Rebecca got in the family way but miscarried. That's when she stopped attending social functions. Kent ended their engagement, though their parents protested. It would be decent to do the right thing and marry her of course. He told his parents that he was going to find you. I suppose he figured that he was free to choose whoever he wanted as his wife since Rebecca was no longer expecting."

"But he knew I married Todd."

"Yes. Everyone knew, my dear. The night you eloped with Todd was a busy night for everyone. We searched for you. The Brothers were furious, but his mother was more understanding about it. I think she sympathizes with Todd, but she's not in the position to do anything about it. His father has made up his mind about the situation. I think Todd may be more accepting of what you want, but some men don't allow their wives to have a say in things that happen. Once Mr. Brothers decided to disown Todd, there was nothing she could do about it."

"What did you and Father think?"

"He was upset. I was too. We had no idea you would even consider a courtship, let alone a marriage, with Todd. We weren't upset that you two married. We were delighted. But we missed out on the fun of our daughter getting married. It's one of those proper things we raised you up to obey. Looking back, however, we realized all the social rules we taught you don't matter. The important thing is that you and Todd are happy."

"Todd treats me much better than Kent ever did. I didn't marry him because I loved him. I married him to get away from Kent and Rebecca. But I got to know him in a way I never could back in Virginia. He's a wonderful man. I love him now." My thoughts drifted to another concern. "Mother, what do you think Father is talking to Todd about?"

"Why, your dowry of course. Mostly though, he will want to welcome Todd to the family."

"But Todd doesn't believe me when I tell him what happened between me and Kent. I tried talking to him, but he won't listen. He even told me to go back to Virginia." My lower lip trembled. The words still stung.

She rested her hand on my arm. "He's afraid he'll lose you. Give him time. When he sees that you aren't leaving, he'll understand."

"What will I do when Mrs. Carson spreads lies about my wanting to kiss Kent? What am I to do then?"

"You wrote to me about Mrs. Carson and how she told everyone that he stole money from the bank. Don't you think he'll realize that she could just as easily spin lies concerning you?"

I hadn't thought of that.

"Everything will work out, especially since you are innocent."

I hoped she was right.

Chapter Nineteen
Todd's Point of View

While Ann took care of changing the bed sheets and blankets in the guest bedroom, I got all the fires started. I couldn't bring myself to go into the guest bedroom while she was in there. It was hard enough to go to her bedroom. I focused so hard on making the fire that I didn't have to think about what almost happened in this room the night before. I couldn't bear that memory at the moment. After I was done with the fires, I fed the horses. Mr. Statesman wanted to examine my barn, and I was glad for his company. I had admired him while I was growing up. I could understand why my father was friends with him.

"This barn is in good condition," he said.

"Mr. Martin owned this land before I got here, and he took good care of everything he had. All I have to do is maintain it."

"Alex Dawson used to talk about farming, didn't he?"

I smiled at the thought of my childhood friend. "He has an aunt and uncle who live in Fargo. They knew some farmers, and they would share some stories with me and Alex when I went over to his place to visit."

Mr. Statesman nodded and walked over to the horses. "I don't recognize this one."

"I bought that one in October," I told him. "I wanted to be sure that two horses were here during the day so Ann could go into town if she wanted. I ride Lightning into town when I go to work." I petted my favorite horse affectionately. "He's always been a good horse."

"I remember you used to take him out and race him with Alex. Your father bragged that you were faster than Alex on any horse." He looked at me. "Your father will come around. He just needs time."

I didn't believe that was going to happen but didn't argue with him.

The snowstorm had finally died down, but the wind was still blowing the snow around. I hadn't taken much notice of the snowstorm with everything that was going on. We returned to the house and sat down in the parlor to talk.

"Are you sure you won't take the dowry? It is yours since you married my daughter," he said.

"No, sir. I wouldn't feel right about it. I don't mean any disrespect."

"I'm not offended, son." He paused. He lit his pipe. "I set aside the dowry when Ann turned sixteen. I knew it wouldn't be long before young men started to court her. I have nothing to do with the money, and it will go to waste if it's not used. May I put it in the bank in her name?"

"That is fine."

He shifted in the chair. "One thing we have always told Ann is the importance of honesty. A person is only as good as his word. I remember when she was twelve and she was playing in the parlor. Later that day, I saw that her mother's favorite vase was broken. This vase wasn't expensive but it was sentimental. It belonged to her great-great-grandmother. We questioned her about the vase and she said that it was still intact when she left the room. We didn't believe her, for who else could have broken it? She had no brothers or sisters. So, we decided that she couldn't go anywhere but school for a month. That was the year she missed Agnes' birthday dinner."

"I remember that. Agnes cried all night." I grinned at the memory of my sister's hysterics.

"Yes. I recall hearing that too. Well, the next week, the servant who had been watching Ann the day the vase was broken returned from her vacation and reported that the neighbor's cat had gotten into the house. That cat ran through the parlor and knocked the vase off the table. Apparently, the letter the servant left explaining this fell off the table so no one found it until we searched for it. It was under the couch. We felt awful after that event, but we learned that we could trust Ann. Believe it or not, she even confessed to sneaking a few cookies before dinner one time. You would think it's easy for someone to admit something good but to admit to a bad behavior... That takes character."

"I understand." He was telling me, in a very nice way, that Ann didn't want to kiss Kent, that Kent had indeed forced the kiss upon her. I sighed. Certainly, he knew when Ann was telling the truth, right?

"We received this from her." He reached into the breast pocket of his suit and pulled a letter out. I took it as he handed it to me. "She is happy here, and for that, we are grateful to you. Now, to change the subject, I want to learn more about tractors. I haven't seen one up close."

I put the letter in my pocket, unsure of whether or not I wanted to read it. "I have a book on the desk over there. Would you like to see it?"

He nodded, so we spent the rest of the afternoon looking through the book together.

***

I did feel better by the time dinner was ready. I still couldn't look at Ann but did participate in the conversation, which was an improvement over my mood earlier that day.

Ann's father beamed at her. "That was delicious. Betsy back home doesn't cook stew this good."

"Oh, Father. She's an excellent cook," Ann argued, obviously pleased by the compliment.

"Which tells you how good this stew is."

He was proud of her, just as I was at times. I wanted to be proud of her again. *If only Kent didn't haunt me...*

"It is very good, my dear," her mother added. "You have done well in learning so much. I don't know how you do it all. You must be exhausted by the end of the day."

"I was at first," she confessed, "but after I got used to it, I hardly noticed how much work it was. You should have seen my first attempt at cooking pancakes. It was a disaster."

I chuckled as I recalled the mess in the kitchen. It took us a good half hour to clean it up. She was endearing as she frantically scurried around the room to clean it up, hoping I wouldn't discover her mishap.

"I don't mean to be rude but I have some dishes to wash," she said.

"Can I help?" her mother asked.

"Yes."

"We'll get out of your way," her father replied.

I wanted to stay with her and ask her again about the events in the mercantile but realized it wasn't the right time, so I followed him out of the room.

***

That night, I sat on my bed. I was exhausted but didn't want to sleep. I stared at the wall for the longest time as the events of the past two days played over and over in my mind. It didn't make sense that Ann would want to consummate our marriage if she planned to leave me. Why would she risk getting a child with me? She had made it a point to never spend a moment alone with any men while she was living with her parents. Even now, I was the only man she let herself be alone with.

She trusted me. She knew I wouldn't force myself on her. But she never allowed Kent to be alone with her. I sighed. It didn't make sense that she would be alone in the backroom of the store with Kent. Then I remembered the missing bell on the door of the store. That bell always made the loudest ring. No one could miss it if they were in the backroom. She would have come out of the backroom if she heard the bell. Had the bell been there on the door, she wouldn't have been in the backroom with him. Then Mrs. Carson would have been in sight and the kiss most likely wouldn't have happened. Could it be true that he forced her to kiss him? Did he take advantage of the situation? The thought was too appealing to my wounded heart.

I stood up and walked to the window. It was a clear night and the moon was full. It was the perfect night to be enjoying Ann in her bed. *Any night would be the perfect night to enjoy her.* I turned from the window and stared at my room. It wasn't as warm as her room, but I knew that it felt lonely because she wasn't here.

I remembered the letter her father handed to me. What did I have to lose? I took the letter out of my pocket and read it. It was written on October 13.

My Dear Mother and Father,

I was glad when I received your letter. In my hasty departure, there were many things I failed to explain. But first, I want to say I miss you both. Even so, I don't regret coming here. There are many things I have learned. I actually cook and clean on my own. There is a good woman who lives on the farm next to ours who has taught me to cook. When I started cooking, I made many mistakes. I couldn't even make scrambled eggs without cracking almost a dozen eggs the wrong way or burning them in the pan. I have gone through five pans already in my pursuit to be a better cook. The laundry is tedious at times but it gives me time to think.

I can't remember what my life was like when I had servants catering to my every whim, and to be honest, I would rather do these things myself. It is fulfilling to do hard work. Every time I see Todd's eyes light up when he tries a new recipe that turned out right, all of my previous failures seem insignificant.

As for Kent, my heart is free of the burden of my anger and grief. Todd has been patient with me during this time, which must've been hard for him. You were right about him. He is a good man. I wish I had taken the time to learn that while we were growing up. I keep wondering why I continually pushed him away in Virginia. I can only come to the conclusion that he didn't stand out as men like Kent did. Todd was shy and quiet. He stayed mostly to himself, though Creepy Alex did bring him out of his shell. I hate to admit it, but Creepy Alex probably wasn't so creepy after all. I should stop calling him 'Creepy' Alex. It's a force of habit. Anyway, it was Alex who realized what a good friend Todd was when so few others did. Not that Todd didn't have other friends, but I don't think any of them took the time to see Todd for who he really was the way that Alex did. It was Alex who encouraged Todd to pursue his dream of farming.

I didn't even know of this until the night you dragged me to the dinner at the Brothers' house. I had wanted to stay home and mope in self-pity, but you insisted I get out, which I am very thankful for. That was the night when Todd and I were on the veranda and he told me he was going to leave for North Dakota. He also professed his love for me and told me he understood that I didn't share those feelings.

It wasn't until the Monday before the dance that I decided to ask Todd to take me with him to North Dakota. I considered asking him to stay in Virginia so I could take the time to know him better, but it didn't seem right to ask him to stay when it meant he had to work at the bank. So I opted to ask him to marry me and take me to North Dakota with him. If Todd left, I would be stuck with settling with someone who most likely would not love me as well as Todd did.

You would be surprised at how he resisted my plan at first. I know he resisted because he didn't think it was in my best interest. I had to threaten to run away if he didn't take me along. We got married by our preacher and you know the rest. I have grown closer to Todd than I have ever been to anyone. He still treats me very well and considers my needs before his own. I can't imagine my life without him and am thankful for his love. I only hope I can be the kind of wife who will bless him. He makes a wonderful husband and he will make a wonderful father.

All My Love,
Ann

I set the letter down. She did love me. This time when I cried, it was with relief. She was still here. She didn't leave with Kent. If she really wanted to run off with him, she wouldn't be here. She didn't know her parents were coming early, so she didn't stay to appease them. She stayed because she decided to fight for our marriage.

I went to her room and lightly knocked on her door. I wanted to talk to her and smooth things over. When she didn't answer, I turned the knob. She was asleep. I wanted to go in bed with her and just hold her, but I knew she was as tired as I was and needed sleep. I smiled and shut the door. I would talk to her tomorrow. At least, I knew she would still be here to talk to.

Chapter Twenty
Ann's Point of View

I woke up past dawn. I looked over at the empty spot next to me. I hadn't noticed how large my bed seemed until Todd had been in it. I was disappointed when he didn't come to my bedroom last night. I laid in bed and stared at the ceiling for a good hour before I finally fell asleep.

I got up and looked outside. The snow sparkled under the intense glare of the sunlight. There wasn't a cloud in the sky. I wondered how deep the snow was. I got dressed and brushed my hair. As I ran down the steps, I was surprised to find Todd and my parents eating breakfast.

"Would you like some cornbread?" Todd offered.

"Why didn't someone wake me? I would have made a hot meal."

"We thought you could use some rest, so we didn't disturb you."

"Thank you." I sat next to him at the table. I was grateful that he seemed more like his usual self.

"We measured the snow and we got three inches yesterday. I found a sleigh under some old blankets in the barn, so we can still hook up the horses to get to town. There is a large snowdrift blocking the large door of the barn. It will take some time to shovel but once the path is clear, we can get the horses and sleigh out."

"I'd like to help," my father offered.

Todd accepted.

"I am eager to see the town," my mother said. "We didn't get a chance to take a good look at it yesterday."

"I would like to introduce you to Mr. and Mrs. Coley," I replied. "They own the mercantile. Of course, you'll have to meet Barbara and John Russell. They're good friends of ours."

It felt strange to say "ours" since I wasn't sure what would become of Todd and me, but I was hopeful from his friendly demeanor.

After breakfast, my mother helped me wash dishes.

"I'm glad you and Father are here. Thank you for being nice to Todd."

"My dear, we have always welcomed him. I think your father is relieved you married well. We had worried you might pick the wrong person."

"I almost did. I almost married Kent."

I put the dirty dishes in a bucket of water and added soap. The clean bucket of water was in the other sink.

"The important thing is you didn't," she said. She picked up a towel and dried the plate I handed her. "You'll never guess who is studying to become a minister."

"Who?"

"Alex Dawson."

My eyes widened in surprise. "Todd's friend?"

"The same. That boy did nothing but play practical jokes all his life. Then he goes off to college and gets serious. Isn't that amazing?"

"Quite. I can't believe it."

"Miracles happen. It will be interesting to see how he behaves when he visits for Christmas. His parents are happy. They worried he might be a troublemaker for his entire life. He has an aunt and uncle out in Fargo, North Dakota who often visited his family. I wonder if they had an influence on Todd wanting to come out here."

"Yes." And for the first time, I was actually glad that Todd knew Alex, for I loved it here.

Two hours later, my mother took me to the guest bedroom so she could give me a photo album and my jewelry box filled with rings, necklaces and bracelets. "I thought you might like these personal mementos of your past," she said.

I took the items and left her so she could take a nap. I went to my bedroom and set the jewelry box on my dresser. I sat on my bed, opened the photo album, and flipped through the pictures. I was surprised to see pictures of Todd with his family. I chuckled at the picture of Agnes making a face at the camera. She hated sitting still for the photographer.

Sitting there, with the pictures in front of me brought back memories from my childhood. My earliest memory was when I was four.

My parents took me over to the Brothers' house so we could see their fourth child who was two days old. While one-year-old Abigail slept, Todd, Agnes and I were in the toy room. A servant watched in amusement as we fought over what game to play.

"Agnes and I want to play dolls," I said, my hands on my hips.

"Dolls is boring," he protested, rolling his eyes. "Let's play with the blocks."

"No. We build towers but you knock them down."

"That's fun!"

"It is not fun. It is rude."

"Fine then. Want to see my new train set?"

Agnes and I looked at each other and nodded.

He took his trains and tracks out of his toy box and we helped him set it up. Agnes couldn't get most of the pieces to fit, so we had to finally tell her to wait until we were done. Then he set up the trains and small wooden people. I grinned at the display.

"It's pretty," I commented.

He gagged. "It's not pretty."

"Here's a Mommy and Daddy and their baby," Agnes said. She took the people and went to the corner to play with them by herself.

"She's a baby," he replied. "We don't need those people anyway."

He moved his train down one of the tracks and I moved my train down another one. We played quietly for a few minutes. Then, to my horror, he rammed his train into mine.

"Bam!"

I shot him a dirty look. "Don't do that."

"It's fun!"

"No, it's not. I'm playing."

"We are playing. Now you crash into me!"

I took his train and threw it across the room.

"What did you do that for?" he demanded, his face red.

"It's fun." I stuck my tongue at him.

"This is my train set. Go play with Agnes."

I grabbed a train and ran to Agnes.

"That's mine! Give it back!" He ran after me.

I giggled as I dodged him. Finally, he knocked me down and grabbed the train out of my hand. I screamed as loud as I could so the world would know the injustice of it all.

The servant calmly took the train from Todd and put all the toys back, except for the people Agnes was quietly playing with. "Todd, go to that corner and face it. Ann, you do the same in the other corner."

"Yes, ma'am," we replied, realizing we would get a spanking if we didn't obey.

I chuckled and looked at more pictures in the photo album. Poor Todd grew up surrounded by girls. He wanted a baby brother so badly but never got one. I used to tell him he should be grateful to have any siblings at all since I was often lonely as an only child. But Alex seemed to be the brother he never had. I shook my head as I recalled the first time I stood up to Alex.

We were ten and I worked on my assignment in class when a pebble hit my head. Startled, I looked back to see who had thrown it at me. My eyes narrowed. I should have known. It was Todd and Alex again. They took an irrational pleasure in throwing things into girls' hair. Our teacher wasn't in the room at the moment, which explained why Todd was involved. He didn't dare do anything wrong when the teacher was in sight. I gave them a "stop it" look and turned back to my work. Of course, they didn't stop. I tried to ignore them as pebbles flew in my hair, past my shoulders and onto my work.

Finally, I lost my temper. I glanced at the door and noticed that the teacher was still talking to a parent. Ignoring Todd and Alex's snickers, I stood up and walked to the jar of sand by the window. It was part of our science lesson, but I found a better use for it. By now, our entire class was watching me. No one alerted the teacher. They wanted to see what I would do. Since Alex and Todd sat next to each other, it was easy to get both of them at once. I took the lid off the jar and dumped the sand on their heads.

They jumped up and screamed. The rest of the class laughed at the hysterical scene.

"Ann!"

I looked up in time to see the teacher rushing to me. "What are you doing?" She shook her head in disbelief. "What got into you?"

"They keep throwing pebbles in my hair," I replied, my voice shaking since I wasn't used to getting in trouble.

Todd and Alex were frantically trying to shake the sand off of their bodies.

"Todd and Alex, you may go outside. Ann, you are going to clean this mess and then put the dunce cap on at the front of the room until I tell you to take it off."

"Yes, Miss Hampton."

Even though I got in trouble, it was worth it. They never threw anything else in my hair again. In fact, they stopped throwing pebbles in the other girls' hair too. I was a hero to those girls that year.

Alex also liked to dare Todd to do disgusting things. I recalled a time during lunch hour when we were twelve. Alex challenged Todd to eat a plate of bugs. As appalling as it was, I joined the other students. There was something mesmerizing about someone eating insects.

Todd seemed hesitant. "You eat them," he said as he pushed the plate to Alex.

"I challenged you first. You can't back out now," Alex replied. He wore that satisfied smirk that drove me crazy.

"You don't have to do it," I argued. "Alex is a coward. That's why he won't do it. Just tell him no."

Alex nodded. "Yes, you could do that."

I frowned. I didn't like the tone in his voice. He was up to something.

"Or, you could kiss Ann." He grinned. "Apparently, you need your mommy to take care of you."

A couple of girls giggled and some boys told Todd to eat the bugs.

Todd took a deep breath. "I'll eat the bugs."

The boys cheered. The girls, including me, just commented on how gross it was. I was secretly relieved to get the focus off of me, and another part of me was fascinated that Todd could sit there so calmly while he ate those bugs. Where did he get the strength? Though he didn't complain about a stomachache, I felt nauseous for the rest of the day.

Todd wasn't always following Alex's instructions. There were times when he was a model student. It helped when his other friends, Jack and Simon, were around. When we were thirteen, a snake got into the classroom. Our teacher, an elderly woman, was terrified. Even Alex wouldn't get out of his chair. Todd, Jack and Simon volunteered to corner the snake. Jack took an empty bag while Todd and Simon chased the snake until it slithered into the bag. Jack immediately ran outside to dump it out of the bag. We cheered for the brave three boys when Jack returned.

Breaking out of my thoughts, I saw another picture of the class Todd and I were in. It was taken last year right before Christmas. I was standing next to Jennifer and Debbie. I looked happy in my pile of seven petticoats and restricting corset. I shook my head. I didn't miss that part of wearing a dress. My dress in the picture was gorgeous, but it would never last on the farm. Todd stood at the end of the line. He was attractive in his dark suit. It was hard for me to think of him in a suit anymore. He wore a suit when he worked at the bank, but as soon as he got fired, he started wearing denim pants and cotton shirts. No one would have guessed he was planning to move out to North Dakota. I sighed. Even back then, he loved me.

My eyes fell on Rebecca who stood next to Debbie. Rebecca wore a big smile. Sympathy welled in my heart. Though I wouldn't have imagined she engaged in improper activities, I felt sorry for her. She must have loved Kent. I shut the album in disgust. He should have married her. It was the least he could have done after dishonoring her.

A light tapping on my door interrupted my thoughts. Startled, I looked up and saw Todd. His cheeks were red from being out in the cold.

"Do you need something?" I asked and stood up.

"No. I'm fine. Your father is reading downstairs. I wanted to talk to you, but I wanted to wait until everything settled down."

My heart skipped a beat. From the way he shyly smiled, I assumed this was going to be a good talk. "Please, come in."

When he walked over to me, his eyes fell on the photo album. "I didn't know you brought some pictures with you."

"Oh. I didn't. My mother did. Would you like to look at them?"

He nodded and I handed the album to him. "Will you sit next to me?"

He sat on the bed. I sat too, but I didn't dare get close enough to touch him. Just being next to him was making me lightheaded.

He opened the album and grinned. "Even as a baby, you were cute."

I groaned. "Those silly ruffles on all those dresses. It's amazing I could crawl around."

"You remember that far back?"

I smiled at his joke. "Of course not, silly." I leaned over and turned the page.

"Oh no! You have a baby picture of me?"

"I like it."

He glanced at me out of the corner of his eye and shook his head. "You take better pictures than I do."

"It's probably because I actually smile at the camera. You look serious in all of these pictures. Well, except for the one of you and Alex." I showed him the picture I referred to.

He chuckled. "I remember that day. After Alex nailed the rug to the parlor floor, we could no longer play unsupervised."

I shook my head. "That was awful."

He shrugged, but I suspected he hid a smile. He turned to another page. "I remember when Agnes brought home this picture." He showed me the picture my parents had taken of me when I turned sixteen. "You were so beautiful I asked her if I could buy it from her. She wouldn't sell it though. She said her friendship couldn't be bought."

"Is that why she asked me for another one? I wondered why she insisted that she have two pictures of me."

"I still have that picture. It's in my top dresser drawer."

I blushed at his confession.

He turned to the final page in the album. It was our school class picture. "You always take good pictures," he softly commented as he stared at my image. "It's easy to see why Kent was taken with you."

The easygoing atmosphere instantly changed as tension settled between us. I waited for him to continue, unsure of where his thoughts were going and unsure if I wanted to know.

He closed the album and turned to face me. "I want you to answer a question that's been bothering me since last night. Please be honest even if you know it's something I don't want to hear."

I took a deep breath. "I will tell you the truth," I slowly replied wondering if this was going to lead to more problems. I clasped my hands together in my lap and braced for the question.

He looked down at the album. "When you saw Kent, did you want to go with him?"

I considered his question. I had been so caught up in the anguish of what Todd assumed happened that I hadn't thought through the actual encounter with Kent. "No."

He looked at me and I noted his relief.

"I kept telling him that I wasn't going to go with him but he didn't listen to me." I shivered as the realization of what happened came to my mind. "When he came toward me, I backed up but the shelves were behind me and I had nowhere to go. I felt trapped. I knew if you were there, he would back away. He just kept talking about all the things he could buy me and then he touched my cheek. That was when I ran to the door. I didn't want him touching me. It all happened so fast. One minute he grabbed my arm, and the next thing I knew, he was kissing me. I was grateful you showed up when you did. I hate to think of what would have happened if you hadn't."

"Ann, I'm sorry," he whispered. He put his arms around me and held me close to him. He lightly kissed the top of my head. "I was a fool not to believe you."

"How could you have known any differently? You walked in at the wrong moment."

He was silent for a few moments. I could feel the beating of his heart. It was very comforting and relaxing. My anxiety over the events slowly faded away.

"I didn't think about it before," he began, "but when I walked into the store, Mrs. Carson was on her way out. I think she was going to get help for you. When she saw me, she said I had to help you. When I saw you kissing Kent, I thought she meant that I had to stop you before you acted improperly. But now that I think about it, she looked scared. I believe she meant that I was to protect you. It all makes sense now."

He finally believes me!

"Can you forgive me?"

I laughed. "Of course."

After another moment passed, I stood up and showed him my jewelry box with the jewelry in it.

"I would like to sell the jewels to Mrs. Coley. She has a couple of merchants who like to stop by and they particularly like these items."

"Ann, those are a part of your past. You don't have to sell them. We're doing fine."

He would never admit the truth, but maybe that was how men were when it came to money. "They're doing me no good here. I don't have any use for them."

He sighed. "They belong to you. Do with them what you will."

I nodded, glad to settle the matter. "I know my father has a dowry for me."

He stood. "Yes. He'll be putting it in your own account at the bank when he can get into town."

I took his hands in mine and looked at him. "I want you to have it. As my husband, it is your right. My mind is made up and you won't change it."

"Alright."

"I need to prepare a snack before dinner."

"I love you, Ann."

I smiled, relieved everything was going to be alright between us. "I love you too." I left the room and turned around. "Aren't you coming?"

"Do I have your permission to move my things in here?"

"It is your bedroom too." I blushed, surprised at my boldness.

He grinned. "I'll be down shortly."

I nodded and floated down the steps.

***

As I prepared dinner later that day, Todd and my father finished shoveling the snowdrift. My mother watched me prepare dinner and offered her services to grab seasonings for me.

She chuckled as she brought me some salt. "I feel lost in here."

"I know how you feel," I agreed. "I was lost when I started cooking. Fortunately, I had Barbara to mentor me. She's going to teach me to sew patches on clothes. I suppose she'll eventually teach me to sew clothes too."

"Why, you are very self-sufficient."

"Actually, it's very satisfying."

She nodded. "I can see that it would be." She put the salt back on the shelf where I kept my seasonings. "I would like to meet Barbara. You've mentioned her several times in your letter."

"You'll get your chance. I'm thinking of paying her a visit tomorrow if Todd and Father manage to get the horses and sleigh ready by then."

"I don't mean to pry but I was wondering if things are settled down between you and Todd? You and Todd seemed happy this afternoon during the snack."

I blushed. "Yes. Thanks to you and Father."

"I don't know what I did but I suppose your father had some words of wisdom. He's good at helping others make amends."

We finished preparing the meal and called the men in to eat.

"You have excellent timing," my father said as he and Todd took off their coats and hats. I noted that Father had borrowed a pair of Todd's comfortable overalls. "We just finished."

"Oh good," Mother replied. "I was hoping to meet Barbara and John."

"John. He's the farmer, isn't he?"

"Yes," Todd answered.

"I would be interested in hearing what he has to say. May I come along?"

"I'm sure they won't mind the company."

As we ate the meal, we discussed some funny incidents during Todd and my childhoods. We laughed so much, it was hard to finish eating, but we managed to get through it.

After desert, Todd offered to help me clean the dishes. "You wash and I'll dry."

Since my parents were in the parlor, we had some privacy. "My father adores you," I confided as I handed him a clean plate to dry.

"I like him too. Your parents aren't stuck on societal expectations."

"They are to a degree, but when they insisted I behave a certain way, they made it clear that it wasn't necessarily because they agreed with it but because it was proper given where we lived. Remember that dance you took me to?"

"How can I forget? You threatened to run away if I didn't take you to North Dakota with me."

I giggled. "Yes, I did. I didn't want to go because of Kent and Rebecca. Though my parents understood and sympathized with me, they felt it best that I go because of how it would look to everyone if I didn't. Then my mother made me wear that horrible pink dress."

"I liked that dress. It showed off your best features."

"It was awful. I could hardly breathe in it. It was so tight."

"I liked the fact that it was tight. You have great curves."

"Why, Todd. I didn't think gentlemen noticed such things."

He raised his eyebrows innocently. "Is it wrong for a man to appreciate the finer qualities in a woman?"

My cheeks grew warm. "No, it's not. It's not like women don't notice some qualities men possess."

"Really?" He set his towel down on the counter and turned to me, interested in what I would say next. When I continued to wash the pan, he said, "Go on."

"Oh no. A lady never tells her secrets," I teased.

"Not even for a kiss?"

I shook my head. "No."

He stood behind me and slowly ran his hands from my shoulders to my hips. "You are very appealing," he whispered in a way that made me forget what I was doing. I held my breath expectantly as he kissed the side of my neck. "I can't wait to see what treasures you're hiding under those clothes."

"Todd, such speech is...is..." I searched for the word but for some reason, I couldn't think straight.

"Appropriate for a husband to tell his wife."

I considered his statement and realized he was right. It still made me blush to talk to him of such things. Determined to overcome my shyness, I turned to face him. I couldn't gather enough courage to look at him directly so I stared at the clock on the wall behind him. "I'm glad you moved your belongings into my bedroom."

"Our bedroom."

He stood so close to me I could feel his breath on my cheek. I nodded weakly. My body was responding to his touch and words in a way that thrilled me. I realized that I longed to explore these new feelings. I noted the time on the clock and wished it was later in the evening so we could go upstairs.

He lightly kissed my cheek. I turned my head so he would kiss me on the lips. His lips met mine and I wrapped my arms around his shoulders, thoroughly enjoying the desire flowing through me. He deepened the kiss. I sensed his pleasure and passion for me as his hands continued their intimate search on my body.

He gently pulled away, his breathing shallow. "If I keep going, I won't be able to stop."

As much as I wanted to keep going, I knew he was right. We would wait until my parents were asleep.

He went back to his side of the sink and picked up the towel. He held out his hand. "I'm ready for the next dish."

I could only nod as I turned back to the sink and finished washing the pan. I handed it to him, surprised that my hands were shaking.

"You didn't answer my question," he stated as he ran the towel over the pan. "What do you find attractive in men?"

"It's what attracts me to you. I like your shoulders. They're strong and broad. Sometimes I watch you as you take care of the horses. I can see your muscles move under your shirt if you're not wearing a vest or a coat."

"You've been admiring me when I wasn't looking?"

I chuckled at his appalled expression. I knew he was joking. "Yes. And not just the shoulders," I admitted, deciding this game was fun.

"What else?"

I glanced at him. "Well, your pajamas are a little tight."

He rolled his eyes. "I know. I picked the wrong size at the store."

"That's your opinion. I take peeks when you're not looking."

"I feel naked."

I could tell he didn't mind being ogled.

"I can't wait for tonight."

I shared his enthusiasm but didn't voice it. Instead, I turned my attention back to the dishes.

Chapter Twenty-One
Todd's Point of View

That night, once her parents were asleep and I finished my usual chores, I quietly walked past my old room. It felt good to not sleep in there anymore.

It felt strange not to knock, but I reminded myself that she was expecting me. It was *our* bedroom now. I opened the door. The kerosene lamp resting on the dresser lit up the room in a soft glow. She stood by the window in her nightgown. Heat swelled in my groin and I resisted the urge to hide my arousal. We were about to make love, so there was no longer the need to hide my attraction for her. I shut the door and smiled at her.

"Should I come to you or would you like to come to me?" I tried to sound playful but it was hard to concentrate on anything but how great she looked. The nightgown didn't hide the curve of her breasts and hips as much as the dresses did.

"I thought I would show you my treasures first." Her voice was soft. "I've been hoping for this night for awhile now."

"Why didn't you tell me?"

"I tried. I didn't come right out and say it. Do you remember that day you lost your job at the bank and we were in the barn?"

I nodded.

"I told you I wanted you to come to my room."

My eyes widened. "I thought you wanted firewood."

"The firewood was nice but it wasn't what I really wanted. I won't make you decode my messages from now on. I should have just said it but wasn't sure how."

I feel so stupid. Why didn't I get that when she said it? "That's it, Ann. I don't care who comes to the door or if the house burns down. I've wanted you for so long, I've thought of little else." I locked the door. "We're not leaving the room until we consummate this marriage."

She smiled. "I wasn't the one who interrupted us before. I want this too."

This I liked to hear. She wanted me. That was the crucial part of this night. I was glad I waited for her to be ready.

She cleared her throat and took off her nightgown, letting the cotton fabric fall to her feet.

I beheld her beauty for a moment. Never in my wildest dreams could I have pictured her like this. Her round breasts with the taut pink nipples, her slender waist, and the patch of dark hair between her legs… She was perfect, and I was about to make love to her. I would finally get a chance to explore her the way I'd wanted to since we got married.

I forced my feet forward, aware that I suddenly felt nervous. I took a deep breath to calm the wild beating of my heart. It didn't work. "You are beautiful."

She gave a soft smile and peered up at me. "It's your turn."

My hands slightly shook as I removed my clothes, aware that she was watching and not sure if that excited me or scared me. I'd never been naked in front of anyone since I was old enough to bathe myself. I stood in front of her, my pulse racing as her gaze swept over me. I cleared my throat and asked, "What do you think?"

Her face turned a pretty shade of pink. "I like what I see."

I cupped her face in my hands and gave her a chaste kiss. "I love you, Ann. I'm going to spend the rest of my life showing you how much."

I lifted her in my arms and carried her to the bed. It suddenly occurred to me that I had no idea how to make love to her. I knew the mechanics of it because of the stories I heard from the older boys in school. But this was really happening to me and it was with Ann. I wondered if she would enjoy it. I hoped so. I wanted to please her.

I settled next to her, lying on my side so I could take in her naked body. She was amazing. Every part of her captivated me. My fingers brushed her cheek. It was a familiar action, and right now a familiar action made me feel like I knew what I was doing.

She turned to me, pressing those wonderful curves into my flesh. She was soft and smooth. My breath caught in my throat. Her abdomen cushioned my erection, sending an unexpected thrill through me. If this was a foretaste of what was to come, then making love had to be the best thing I was ever going to experience.

"Tell me what you want," I said in a husky voice I didn't recognize.

"Kiss me."

She didn't have to make that request twice. I lowered my head to hers and obeyed. The kiss started out as a gentle one. I parted my lips and she did the same, allowing me to taste her. Our kiss deepened and I shifted against her. She was, without a doubt, the most exquisite woman in the world. I could happily kiss her for the rest of my life, but my body wanted more. I wondered if hers did too.

I slid an arm under her to support her weight. Her hands rested against my chest, her fingers a bit ticklish but also sensual. My hand cupped her breast, which was just as soft as I remembered from having touched it before. I groaned. My shyness was slowly slipping away as my desire for her intensified. I traced the length of her side, covering the dip of her waist and the rise of her hip and the strength of her thigh. She was incredibly made, and she was mine. All mine to cherish and enjoy.

She moaned and rubbed her leg against mine, sending shivers through me. I wanted to enter her right then. But I was determined to take it slow, to learn her and savor each moment. All of it was terrific.

I turned her on her back so I could have better access to her body. My mouth left hers and descended to her neck. Her arms wrapped around me, the palms of her hands pressing into my back. I nuzzled her neck, taking in the wonderful smell of the lilac soap she used when she had bathed after dinner. I groaned as I pictured her wet and naked in the metal tub. Now that I knew what she looked like naked, I could visualize it. And I liked it.

"Oh Ann. You're so very beautiful."

My words barely came out as a whisper. I wanted to both feel her and taste her. I took the time to study her curves, taking time to caress the full length of her body, spending more time on her breasts. I kissed them and cupped them in the palms of my hands, my thumbs brushing the hardened nipples. With a soft sigh, she shifted and spread her legs. I took the invitation and settled my anxious body between her thighs. I leaned back so my hungry eyes could take in her figure.

I massaged her legs that rested against my waist, and I worked my hands up her thighs, pausing a moment over the center of her womanhood. Holding off on entering her, which was proving more difficult with each passing minute, I knelt in front of her. I wanted to taste this part of her and see it up close. I bent down. With feathery touches, I traced the yielding folds of her flesh. She was a wonder to learn. I ran my tongue along her, enjoying her unique taste and scent. It was her. A very intimate part. And I liked it.

I gave a slight smile as she squirmed against me and ran her fingers through my hair. I realized that she enjoyed this. I returned to sitting in front of her so that I could better explore her with my fingers, to get an idea of how I should enter her. I didn't wish to hurt her. I heard the first time could be difficult for a woman. I wished to give her as much ease into the consummation as possible. I found the flesh beneath the curls and fingered it.

She encouraged me to explore her, and I was more than happy to oblige her. I slipped a finger inside her and groaned at how warm and wet her flesh was. It was more amazing than I imagined. I knew it would feel good but had no idea just how incredible it would be.

She arched her back. "Don't stop."

Excited because she liked what I was doing, I slid in a second finger and stroked her. Her whimpers of pleasure served to push away the lingering doubts I had, and I became firm in my movements. I explored the area around the opening. When my thumb found her sensitive nub, she gave out a louder moan. I slid a third finger into her, noting the tightness at what I suspected was her hymen. I glanced at her, wondering if I should take the third finger out but she moved her hips against me, giving my three fingers full access into her.

I watched her as I caressed her nub with my thumb while my fingers continued to stroke her. Seeing her naked and touching her was sexually pleasing but seeing her receiving pleasure from what I was doing proved to be the most stimulating thing I'd ever witnessed. Her breathing came faster and she moved against me in a rhythm until she let out a final cry. Her tender flesh clenched around my fingers. I stilled my movements and waited as the contractions lessened. Her body relaxed.

Having satisfied her, I removed my fingers and entered her. She was a little tight, and her stiffening against me made me go still.

"Ann?" I asked, forcing myself to remain still in case she was hurt.

"Keep going," she whispered. "Fill me."

I didn't need further prompting. Wishing to prolong the tingling sensation mounting in me, I slowly moved back only to slide further in. Her flesh yielded to me, surrounding me and clenching around me. She groaned again and tightened her hold on my arms. Her legs wrapped around my waist and drew me in as far as I could go. Any semblance of self-control departed. All I could think of was how amazing she felt. I increased the momentum of my movements, each thrust driving me closer to the brink of heaven. Her moans blended with mine until she let out another cry, her flesh clenching around my arousal, and I gave into the urge to let go. I shuddered as the intense pleasure consumed me. I stayed still as my throbbing died down, feeling complete in having emptied my seed inside her.

I collapsed on top of her with more force than I intended. I pulled back to relieve her of my weight, but she stopped me by tightening her legs around me.

"Don't go," she softly spoke.

I looked into her eyes and saw that she was happy. Thrilled at the realization, I smiled and settled over her, making sure I didn't make her uncomfortable. I liked being inside her. It felt as if we were one. I wanted to prolong the experience. We were closer than ever before, and it was a wonderful feeling. She was mine. I was hers. Together, we were complete.

I touched my lips to hers. "I love you."

She let out a contented sigh and returned my smile. "I love you too."

I dropped kisses along her cheeks and forehead and back to her lips. Knowing this was the first of many times we'd come together to celebrate the marital bed filled me with a sense of awe and satisfaction. And there was no one else I would rather be with than her.

***

The next morning I woke up with my arms around Ann. It was the moment I had hoped for every morning since we married, and it was finally here. She was fast asleep. I gazed at her, loving how she looked first thing in the morning. I didn't think it was possible to love her more than I had, but I did. I softly kissed her and eased out of bed. It was still early but I wanted to take care of the horses so we could head out to the Russell farm. I knew Ann wanted to introduce her mother to Barbara. And I wanted to do what I could to please Ann.

I noted the chill in the room so I added another piece of firewood to the box stove. I wrapped the blanket around her body so she would be warm. Then I got dressed and shaved. I felt different. It was a good feeling. I recalled how she felt, how she smelled and how she tasted. Everything about her was wonderful. I couldn't stop smiling. I almost felt comical running down the steps with a big grin on my face, but I was too happy to care.

As I put on my hat and coat, her parents came down the stairs.

"Good morning," I called out.

"Good morning," they replied.

"Can I see your barn?" her mother asked. "I wasn't able to check it out before."

"Sure. I'm on my way to feed the horses," I replied.

"Lightning is out there," her father told her mother.

"Lightning? That is your best horse, Todd. I'm glad you were able to take him with you."

I waited for them to put their coats and boots on.

She continued. "I remember the first day you got that horse. You had just turned fifteen. Even Ann was excited about that horse. She thought it was the most beautiful shade of brown she ever saw. She asked us if we would ask you if she could ride it. Maybe we should have said yes. We weren't sure that it was a good idea since she had never ridden a horse before. Who knows? It could have started something between you two sooner."

"Lucille, things are fine. There's no sense in dwelling on the past," he said.

"Mr. and Mrs. Statesman, I would like to thank you for raising Ann as well as you did. She's a wonderful wife. She brings a lot of happiness to this place. It wouldn't be the same without her."

They smiled at my compliment.

"Thank you, Todd. That means a lot coming from you," she replied.

"We're glad to have you in the family," her father added. "Your father will come around. He's a good man. He does miss you."

"I miss him too," I admitted. But even he couldn't bring my mood down today. "Are you ready?" I opened the door for them and led them to the barn.

When we came back, we were hungry. I decided to get the rolls that Ann set aside for breakfast when we heard a knock at the front door. Leaving the kitchen, I went to the front door and opened it. To my surprise, it was Mrs. Carson.

"Good morning," I greeted.

"Good morning, Todd." She wrung her hands on her scarf. "May I please come in? I have something very important to tell you."

I stepped aside to let her into the parlor. Turning to Ann's parents, I made the introductions.

As soon as the usual pleasantries were done, I invited her into the kitchen. "Would you like something to eat or drink?" It was breakfast time. I wondered why she felt the need to come out this early.

"No thank you. I had to tell you that what you saw in the mercantile the other day wasn't what really happened." She looked frantic as she sat at the kitchen table. "I feel terrible. I wasn't able to eat or sleep. I tried to get here two days ago but the storm prevented me from leaving town. Then yesterday, I had to make arrangements for a sleigh. I wanted to come and explain what happened."

I sat next to her and Ann's parents sat on the other side.

"What did happen, Mrs. Carson?" I asked.

"It wasn't the way Kent said, Todd. Ann was trying to get out of the backroom. She kept telling him she was married and loved you but Kent wouldn't listen to reason. I still remember how patronizing he sounded. It was as if he thought her love was a childish thing. I was ready to step into the room, but she screamed and I heard footsteps. When I didn't see her emerge from the room, I knew he had physically stopped her. I realized I was just a woman and I didn't have the strength to stand up to a man. So I ran to the front door of the store. My intention was to go next door and get a man to help me. Fortunately, that's when you showed up. I was relieved to see you. I wanted to explain what happened when I realized you misunderstood the situation, but you ran out of there so fast, I didn't have a chance. Then Ann came out, and she looked distraught. Kent finally left, but he promised to come back for her."

My ears perked up at this announcement. Why hadn't Ann mentioned this? *Probably because she forgot it during the ordeal with me.*

"I think he meant it," she continued. "It would be wise for her to be careful. I still get chills when I recall the look of satisfaction on his face, as if he enjoyed putting a wedge between you and Ann. Then I told Ann I heard everything." She sighed, looking sheepish. "I don't think she took that the right way, which I can understand, given my history of spreading gossip. This brings me to another reason why I am here today. I want to apologize for telling the town you stole money at the bank. I had no proof but found it such a tasty morsel of gossip, I didn't resist spreading it. I don't know who did it. But I am a changed woman. I have learned the error of my ways."

"Thank you, Mrs. Carson," I said. "I appreciate your coming out and telling me this."

Ann opened the kitchen door. "Good morning."

Her father and I stood up at her arrival.

Her father waved her forward. "Come on in."

Mrs. Carson smiled at her. "I'm sorry I came so early. My spirit would not rest until I told your husband that you didn't want to be with that man in the mercantile."

"Thank you, Mrs. Carson," she replied.

"I feel much better. Now I can go home and sleep."

"I will see you at the store next week when I go in to help Mrs. Coley."

She nodded, said good-bye and left.

My thoughts turned back to Mrs. Carson's warning. Having her account of the events match so clearly with Ann's made me aware that Kent did indeed plan to return. I recalled the way Ann explained her encounter with him in the store. She had been afraid of him. And for good reason. What if he didn't come for her when she was in the store next time? What if he came to this house? What if I wasn't here when he did come? Who would protect her?

It occurred to me that Ann was talking to her parents but I didn't hear anything they said. I turned to her father who seemed to understand what was bothering me.

"What should I do?" I asked him.

"I wonder..." he pondered. His eyebrows furrowed. "Let's discuss it outside. We may be overreacting so I'd rather not worry the women." Turning to Ann and her mother, he said, "We will return soon."

I kissed Ann on the cheek before I followed her father out of the house.

Chapter Twenty-Two
Ann's Point of View

After breakfast, we decided to visit John and Barbara. My father insisted on getting the sleigh and horses ready while my mother went to the guest bedroom to find some suitable jewelry to wear. She loved her necklaces and rings.

Todd helped me with my coat. He paused, his hands on my hips. "I'm glad you're here," he whispered. He leaned over to kiss me.

I loved the feel of his hair as I ran my fingers through the silky strands. When he pulled away, I realized my impulsive behavior had messed up his neatly combed hair. I smoothed his hair the best I could, but it was still messy. He didn't seem to mind. When I saw we were still alone, I allowed my hands to descend from his neck to his chest. I found that I enjoyed our newfound intimacy.

By the smile on his face, I could tell he liked it too. "Just wait until tonight," he promised.

I blushed, recalling how wonderful lovemaking was.

Turning serious, he kissed me again. "I will do everything I can to keep you safe."

I frowned. "What is it, Todd? What's wrong?"

"We'll discuss it later. I want to enjoy the day."

I nodded. I wondered if Todd would mention what he and my father discussed in the barn. As long as he wasn't upset with me, I was content to wait.

My mother came down the stairs. We waited for her at the door before we headed out to the sleigh. The ride to John and Barbara's was spectacular. The sunlight glistened off the snow. The weather was warmer than the day before, so we didn't have to bundle up with as many blankets. It was a perfect day for a ride through the country. My father and mother sat up front, so Todd and I had the back to ourselves. We sat close together and held hands. I couldn't believe I spent so much time trying to avoid him while we were growing up. Now all I wanted to do was be near him.

When we reached John and Barbara's house, their children were playing in the snow. Calvin was beating Bruce at their snowball fight, though Bruce tried his hardest to hold his own. Molly was eating the snow, obviously enjoying the cold white stuff.

"Why do boys play rough?" I asked Todd, recalling how he wanted to bang his trains into mine when we played together as children.

He grinned. "It's fun. There's action and adventure. All you girls seem to do is sit down and stare at your dolls. That's boring."

"We didn't stare at the dolls. Agnes and I made up stories with those dolls."

"And you wonder why that's boring?"

"I suppose girls and boys find different things interesting. Our parents never should have made us play together."

"Growing up with sisters, I didn't have a choice but to play with girls. At least you fought back when I rammed my trains into yours."

"What did your sisters do?"

"They ran to my parents. Since I was the boy, they usually took their side. My sisters used that to their advantage."

"So what happened?"

"I either had to go to my room or play whatever they wanted. I spent most of my time in my room."

"If we were boring, why did you want to be around us when I came over?"

"Isn't it obvious? I thought you were pretty."

I guessed as much but it was nice to hear.

We got out of the sleigh and introduced John and Barbara to my parents. As Todd was about to join John and my father out to the Russell barn, I quickly asked Todd why men liked to separate themselves from women.

"Because, you're still boring," he good-naturedly replied. "When you get together, you talk about cooking, cleaning or children. God forbid you should mention a female problem. Those are the scariest of all talks, and I've heard enough of those from my sisters."

"So what do you men talk about?"

"Work. Sometimes we discuss how to fix things."

"Oh. Now that's boring." Thank goodness I didn't have any brothers to listen to while growing up.

"At least when we get together, the conversation is better for both of us." He kissed the top of my nose. "Just so you know, I enjoy our time together the most."

"Me too."

I smiled as he walked to Calvin, John and my father. As much as I looked forward to spending time with Barbara and my mother, I knew my thoughts would be on Todd and how wonderful he was. Barbara was delighted to see that things were better between Todd and me.

"I prayed day and night that you two would be alright," she confided while my mother talked to Molly and Bruce. "But today, you are glowing."

"I appreciate your prayers. They worked."

"Thank goodness."

"How are you feeling?"

"Tired but happy, especially since you and Todd are alright."

Bruce led my mother to us. "Can Mrs. Statesman see my jacks?"

"Yes, she may," Barbara replied.

He ran into the house.

"Would you like to come inside?" Barbara asked my mother and me.

We nodded and joined her.

***

When we decided to go to town, I was surprised that Todd, John and my father went to visit Mr. Fields who had puppies he was eager to give away. I wondered why they brought two light brown and white puppies. I soon discovered that one was for John's children and the other one was for Todd and me. I wanted to ask Todd why we needed a puppy but knew he would tell me later. While the men stayed to talk to Mr. Fields, Barbara took me and my mother to visit her mother and to meet Mr. and Mrs. Coley.

Afterwards, we returned to the Russell house to prepare dinner. My mother insisted on playing with the children since she made a better nanny than a cook.

"She enjoys the children as much as you do," Barbara commented as she rolled the dough.

I stuffed the dough with cheese and folded the dough to make ravioli. "She spent a lot of time with me when I was a little girl. I suppose since I was the only child, it was easy to devote most of her time to me."

"She seems like a compassionate person."

"She is. I think she took my heartbreak over Kent worse than I did. It wasn't that she liked him. She liked Todd more, but it hurt her to watch me in pain." I sighed thoughtfully. "She'll make a good grandmother."

Barbara looked at me. "Is that a possibility?"

"A lot has changed in two days," I simply replied, my cheeks hot from embarrassment.

"What great news! Maybe you'll be expecting soon and we can have our babies close together. They could be good friends."

I smiled. "What if I have a girl and you have a boy?"

"Then maybe they'll marry someday."

"You're horrible!"

She shrugged. "It's fun to imagine."

I grinned. Yes, it was.

***

After my parents settled into bed for the night, Todd said he wanted to talk to me, so I sat next to him on the couch. The puppy quietly played in the corner with an old shoe. I hoped this talk would explain the sudden need for a dog.

"I know this is something you don't like to think about, but I need you to remember something for me," he said.

I frowned. This didn't sound promising.

"When I saw you and Kent in the mercantile, did he say anything after I left?"

I blinked in surprise. I stared at the fire as I processed the events through my mind. I had focused so much on the fact that Todd saw us kissing that I hadn't considered what happened afterwards. A feeling of dread washed over me. "He said he would be back."

"That's what Mrs. Carson said. You didn't mention it before, so I couldn't be sure that is what happened but now I know. Your father recommended that we get a dog for protection. I can't be here all the time."

I sat up straight. "You think he'll come here? To our home?"

"I don't know but I'd rather play it safe. I want you to come with me to the barn."

I reluctantly put on my coat and followed him outside. Once he set the lantern on the ground, he picked up his gun.

"What are you doing?" I asked, though I really didn't want to know.

"You may need to use this. The dog won't do enough damage to stop him. It will just buy you time. If Kent's serious, he'll still come after you. Ann, shooting someone to protect yourself is not murder."

I shivered. I didn't feel comfortable using a gun. "Can't I use something else?" Did I really want to be out here, having this conversation?

He thought for a moment. "I guess the gun is intimidating to a woman."

This whole conversation was intimidating to a woman. Was Kent going to drag me off and force me to be his wife? Did Todd think that would actually happen? I recalled the way he kissed me, the force he used and how he wouldn't go away when I told him to. I quickly turned around so I could regain my composure.

Todd wrapped his arms around me. "Ann, I hope I'm overreacting, but I can't afford to take my chances. You said you were afraid of him. I can only do so much to protect you. As long as you're with someone in town, I think you'll be safe. But if you're alone here, there's no one to help you. Your father is going to discuss the situation with Kent's father. Hopefully, they can resolve the issue. In the meantime, I need you to be strong for me. Please?"

I took a deep breath. "I'll learn to shoot the gun."

He smiled. "There's the girl that threw sand on two class bullies."

I laughed, glad to have the mood lightened. I didn't want to think of Kent. I wanted to focus on Todd and how wonderful it felt to be loved by him.

"We won't practice tonight, but I want to show you where to find the gun in case you need it."

I watched him put it behind the pile of chopped wood.

He continued to explain, "I figure that if you're at the house, the dog will attack Kent and it should give you enough time to get the gun. I'm going to install door locks on the front and back doors of the house." He picked up the axe that had been behind the chopped wood and placed it on the shelf above the wood. "We'll start practicing after your parents leave."

As he took my hand and led me back into the house, I hoped that I would never have to follow his plan.

***

My parents stayed for two weeks before they went back to Virginia. Todd and I spent Thanksgiving with the Russells and their relatives. For Christmas, I gave Todd a new pair of boots that would be durable for farming. He gave me a wedding ring.

"Todd, it's beautiful," I said that night as we sat together in front of the fire in the parlor. "I think it's the most beautiful ring I've ever seen."

"You've owned fancier rings than that one."

"Maybe. But none of them were from you."

He put his arm around me. "Is it any wonder that I love you?"

I finally stopped staring at the ring and turned to him. "I would like to go into town tomorrow and help Mrs. Carson take down Christmas decorations at the church. She's really a different person now. Even Mr. Carson decided to go to church. He wanted to know what caused the big change."

"It's nice to know you two are friends." He held my hand. "You don't have to keep working for the Coley's. We have plenty of money."

"I supposed that was the case when I gave you the dowry. I still get food and cooking supplies, but I also enjoy being there. I've made some friends in town and it's a great way to visit them. You would be surprised at how many women go shopping during the day."

"More boring women talk. No wonder men rarely enter the mercantile."

I didn't take offense at his comment since I knew he was joking.

Someone knocked at the door so I jumped up to answer it. I blinked in surprise. What was Mr. Richard doing here?

He took his hat off. "Good evening, ma'am. May I speak with your husband?"

I glanced over my shoulder at Todd who hopped off the couch.

"Mr. Richard, it's a pleasure to see you. Come in," he invited.

I moved aside and took his coat and hat, which I hung on the nail by the door. "Would you like some hot cocoa?" I asked him.

"No thank you, Mrs. Brothers."

I looked at Todd to see if he wanted something to drink.

He shook his head.

"If you'll excuse me, gentlemen," I said and left the room.

I went upstairs and changed into my nightgown. As soon as I got into bed, I realized how tired I was and fell asleep. I didn't wake up until the next morning. I squinted as I lifted my head off the pillow.

Todd smiled at me. "Good morning."

"What time is it?"

"Almost seven."

"I must have been more tired than I thought."

He chuckled. "Would you like some good news?"

"Sure. It's a good way to start the day."

"Mr. Richard discovered who stole the money."

"Really? Who did it?"

"Mr. Randolph. He's been working at the bank for ten years. Shortly after I began working at the bank, his wife got sick. Since there wasn't anyone to take care of her, he missed a lot of work. He took some money when they ran out of food. He thought that he could make up the work by doing overtime, but her health kept getting worse. Mr. Richard caught him taking some money out of the safe yesterday."

"But the bank was closed."

"That's why Mr. Richard went to investigate the bank. He noticed someone was inside it. Mr. Randolph knew where Mr. Richard put the key, so that's how he got in without being noticed."

"So did Mr. Randolph plant the money and the combination to the safe in your desk?"

"Yes. He was desperate and scared. He was afraid if he lost his job, then he wouldn't be able to support him and his wife at all." He reached for my hand. "Mrs. Carson happened to be passing the bank and heard what was going on. She volunteered to watch Mrs. Randolph so he could go back to work. He'll be working some overtime to pay back what he stole, but I think everyone is happy with the outcome. Even though stealing is wrong, I can understand why he did it. I'm glad he'll be paying Mr. Richard back, and it's great that Mrs. Carson is doing so much good for people in town."

I nodded.

"Mr. Richard offered me the job back, but I said I was happy working for Mr. Fields. Isn't it amazing how things work out? Mr. Richard gave me some money for what he did to me. I told him he actually did me a favor because I hated that job."

"That's wonderful news for everyone."

"I had to resist the urge to wake you up last night and tell you. You were just too tired. I couldn't wake you up."

I snuggled up to him and smiled.

Chapter Twenty-Three
Todd's Point of View

The next month and a half passed by swiftly. Ann and I fell into a very comfortable and pleasant routine. As much as I enjoyed my work, I couldn't wait to come home. She would wait for me at the door and give me a big hug and long kiss to let me know she missed me when I was gone. We continued in our book readings, and I took her out to the barn twice a week to practice shooting at bottles. She was terrified when she first fired the gun, and it wasn't easy to get her over the discomfort of using the weapon. But she pressed through her anxiety and became a good shot. I mastered my own shooting skills and had no problems shooting each bottle.

The puppy grew into a big hairy dog. We finally decided to call him Patches since his brown and white spotted fur reminded Ann of a mended garment. I built a doghouse for him in the front yard, and we gave him some old blankets to help add to his comfort in the cold winter months. January and February were the coldest months, and we spent most of our time indoors whenever we had a snowstorm. I liked these days the most because we would spend all day in bed, enjoying each other. Farming couldn't compare to the joy of being with her.

***

One unusually warm day in mid-February, I took Ann to town. Since enough snow melted, I was able to take the wagon. She sat close to me and wrapped her arm around mine. She rested her head on my shoulder. I smiled, enjoying the moments I had with her before we went our separate ways. She went to the Coley's store to help Mrs. Coley while I went to Mr. Fields' to work. Ann planned to go to Barbara's mother's house during lunch, so I took that time to purchase Ann's gift. It was another idea I got from Calvin. I smiled as I hid it in the back of the wagon. I loved to give her things I knew she liked but wouldn't buy for herself.

The rest of the day went by slowly as I waited for the end of the workday. Finally, I got off of work and went to Barbara's mother's house to pick Ann up. She was helping Barbara with some last minute cooking. I watched Ann as she took a pie out of the oven.

"Would you like a piece?" she asked me.

"There's plenty," Barbara added.

"No thanks." I was eager to show Ann her gift.

"Can I have a piece?" Calvin and Molly asked as they hovered around Barbara who was showing in her pregnancy. Bruce was too busy chasing a cat to notice the pie.

We said good-bye to them and left. As we strolled to the stable, she put her arm through mine and whispered, "I stopped menstruating."

Had it been any other woman, this comment would have repulsed me, but coming from Ann, I knew it meant that we could be physically intimate that day. I grinned and quickly pulled her into a small alley where we would be out of sight. I gave her a long kiss, my hands running down her back. "Just you wait until I get you home," I said.

"We'll see," she slyly replied.

I raised an eyebrow. "What do you mean by that?"

She shrugged and left the alley. Glancing over her shoulder, she said, "I don't think you'll make it that long."

I chuckled. She was shy in the beginning, but I liked the way she grew more assertive as she got more comfortable in our lovemaking.

We went to the stable and I paid the owner before helping her into the wagon. As she hopped up into her seat, she brushed her body against mine. *Did she do that on purpose?* By the expression on her face, it was hard to tell. She appeared to have nothing on her mind. The ride home, however, soon proved that she did do it on purpose. She sat close to me again, but as soon as we were out of town and alone, her hands caressed parts of me that made it difficult to properly lead the horses. Her kissing on my neck didn't help much either.

When I couldn't take it anymore, I stopped the horses and set the brake on the wagon. "I have a surprise for you," I told her.

"Are you going to show me?" She took my hand and urged me to follow her into the back of the covered wagon. She began to unbutton my pants. "I've been desiring you all day." She kissed me.

I almost forgot what the surprise was but suddenly remembered it was breakable. "It's right behind you. Watch out or you'll sit on it," I warned.

She turned around to see what I was talking about. *Two can play this game. You're not the only one who can catch the other one off guard.* She let out of shout of glee when she saw the box. She opened it.

I enjoyed her excitement as she pulled out the matching dish set decorated with various fruits. "How did you know I wanted this?"

I sat next to her. "I can read your mind."

"You seem to do that, you know. It's almost spooky the way you know exactly what I want. Did Mrs. Coley or Barbara tell you?"

"No and you can't ask any more questions or I can't surprise you anymore."

"Oh. I love your surprises. You are so thoughtful."

"I like buying you things."

She put the cups and dishes back into the box. "This will go perfectly with the new kitchen towels you got me. I think Mrs. Coley likes to see you. You're a faithful customer. How can you afford all of this? Don't you need some money for your farming supplies?"

"I knew you would ask me that question, so I brought you a written account from the bank. This is what is in our account. I keep your dowry money in the investment account. You'll see that I take the interest we earn from the dowry and use that to buy you gifts. Mrs. Coley gives me discounts on anything I buy you. Apparently, you don't take enough food for the amount of work you do."

"No, I don't. I like being there so much that it doesn't seem like work. It almost seems like I'm taking advantage of her."

"She said the same thing about you. I think when I buy you things at a discount, it makes her feel better."

She examined the papers. "So, we have been doing well all along."

"That's what I've been trying to tell you."

She grinned. "I suppose I haven't taken the time to listen to you."

"You wanted to help me. I love you for that, Ann."

"You're doing well. That's a good thing. But why did you spend so many nights last fall pacing the floors at night? I thought you were worried about money."

"You were in the room next to mine and I wanted to be with you."

"Oh. Then you spent a lot of time desiring me and I had no idea."

I took off my hat and laid down. "Yes, but I wanted to be sure you were ready. I didn't want you to have sex with me because you felt obligated to."

She looked at me with her compassionate expression. "You poor thing. What you must have gone through."

I was ready to reassure her that I was fine, but the moment seemed too good to pass up. I loudly sighed. "It was hard. A man has needs."

"I want to meet those needs." She leaned forward and kissed me.

My thoughts shifted in another direction. "Ann, when I was working at the bank, I overheard two women telling each other that they considered sex a chore. You don't think that, do you?"

"I spent all day in anticipation for this moment and you ask me a silly question like that? Couldn't you tell how much I wanted you?" Her hand slid from my shirt and under my pants until she caressed my erection.

I raised an eyebrow. "You do have your hands all over me."

She chuckled. "You are irresistible." She paused and grew thoughtful. "I suppose if a man doesn't treat his wife with respect and love, then it's hard to get excited about being intimate. I don't have that problem with you. You've always been good to me. How can I not desire you?" A wicked grin crossed her face. "Can we stop talking and get to the fun part? I've been waiting for this all week."

"I'm all yours." I pulled her on top of me and let her make love to me.

***

We did have another snowstorm in late February, but the snow didn't stay on the ground for long. In early March, Ann received a letter from her parents. She told me what was in it while we sat on the porch swing. She seemed as sad as I felt when she informed me that my father had forbidden Agnes to communicate with us. It was apparent that he was determined to hold onto his anger, though my mother was sympathetic and wished to talk to us.

"Onto better news," Ann continued. "My parents are moving to Jamestown in August. I do miss them. It will be good to have them nearby."

I nodded. I had always thought her parents were good people.

"Also," she went on, "Alex and Agnes seemed to get along well when he came by for a quick visit during Christmas vacation. They're writing letters now, and it appears that they are fond of each other. I hope this won't lead to where I think it's leading."

"You mean marriage? What's wrong with that?"

"Alex will be related to me."

I laughed. "It will be good to have him as a brother. Besides, Agnes seemed to think he was attractive, though they didn't take the time to talk. I suppose with me out of the way, it gave them a chance to get to know each other."

She groaned. "Maybe we should have stayed in Virginia."

"Then we wouldn't have gotten to know each other as we have."

She sighed miserably. "I am trapped either way I go."

I kissed her. "Is it that bad? He won't be living near us. He'll be states away."

"That does help ease the pain."

I shook my head, unable to understand how two people who had such a big impact on my life could be at odds with one another. "You don't have to worry about him. If he pulls any of his pranks on you, I'll slip a squirrel in his shirt."

Her face lit up. "You would do something like that for me, wouldn't you?"

"Of course. I can't have him pulling pranks on you."

She snuggled against me. "I love you, Todd."

"I love you, too." I put my arm around her shoulders and enjoyed the gentle breeze. "Did your mother say anything else?"

"Yes, she did. You'll like this news. Once she and my father got back to Virginia, he had a long discussion with Kent's father. Kent's been warned not to see me again. Mother said he won't be a problem anymore."

I sighed with relief. Thank goodness that was over.

Chapter Twenty-Four
Ann's Point of View

It was mid-March when most of the snow melted and my trips to town with Barbara picked up to twice a week again. Since Thanksgiving, I stopped going to town as often. Barbara was six months pregnant by this time and over our talks, I became adequately educated on the subject of expecting and babies. I supposed that Todd was relieved he wasn't around for such talk. He would surely consider it boring. Bruce had turned six and Molly had turned three in January. Calvin was anxiously expecting his birthday in April. Mrs. Carson came in to pick up food for Mrs. Randolph who was still ill but steadily getting better. Mrs. Carson signed up at the town's church to clean and cook for the elderly who didn't have any relatives to care for them. Rumor was that the elderly loved her stories of what good things people were doing for others in the town. She was, in a sense, the town angel. Even Mr. Carson couldn't stop praising his wife.

When Barbara stopped the carryall at my house, I thanked her for taking me to town and got out of the carriage. I took the bag of goods the Coleys had given me into the kitchen. When I entered the parlor, I was surprised to see Todd sitting at the desk with some papers in front of him.

"I thought you were going to Mr. Fields' today."

He looked up from the papers and smiled. "I don't need to work there anymore. I just brought home our own tractor. Soon I'll start working here."

"That's wonderful! Can I see it?"

"I was hoping you'd ask." He quickly grabbed his sweater and led me to the barn. "It's used but the parts work. I should know. I helped him repair it."

"You worked on this?" I stepped around to examine the red machine that would sit one person. It looked large and intimidating.

"It's a John Froelich tractor. It runs on gasoline."

"Instead of steam?"

He nodded. "I'm going to buy a threshing machine. This tractor will pull it during the harvest season. It'll cut my time down because it'd take longer if I used the horses."

I was impressed he could use the tractor, let alone understand what to do with it. "You must know a lot about farming."

"I learn a little more each day."

I hugged him, laughing. "Your dream is finally coming true! You're a farmer, Todd."

I could tell he was pleased, and I was pleased for him.

***

By the end of March, I woke up in the middle of the night not feeling well. It was a mild nausea so I thought I could ignore it and go back to sleep, but it bothered me enough that I had to get up. I tried not to wake Todd as I took the kerosene lamp and went down the steps. I waited until I was in the kitchen before I lit it. I turned the knob so the flame was low.

I sat at the table. The mild illness wasn't anything I had experienced before, so I tried to decide what could be causing it. After a few minutes, I stood up and went to the calendar that hung on the wall. In the news of my parents' plans to move to town, I had forgotten to keep track of the days in my cycle. When I realized I was late for the month of March, my heart fluttered with excitement.

"Is everything alright?"

I turned to the kitchen door. I hadn't heard Todd come in.

"When I woke up, you were gone. I came to see if anything is wrong."

I couldn't stop smiling. "No, nothing's wrong. I think I'm expecting."

"Really?" Suddenly he was wide awake.

"I'll have to see the doctor to make sure, but I'm pretty sure. Barbara told me everything I need to know about it."

He walked over to me and kissed me. "Ann, this is great news. I never imagined my life would change so much in a year."

"I can hardly remember what life was like before we came out here. Isn't that strange? I'm glad you took me with you."

"Me too."

***

I couldn't wait until Thursday to go into town, so I went to Barbara's house the next day and we went to see the doctor. She was as excited as I was when he confirmed my suspicions. "It looks like you'll be having an early Christmas gift this year," he said.

Of course, I had to stop by the mercantile and tell Mr. and Mrs. Coley the news. I even told them to let Mrs. Carson know the next time she came in. I sent a telegram to my parents. I knew they would be thrilled. The ride home was longer than usual, for I couldn't wait to confirm the news with Todd. After I took Barbara and Molly home, I put the horses and buggy in the barn.

I noted that Lightning was gone. Todd must have gone out to the fields to make plans on where he would plant his crops. He had mentioned needing to do that. I dismissed my disappointment. It wasn't like he didn't already know.

I went to the house and gathered food for the dog. Sometimes the cats liked to eat with the dog, so I put the food in an extra large bowl. I walked out to the front and set the bowl on the porch where the dog and cats quickly ran up to me. I grinned. The only time they seemed to care about me was during mealtime. I sat on one of the chairs and watched them enjoy their meal. As I rocked back and forth, I felt tired from the day's events. In all the excitement the night before, I couldn't sleep. I went over to the porch swing, laid down and took a nap, wrapping a warm blanket around me.

Patches' barking woke me up. I tried to ignore it but the dog's persistence paid off so I sat up to see what was bothering him. Perhaps Barbara was coming over. He often barked no matter who came to visit. I frowned as a man on a black horse rode toward the house. I didn't recognize the horse, and it was too soon to recognize who the visitor was. John didn't come over unless he brought his wagon. He usually brought some tools to work on Todd's farming equipment. Perhaps it was Mr. Fields coming to check the condition of the tractor. Did he have a black horse? I wished I had paid more attention when I visited him and his wife a month ago. But Todd would be here if he expected Mr. Fields. He wouldn't be out in the field.

Feeling uneasy, I pushed the blanket aside and stood up. I grabbed the empty bowl and took it into the house. After I placed it on the kitchen table, I hastened to the parlor and peered out the window. A feeling of dread came over me. It was Kent! Why was he coming here? He wasn't supposed to come back. He even made it a point to apologize to my parents. So why was he here? I couldn't dismiss the feeling that something was wrong. I quickly locked the front door and backed up.

Patches' barking grew more persistent. Kent was getting closer. I stopped walking when I reached the back door of the house. I looked out the window by the door. Could I make it to the barn in time? Should I stay here or go to the barn? My heart pounded fiercely in my chest. Where was I safer? The distance to the barn seemed to span an eternity.

The sound of someone knocking on the front door made me jump. I knew it was him without looking out the window. I quickly locked the back door and ran up the steps. I didn't consider that my movements would be loud enough for him to hear from outside. In my panic, I thought if I stayed in the house, he would assume I wasn't home and go away. I breathed heavily when I made it to the guest bedroom, which was the first bedroom upstairs.

Just stay quiet and he'll go away.

Patches continued to bark but I could still make out the sound of knocking from downstairs.

I forced myself to take deep breaths so I could calm my nerves. He would go away. He would have to go away. *He doesn't know I'm here. Does he? Did he hear me running up the steps? Oh God, why wasn't I more quiet?*

I stood in the doorway. I couldn't see the front door but I could hear what was going on. The sound of glass smashing nearly made me scream. I put my hand over my mouth before the sound could escape my throat. Was he really going to break into my house?

What should I do? What should I do?!

Patches was growling and Kent screamed at him. Sounds of a struggle made its way up the stairs. I took the moment to take my shoes off since they made the loudest sound possible on the hardwood floors. My feet were quiet as I anxiously made my way across the room. I looked out the window. I groaned when I didn't see a tree to climb down.

Todd's old bedroom had the tree in front of it. Downstairs, the struggle between Patches and Kent ended. Was Patches dead? The sound of Kent walking across the parlor moved me to action. I slid under the bed. The bed was high but the blanket was so long it was inches from the floor. I readjusted it, praying that it would hide me. I set my shoes at my head and closed my eyes, forcing my breathing to slow down. *Pretend you're wearing one of those horrible corsets.*

It wasn't long before I heard footsteps coming up the stairs. "Ann? Are you here?"

I cringed at the sound of his voice. *Go away!*

"Ann, I know you're here. I saw you from the porch when I was coming here."

I squeezed my eyes shut. That was my mistake. I should have gone to the barn. He would be searching the house and I would be safe out there.

He casually made his way up the steps. *Don't look under the bed!* He stopped at the guest bedroom. I saw a drop of blood fall to the floor. Was it his blood or Patches' blood? He walked in and looked around the room. I held my breath as his shoes stopped in front of the bed. He left the room and went to Todd's old bedroom.

I had to get out of the house. When he didn't find me in the other bedrooms, he would surely start looking under the beds. I had to move quickly but quietly. I slid out from under the bed and tiptoed to the door. I peeked around the corner. He was inside the room.

He laughed. "I don't understand why you're hiding from me." Then he grew serious, "Is Todd here too? Is he keeping you quiet?"

I made my way down the stairs as quietly as I could. Since he was talking, it made it easier to hide the squeaky sounds my footsteps made on the steps. Just as I made it downstairs, he came out of the second bedroom. I stopped, pressed my back to the wall, and waited to see if he would look in my direction. I noted his bloody arm. It looked like Patches bit him. Kent didn't look at me. He went to the third bedroom.

His voice turned sour. "Hmm... It looks like you two got friendly. I thought you were going to stay pure for me. I told you I'd be back for you."

I didn't listen to him. Every instinct in my body told me to get to the barn. I ran as slowly as I dared, hoping he wouldn't hear my footsteps as I made my way through the house. I unlocked the back door and opened it. Since he was still talking, it was easy to avoid being heard.

Once I was out of the house, I ran as fast as I could to the barn.

"Ann? Are you running away from me?" he yelled out of my bedroom window.

I didn't look back. I just kept running, my heart pounding loudly in my ears. I knew Kent would be able to outrun me. I just hoped I had enough of a head start to make it to the barn first. Once I got the gun, he would have to leave me alone.

I heard the back door slam shut. That meant he had left the house.

"Ann! Wait! I can forgive you for sleeping with Todd," he yelled as he pursued me.

Where was the dog? Where was Todd? What did Kent plan to do to me? I recalled my encounter with him in the mercantile. *What am I supposed to do when he won't listen to me? I can tell him no but he won't accept it. Do I have to point a gun at him to make him listen?*

I made it to the barn. I ignored my shaking hands as I went to the pile of chopped wood. I nearly cried in alarm when I saw that the gun was gone. I glanced up on the shelf and saw the axe. I grabbed it and frantically looked around. I needed to get to Todd. He would know what to do. My breathing was so fast that it made me lightheaded. I forced myself to take a deep breath. I needed to think clearly. Now wasn't the time to faint.

Just talk sense into him. Did I really expect him to think I was trying to talk sense into him when I was holding an axe in my clammy, shaky hands? I considered laying the axe down but something stopped me. What if he didn't just kiss me? What if he went further than that? With Todd and the dog out of sight, I had no guarantee that anyone or anything would stop him before he did something rash. So I decided I would hold onto the axe. Todd was right. It was better to overreact if it meant I increased my chances of being safe. I glanced at the two horses in their stalls. The smaller one would be easier to ride bareback. I wished I had taken the time to learn to ride a horse, but now was not the time for regrets. It was time for action. The smaller one would have to do. I hurried over to the stalls.

Kent ran into the barn and came to an abrupt stop when he saw me. In the stall beside me, Storm neighed at the sight of the stranger.

Kent shook his head. "Ann, I came back for you. Aren't you happy to see me?"

"Go away!" I yelled.

He looked shocked.

"I want to be here," I continued. "I love Todd."

"What has happened to you out here? Have you gone mad?"

Why doesn't he leave? I felt the tears welling up in my eyes but forced myself to stay focused. *I'm so scared!* I gripped the axe. *I don't want to use it. Lord, please don't let it come to that. Just send him away.*

"Please, leave," I sobbed despite my best effort not to.

"Ann, I wouldn't hurt you. I love you. I want to marry you. It should have been you. Rebecca got in the way. She seduced me, as I'm sure Todd seduced you. Can't you understand that I never wanted to end our courtship?"

"It doesn't matter what happened, Kent," I said. "We've already made our choices. You have to move on."

He glared at me. "Are you preaching at me?"

What?

He moved forward a step.

I moved back.

The horses neighed.

"I've had enough of people reminding me that I need to move on," he spat. "What I need is to get back to the way things were a year ago. You can't honestly stand there and tell me you like it here."

"Yes, I can."

"No, Ann! You're not supposed to like it here. Todd forced you out here and kept you a prisoner against your will. I'm here to save you."

I shook my head and rapidly blinked through my tears so I could keep track of him. "I want to be here."

"No!" He lunged for me.

I shrieked and swung the axe. I wasn't aiming at him. I was trying to stop him from getting closer to me. It worked. He immediately backed away. I had to get out of the barn but how? I glanced at Storm. If I could get on her back, I could ride out of here. Trying to steadily my hold the axe in one hand, I reached for the latch on the stall door with my other hand. My hand shook so badly, I couldn't open it.

To my shock, he grabbed the axe. I tried to hold onto it. I gripped it with both hands and leaned back, hoping gravity would work to my advantage, but he was too strong for me. He pulled the axe toward him and I fell back when he yanked it out of my hands. I sat on the ground in shock. I watched as he held the axe. *Oh God, what is he going to do?*

He shook his head. "Do you think I'm going to use this on you?" He put the axe gently on the ground. "I don't want to hurt you, Ann. I want to marry you."

"I'm not yours."

"We can change that. You ran away with Todd. Run away with me."

"No."

My fingers felt a solid object. I gripped the rock in my hand. I managed to stand up. I had to get out of here!

"You have to love me, Ann!" He grabbed me by the arms and tried to kiss me.

I threw a rock at his head with as much strength as I could muster.

He screamed and let me go.

I turned to the stall and tried to shake the door open. It wouldn't budge. I wasn't thinking clearly enough to unlock it. I swung my leg over the side of the door. If I could hop on the horse, I could get out of here. Just as I made it halfway over the door, Kent grabbed my foot. I slipped and grabbed onto Storm's neck. The horse bucked back in protest, but I managed to hold onto her. Kent lost hold of my foot but held onto the hem of my dress.

He started to climb the stall.

"Let me go!" I screamed, kicking at him.

Suddenly the sound of a gunshot pierced through the air. Startled, Kent let go of me, and I fell into the stall with the horse. Storm bucked again but I rolled away from her in time to avoid being stepped on.

"Get away from my wife."

I was so grateful to hear Todd's cold voice that all of my energy departed. I just cried silently in the stall while I watched them.

Kent grabbed his ear. Blood seeped through his fingers. He slowly backed away from the stall, his hands up in the air. "It's not what it looks like."

Todd's horse moved closer to Kent. Kent continued to walk back until he was against the wall. Todd sat on Lightning, his gun trained on Kent. He shot an anxious glance in my direction. "Are you alright?"

I was so relieved to see him that I could only nod.

Turning his attention back to Kent, he clenched his jaw. "I ought to kill you for attacking my wife."

"Don't...I..." Kent's voice shook. "I won't come back. I promise."

The next sound I heard was Patches' barking.

"How do I know you'll leave her alone?" Todd demanded over the barking.

"Look at you. You're ready to kill me. I don't want to die." Kent touched his bloody ear. "I understand now. She wants to be with you. I thought I was rescuing her but I wasn't."

Patches quieted down.

"You told her parents you would leave her alone. But here you are. I don't believe a word you're saying. I think you'll say anything to get out of trouble."

Someone called out, "Mr. Brothers?"

I stood up to see who it was. I blinked in surprise. It was Kent's father. Kent hustled over to him. Todd finally relaxed his hold on the gun.

"Son, you have caused much grief to your mother and I," his father sadly said. "Mr. Brothers, I apologize for trusting my son to stay away from your wife. Kent, get your horse. I want to talk to Mr. Brothers."

Kent nodded and left the barn.

Todd leaned over and helped me out of the stall. He slid off his horse and set the gun aside on the ground. With one arm around me and one hand on the horse's bridle, he led us to where Kent's father stood.

Mr. Ashton's face was glum. "I'm sending him to my brother in Ireland. My brother is tough. He won't let Kent get away with anything, and if Kent hopes to get his inheritance, he will have to abide by my brother's rules."

"Do you believe he'll stay away from here?" Todd asked.

"If there's one thing Kent loves more than women, it's money. He won't give up that inheritance for anything or anyone."

"I believe you, sir."

"I'm sorry. He was raised better than this." He shook his head. "Good day, Mr. Brothers, Mrs. Brothers."

I nodded to him. I was speechless. A year ago, I wanted to be with Kent. Now, I couldn't imagine being with anyone but Todd. I leaned against him, grateful he was mine and I was his.

We watched Kent and his father leave. Once they were out of sight, Todd returned the horse to its stall. I hugged the dog, grateful that he went to find Todd for me. The dog did have blood around his mouth, but he looked unharmed. Patches must have bitten Kent's arm and when he couldn't stop Kent, he ran to get Todd. When Todd saw the blood on Patches' mouth, he knew something was wrong. The pieces of the events that occurred were easy to put together.

Todd walked back to me.

"He got you for me," I said.

I stood up and hugged him.

He held me tightly against him. "I was never so scared in my entire life," he whispered. "I almost killed him, Ann. I came so close to pulling the trigger."

I tightened my hold on him.

We stayed there for the longest time, just holding onto each other, still shaky but relieved.

Chapter Twenty-Five
Ann's Point of View

One night in late April, I had a nightmare that I woke up and was next to Kent.

He smiled his usual charming smile at me. "I will never go away, Ann. I won't take no for an answer. You belong to me."

I bolted up in bed, my pulse racing as I struggled to determine whether or not I was still dreaming. It was disturbing to have a dream where I kept waking up only to realize I was still dreaming. That had been happening a lot lately. I glanced next to me and saw someone right there. My mind, still caught up in a dreamlike state, couldn't register who it was. For a moment, in the moonlight, the person almost looked like Kent.

"Ann, are you alright?" he asked, sitting up.

I screamed and fell off the bed. I quickly squirmed under the bed and closed my eyes. *Make him go away.* I held my breath, willing him to leave the house.

"Ann? It's me. Todd."

Todd? I opened my eyes and saw Todd kneeling by the bed, his concerned expression immediately bringing me relief.

I released the sobs I had been holding in. "I thought you were Kent."

He moved close to me and held me in his arms. "What did he put you through?" I could hear the anger and pain in his voice. Though he tried to hide it, I knew he was furious at

Kent for what he did. "I'll never forgive myself for not leaving that gun behind the woodpile."

I held onto him and continued crying. "We didn't know he would come back. There was no way to know."

He kissed the top of my head and tightened his hold on me. "I promise that the gun will always be there for you in the future. I'll get a gun for the house and another one for when I'm in the fields."

The next day, he did just that.

Sometimes, I went to the barn with him while he worked to make necessary repairs or to take care of the horses. I didn't know what I could do to help him, so I mostly sat and watched him work. He taught me how to ride Storm since she was a gentle horse. If I ever needed to ride a horse to escape, I would know how. Lovemaking took on another dimension. It was one of the few things that took my mind completely off of Kent. I discovered that the simple act of being intimate with Todd wasn't only exciting and pleasurable but it was also comforting because I knew he loved me and did everything he could to keep me safe.

***

Fortunately, Barbara came over as often as she could. Her presence and words brought me great comfort.

"I don't understand why I'm still afraid," I told her in May when we sat at the kitchen table while Molly played with her doll.

"Give yourself time, Ann. What happened to you was traumatic for any woman. It will take time before you can feel safe when you're alone."

"I'm glad you're willing to spend so much time with me," I admitted. Mrs. Carson had made regular trips to visit, and my trips to town with Barbara to help out at the Coley's store did much to alleviate my anxiety, but I felt closer to Barbara than anyone, except for Todd.

"This time of year, the men are out in the fields a lot," she replied. "It can get lonely, so it's really no trouble for me to be here. As busy as children keep me, it's still nice to have another adult to talk to."

"You're due next month. Is your mother coming to your place to help you?"

"She will stay for a month to help out, yes. It would be nice to have you come by for a visit too, and I should be healed enough in a couple of weeks to come out here."

"I do want to be there when your baby is born. I would like to know what to expect. I know you've described it but I want to see the birth, if that is alright?"

"You are certainly welcome. In six months, you'll have your own experience. It will be painful, but when you hold your baby in your arms for the first time, you won't even think of the pain. Just be sure you spend some time alone with Todd. Sometimes husbands can feel left out after the baby is born."

I took note to be sure to follow her advice.

A knock at the door interrupted our conversation. I opened it and smiled at Mrs. Carson who brought in a box of food.

"I hope it's alright that I came here unannounced," she greeted.

"Certainly. It's always good to see you," I replied.

She followed me to the kitchen and gave the box to Barbara. "This is for you, so you won't have to worry about cooking once the little one arrives."

"Thank you, Melanie," Barbara responded, obviously pleased. "How do you find time to do so much for everyone?"

"Oh, that's easy. My children are grown and have yet to be married, so I just have my husband to care for. I have too much time on my hands and will linger a little too long where I shouldn't be if I don't keep busy. Though I don't gossip anymore, I like to avoid temptation when I can."

"If I have a girl, I'm naming her Melanie in hopes she'll be as thoughtful and caring as you."

"Well, I don't know what to say." She took her handkerchief out and dabbed her eyes. "I've never received such an honor before."

"Now, don't go crying. Barbara and I are so emotional these days, we'll start crying too," I joked, though there was some truth to it. I wasn't prepared for the frequent urge to cry at the slightest provocation.

She laughed. "We can't have a room full of crying women." She sat down next to us. "So, did you receive a letter from your mother yet?"

I nodded. "Yes. It came just the other day. They should be arriving at the end of August. They are coming out to buy a house, and after that, they will move their things here. I think you will get along very well with my mother."

"Will they bring their servants with them?"

"Just Ginny. Ginny is almost like a sister to me, and she is close to my mother. She said she wished to stay on as their servant. She has no family keeping her back in Virginia."

"How are you feeling these days?" Melanie asked me, suddenly serious. "Are your nightmares going away?"

"Slowly. It's not so bad anymore. My mother confirmed that Kent is in Ireland with his uncle. He's under constant supervision."

We sat in silence for a few moments.

Barbara looked at me. "Have you heard anything about Agnes? I often wonder how she is doing since she graduated."

"Actually, I did receive a letter from her too. She will marry Alex next month. They are going to stay in Virginia while he finishes up his schooling. Alex has become close to her parents. I think Todd's father is starting to come around to accepting Todd again. Agnes says that when her father sees Alex, he sees Todd. I guess since Alex and Todd are friends, his father can't help but remember Todd whenever Alex is around."

"Wouldn't it be wonderful to see your parents and Todd's parents visiting for Christmas?"

"We must not give up hope," Melanie said. "After all, if a gossiping, crabby woman like me can change, then anything is possible."

Barbara and I laughed.

"I can't remember what you were like before," I admitted.

Barbara nodded her agreement.

***

Later that day as I was making dinner, Todd came in from the fields. After he washed up, he joined me in the kitchen and gave me a big hug.

"Are you excited about seeing Agnes and Alex when they visit in July?" I asked him.

"Of course, I am. But are you? I do recall you being upset whenever Creepy Alex was nearby."

"I'll just have to get used to him, I suppose. Despite my best intentions, it looks like he'll be my brother-in-law."

"When you get to know him, as I know him, you'll be alright with him."

I turned my attention to the stew on the stove. "One can only hope." Though I gave Todd a hard time about his childhood friend, I did expect to enjoy his company.

"He will never admit it but you intimidate him."

"That's hard to believe."

"It's true. But you can't tell him I told you that."

"Why weren't you ever intimidated by me?"

"Growing up with six sisters who picked on me gave me amazing strength to withstand female hysterics."

I stared at him in disbelief. "What?"

"Poor Alex had two brothers. He didn't know what to do."

"Female hysterics?"

He paused and looked at me. Despite his joking, I could see the admiration and love he had for me in his eyes. "I wouldn't change anything about you."

He took me in his arms and kissed me with so much passion, I felt my face flush.

"I think you're done with dinner," he whispered in my ear.

"No. I have to keep stirring it or the meat and vegetables will stick to the pot."

"I'll help you with that." He leaned against me and took the pot off the stove. Then he looked at me with a mischievous glint in his eye. "Now, where were we?"

"You were just telling me that women are better than men."

His eyes widened. "I was?"

I wrapped my arms around his waist and kissed his neck. I loved the way he smelled. He had such a masculine scent. It spoke of the freedom of the fields and fresh air. "Yes."

"You could almost talk me into that." He gently pulled me away and smiled at me. "Did you know you grow more and more beautiful every day?"

"You keep talking like that and your dinner will get cold," I whispered, my heart pounding in anticipation at his words and the way his hands caressed my body.

"I'm not hungry. Not for food anyway."

I gladly responded to his kiss. An all too familiar ache formed between my legs, reminding me how wonderful it felt when he was inside me. He pulled me tightly against him, his solid chest crushing my breasts. I didn't mind. In fact, I liked it. I liked everything about making love to him. I especially enjoyed the feel of his arousal and pressed my abdomen closer to it. Groaning, he stroked my back, sending unexpected chills up and down my spine. My skin flushed with desire. I wasn't new to lovemaking anymore, and knowing what to expect made me eager for him.

"I can't wait. I need you now," I confessed as I pulled far enough from him so I could undo the buttons of his cotton shirt.

I slipped my hands under the shirt. He'd developed muscles in the time we'd been out here. I found him especially sexy when he chopped wood, and as I traced the hardness in his chest, I pictured him out in the barn with his axe. Why didn't I realize he was sexy when we lived in Virginia?

He shrugged out of his shirt and kissed my neck. I giggled at the tickling sensation that played along my skin. His hands traveled from my shoulders and caressed my arms. I closed my eyes and tilted my head to grant him better access to my neck. The tickling sensation faded into a more urgent demand for him. My hands dropped lower, tracing his lean abdomen and down to the belt holding his pants up. I always had trouble with the leather belt. I groaned in aggravation.

He chuckled. "I'll help."

"Well, hurry up. I don't know how much longer I can wait," I teased.

"You can help by taking your things off too."

I smiled at his playful tone and removed my clothing, no longer shy in front of him. It was strange but being naked in front of him felt as natural as if I were alone. He truly was a part of me, though a more exciting part. I liked his body and had fun exploring him and learning what he liked. When his pants fell at his feet, I let my hands caress the male part of him. Leaning into him, I stroked him, closing my eyes so I could focus on how it felt. Hard and thick. The ache between my legs increased. I longed to feel it in me again.

I didn't know why a couple of the girls in my class seemed horrified by the notion of touching their future husbands intimately. But having learned Todd as I had, I also discovered that the girls really didn't understand the male body, or the beauty of it. Broad shoulders and narrow waist. Strong arms and legs. The intimate touching was one of my favorite parts of lovemaking, whether he touched me or I touched him.

He led me to the kitchen table, which he had fixed so it no longer wobbled. Taking me by the waist, he picked me up and set me on it. He moved closer to me. He didn't enter me but his erection settled against me. I moaned and kissed him, enjoying the way his hands traveled my body. My skin responded to his touch, feeling as if it had caught on fire.

I didn't have the patience to wait any longer. I laid back on the table. I wrapped my legs around his waist and pulled him to me. "I need you."

Still standing, he entered me. I moaned. The initial contact always felt wonderful. I liked how he filled me. It made me feel very feminine, and I was glad I was a woman. He found my sensitive nub and rubbed it. Closing my eyes, I gave into the sensations his fondling produced, aware that my body clenched around his erection as he made slow, purposeful movements in and out of me. I shifted my hips to heighten my pleasure. I grabbed the back of his thighs and pulled him closer. Not that we could get any closer, really. But the contact was incredible.

He continued his slow and methodical movements, which drove me crazy since my body was screaming for release. When I finally reached the peak, I cried out and tightened my hold on him. He leaned over and kissed me. I wrapped my arms around his shoulders and kissed him back, returning passion for passion. His skin felt slick and he smelled wonderfully masculine.

Clinging to me, he moved inside me, gradually increasing the momentum of his thrusting. He brought his lips to my neck, and I could hear his ragged breathing. I moved with him, eager for him to experience the same pleasure he brought me. He arched his back. I felt him throb inside of me and knew he found his release. Knowing he found such ecstasy with me made my heart flutter with joy. I wanted to give him pleasure. He treated me so well, cherished me so well, and loved me so well. How could I not want to satisfy him? Not just with my cooking or cleaning, but also by opening myself completely and freely to him. Loving him as he had loved me for all those years.

He rested on top of me, his breathing still rough. I kissed his neck and held him. When he rose up on his elbows, he kissed me, a lingering kiss that delighted me.

I smiled. "Dinner might be cold this evening."

He grinned back. "I'll survive. Besides, this was worth it."

Yes, it was. It definitely was.

***

In early June, I decided to make lunch while Todd washed the horses. He offered to join me in the kitchen, but I wanted to be able to do something in the house alone. I wanted to do my chores without being in constant fear. I chose to make sandwiches, and I was chopping a tomato when I heard Patches bark. I froze. For a moment, I couldn't breathe as images of Kent breaking into my house flashed through my mind. I didn't want to look out the window but I forced myself to go to the parlor and check the front yard. I cried with relief when I saw that Patches was playing with the two cats.

I stumbled back to the kitchen. My tears fell down my cheeks as the reality of my fear consumed me. I had been paralyzed when I thought he was coming. I knew I was safe but I wanted to feel safe too. I hated Kent! I knew he was terrified of Todd now that Todd had pulled a gun on him. I knew he wouldn't come back because Todd would kill him if he ever saw him again. But I didn't *feel* safe!

Struggling to complete the lunch, I set the tomato onto its side. My hands shook. *Stop it. You're safe. He's all the way in Europe. He can't harm you anymore.* As much as I repeated these things, my shaking and crying wouldn't stop.

I angrily sliced the tomato until I realized I was cutting the board too. I threw the knife in the sink, picked up the board and banged it against the table, pretending I was hitting Kent with it. If I pounded the table enough, I could erase Kent completely from my mind. *I hate you, Kent! I wish I never met you! I won't live my life in fear anymore.*

The board finally gave and split in half. The table had suffered damage as well but was still intact. I curled up in the corner of the room and sobbed hysterically into my hands. I couldn't keep living this way. I had to get past this or else I would be a prisoner forever. *Maybe I'll never feel completely safe again. Maybe the fear will always linger in the back of my mind, but I should be able to do something to ease that fear enough so I can be comfortable when I'm alone.*

Out of the corner of my eye, I caught sight of the closet by the door. The kitchen door was open. I had a good view of the parlor. I hated for any door to be closed since I wanted to know what or who was in the next room at all times. The closet door was open as well, and I saw the rifle sitting under the coats. *I may not be able to control the circumstances around me, but I can control how I respond to those circumstances.* I wiped the tears from my eyes and stood up. My anger returned with newfound energy. *I can control some things in my life, and I can make every effort to protect myself.*

I recalled the stack of empty glass bottles under the kitchen sink and grabbed an armful of them. *You don't win, Kent! I'm taking my life back!* I stormed out of the house and to the barn. I didn't see Todd, so I went to the shelf in the corner of the barn and set the bottles on it. After the bottles were in a row, I went to the woodpile and picked up the rifle from behind it. I made sure it had bullets in it before I turned my attention back to the bottles. *I will defend myself. I will kill Kent if he ever comes near me again. I have every right to protect myself.* I shot at each bottle until I succeeded in blowing them all off the shelf. When I was done, a sense of relief flooded over me. I knew this was the answer. I was going to overcome my fear and anger by equipping myself with the skills necessary to protect myself.

I turned to put the gun back when I saw Todd who silently watched me. He was washing Thunder by the large door of the barn. No wonder I didn't see him when I came in. The storage shed had blocked my view of him. I walked over to him.

"I'm tired of being scared all the time," I told him.

He nodded. "I'm tired of being angry."

By the look in his eyes, I knew that we had just agreed to put the past behind us and move on. Relieved, I returned to the kitchen to finish making the sandwiches.

***

Two days later in the late morning, John came over to announce that Barbara went into labor. I told Todd that I was going to help out, and after I got into the buggy, I rode over to the Russell house where a flurry of activity greeted me.

"She went into labor yesterday afternoon," her mother told me as soon as I walked through the front door.

John took the children out to the barn so we could help the doctor without them running around us. I followed her mother to the bedroom where Barbara was trying to breathe through the pain. She gripped the newspapers under her and groaned.

"The baby will be here soon," the doctor said.

"Does labor always take long?" I asked.

"Sometimes it can. Barbara has had long labors in the past, but she progresses smoothly along and has little trouble with the actual delivery."

So I could expect to be in labor for a long time as well.

"The beginning of labor involves minor discomfort," her mother continued as the doctor turned back to Barbara. "It's not like she spent the whole night in pain. Now that she's ready to give birth, things are intense."

I was glad to be here so I knew what to expect when my time came. I took a deep breath. It was difficult to watch Barbara in pain but I was determined to help. "Is there anything I can do?"

"It would be a good time to get some hot water, clean towels and more newspapers," the doctor replied.

I nodded and boiled some water on the stove while her mother gathered the towels and newspapers. By the time we finished getting everything ready, the doctor announced that it was time for Barbara to start pushing. Her mother held onto her hand while I sat and waited with a towel.

I was aware of the movement in my womb. Soon it would be my turn. I had to admit that the process of giving birth was unpleasant and I felt queasy as I watched the baby's head come out, followed by the rest of the body. *There's no way*

I'm going to let Todd watch me give birth. I could understand why the husband and children were sent outside. I didn't relish the idea of going through it myself.

"It's a girl!" the doctor announced.

Little Melanie cried and we all laughed. The doctor handed her to me and I gently held her while I did my best to clean her up with water. She was tiny but amazingly strong and loud as she struggled to squirm away from me. I handed Melanie to Barbara while the doctor took care of the afterbirth. Her mother leaned over and smiled at her new granddaughter.

I smiled. "She's a cute little girl. I bet Molly will be delighted to have a sister. And I can't wait to tell Mrs. Carson that you had a girl."

Barbara laughed. "Yes, she will be pleased."

"It was scary to watch," I confessed. "But when I saw Melanie, I realized you were right. It is worth it."

"I'm glad you were here."

"I wouldn't have missed it for anything."

"Everything looks good," the doctor said. He checked Barbara's temperature and heart rate. Then he checked Melanie to see how she was doing. "I'm giving both of you a clean bill of health. You've been through this before, so you know what do but remember to get plenty of rest."

Melanie continued crying.

He chuckled. "Well, get as much rest as you can. I'll tell the father the good news and be on my way."

Her mother and I finished gathering the towels and blankets and took them to the laundry. John came in shortly after the doctor left and Calvin, Bruce and Molly got to meet their baby sister. After her mother and I were done washing the laundry, I hung the things up to dry and asked if there was anything else I could do. I was anxious to go home and tell Todd that Barbara and John had a girl. They said that there was nothing more they needed, so I went home to tell Todd the good news.

Chapter Twenty-Six
Todd's Point of View

Alex wrote me a letter to tell me that he and Agnes would be visiting for a couple of days in July. I thought that Ann pretended to be upset that they married since she had vowed to never let him become her brother-in-law, but Alex's hesitation to stay in our guest bedroom gave me an idea to have a good time with my childhood friend.

Ann offered to come with me into town to pick Alex and Agnes up from the train station, but I asked her if she would practice her shooting in the barn by the time we returned. She asked me why I wanted her to do this, but I told her it would become obvious soon enough. She shrugged and agreed to my strange request. It felt good to leave her alone and know she was comfortable with it.

Alex and Agnes looked very happy together, and I couldn't believe how much he had changed. He was more serious, though he did tell some good jokes. He had matured in college. I noticed how Agnes' face glowed whenever he looked at her. I was glad he was treating my sister well.

Ann kept her word and was in the barn practicing her shot with the rifle by the time we entered the barn. I grinned as soon as I saw her. She was starting to show in her pregnancy, so she looked especially feminine even though she was holding a gun in her hands.

She stopped shooting and came over to us. "Hello, Agnes and Alex."

Alex ducked when she swung the gun his way.

I bit my lower lip so I wouldn't laugh. She was so used to the gun that she didn't notice she was waving it around.

"When are you due to give birth?" Agnes asked, delighted to see her.

"Either late November or early December deciding on when the baby's ready to come out." She hugged Agnes. "You'll be an aunt soon enough."

"Good. I can't wait to spoil my niece or nephew."

This was beginning to get boring. I cleared my throat and nodded at Alex.

"Oh. Hello, Alex. Did you enjoy your trip?" Ann asked. She waved the gun in his direction.

"Watch where you're pointing that thing!" he squeaked as he hid behind me.

I burst out laughing. It was fun to watch him run from her like that.

Her eyes grew wide. "I forgot I had this in my hands." She quickly went to put it away.

"How could she forget something like that?" he whispered.

I noted the sweat on his brow.

I told her he was scared of her. Ever since she dumped sand on us, he had been on his guard around her. But she wasn't aware of his reaction to her, which made it even more humorous.

She walked back over to us. "Did you have a good trip?"

"It was wonderful," Agnes nodded, also unaware of Alex's hesitation around Ann. "It's much more fun to travel when you're with someone you love." She glanced at Alex and smiled.

"Alex, I'm looking forward to getting to know you as Todd's friend instead of the annoying boy who pulled pranks on everyone," Ann said. "I better get started on dinner. You two must be famished."

Agnes hastened to her. "Can I help? There's so much I want to tell you."

"Sure."

I watched Alex gulp nervously as Ann and Agnes went to the house. Of course, I could only hear Agnes talking. My sister rarely stopped to take a breath.

"Why don't we eat in town?" he asked.

I shook my head. "What's wrong with you? Ann's going out of her way to be nice to you. She never would have done that in Virginia."

He followed me as I brought the horses and wagon into the barn.

"She's only being nice to make me feel safe until she can spring her revenge on me," he insisted.

"You're paranoid."

"Am I? Agnes told me that Ann called me 'Creepy Alex' while we were growing up. She even said that Ann once told her that she'd kill me if I ever became her brother-in-law. Do you think she's going to do something to the dinner?"

After the wagon was in its proper spot, I unhooked the horses. I knew I shouldn't increase his anxiety but the moment seemed too good to pass up. "I'll tell you what. You ride Thunder and I'll ride Lightning." I got the horses ready while I talked. "We'll take a race. If you win, we'll eat in town. If I win, we'll eat here. Deal?"

He shifted from one foot to the other. "I don't like to make bets anymore."

"Just because you're going to be a preacher doesn't mean you can't have some good old fashioned fun. I promise you that Ann will not do anything to your food."

"I don't know."

"Wouldn't it be good to have a race for old time's sake? We used to have a lot of fun. Sometimes I miss it."

He sighed. "I do too. When you go off to college, everyone expects you to be serious."

"Great. So throw off your hat and let's have some fun!"

"Alright. But if I win, we're eating in town."

"Agreed."

As we got up on the horses, I asked him how long he planned to stay.

"Two days," he said. "Agnes and I still have to visit my aunt and uncle."

"How are they doing?"

"They're doing well. They wanted me to stop by here first so I can give them an update on your progress out here."

"Then I'll have to give you a tour tomorrow."

We urged our horses forward. I pointed to the route we should use in our race. "Are you ready?"

He grinned. "On the count of three. One, two..." He took off.

"You cheater!" I spurred my horse to action.

The ride felt wonderful, and I won despite his effort to gain a head start.

"We eat here tonight!" I cheered. "Ann's making your favorite dish. Pot roast with vegetables. She's going all out for you and Agnes. She'll make Agnes' favorite meal tomorrow."

"I can't wait." He didn't sound enthusiastic.

By the time we went into the house, Ann was almost done with the meal. Alex sat next to Agnes on the couch so I slipped into the kitchen, wrapped my arms around Ann and kissed her on the side of the neck.

She jumped. "Why don't I ever hear you when you come into the kitchen?"

I chuckled. "Alex and I had a race to see if we were going to eat here or in town. I won so we'll be eating here."

She frowned and turned from the sink where she was washing some bowls. "Why doesn't he want to eat my food?"

"He's afraid you're going to put something bad in it. I told him you wouldn't but he believes the worst."

"I can't believe this. I went to great lengths to be nice to him in the barn, and this is how he thanks me?"

For Ann, it probably was a big effort on her part. "I know. You were wonderful." I kissed her soapy hand. "I think Agnes told Alex the 'Creepy Alex' rants you had while we were growing up. It's got him paranoid."

She seemed ready to protest but then she looked out the window and slyly grinned.

"What are you planning?" I liked it when she had that twinkle in her eye.

"You'll see." She kissed me on the cheek. "I don't want you to have to share the blame."

"Is there anything I can do to help?"

"Just keep Alex and Agnes out of here. I want him to know that no one was in here with me."

I couldn't wait to see what she was scheming. And fortunately, I didn't have to wait long. As soon as we sat at the table, Alex led us in prayer.

"Lord, we thank You for the chance to get together," he began. "Most of all, we thank You for Your protection from things we cannot see that may be out to harm us. Please watch over us while we eat this meal and give us long life afterwards. Amen."

I struggled to hold in my laughter, but Ann's own quiet giggles didn't help. She nudged me in the side, which only made the situation that much more funny.

"What is so funny?" Agnes wondered, bewildered. "I thought that was a lovely prayer."

I couldn't look at Ann. I knew I would burst out laughing if I did. Instead, I focused on my little sister. "We're just so happy you two are here."

"Oh, that's nice." She smiled, content with the answer.

Alex hesitated to eat the food on his plate. He glanced around the table and sighed.

Agnes brought a fork full of pot roast up to her mouth.

"Agnes, stop!" Ann cried out. "I gave you the wrong plate." She ran over to the other side of the table and switched Agnes' and Alex's plates. "There. That's better. I wanted to give the bigger potato to Alex. I know how you men need your strength." She sat next to me and took a bite of the food on her plate. "Isn't anyone else going to eat?"

I stared at her in awe. How could she do that with a straight face?

I tried to eat but I was too busy fighting off my laughter to do so.

"This is delicious," Agnes said after she took a bite. She glanced at Alex. "You should eat some. It's your favorite dish."

"I'm not that hungry. Maybe I should just share your plate," he replied.

"You haven't eaten anything since this morning."

"Traveling affects my appetite."

"You ate just fine last night."

"Are you lying, Alex?" I pretended to be shocked. "You can't preach the Bible and lie."

"I'm not lying. I really don't have much of an appetite."

Ann groaned. "Alex, I did nothing to your food. I must admit I'm disheartened that you would think I would do such a thing."

"Well, you did put a squirrel in my bag during the Christmas performance when we were fifteen," he told her.

"I did not."

"Sure you did. There wasn't anyone else who could have done it."

"Oh no?" I spoke up.

He gasped as he turned his attention to me. "You did it?"

"Yes," I admitted.

"But why? We were supposed to play pranks on other people, not each other."

"Do you remember that day you made me eat bugs when we were twelve? Ann said I didn't have to eat the bugs but you told me to either eat the bugs or kiss her?"

He grinned. "That was great. I actually wondered which one you'd pick. You were always praising her. It would have been more fun if you had kissed her in front of the whole school."

"No. It wouldn't have been fun. I was twelve. Kissing girls was embarrassing back then."

"So you waited for three years to put a squirrel in my bag?"

"I have a lot of patience."

Ann placed her hand on my thigh and smiled at me. "Thank goodness for that."

I returned her smile.

"So you see, you're perfectly safe," Agnes said. "I swear, all the way out here, he kept fretting over all the things he was afraid you were going to do to him. Now he knows who he really has to watch out for."

"Then explain why she changed our plates around," he insisted.

"She wanted to give you the bigger potato."

"I was just playing with you, Alex," Ann interrupted. "I didn't touch your plate."

"If it makes you feel better, you can have mine," I offered as I exchanged my plate with his. "Now if I die in the morning, you'll know you were right." I took a bite. "This is really good, Ann. Once again, you outdid yourself."

She blushed from my compliment. "Thank you."

Alex slowly picked up his fork. "I guess I was wrong. I'm sorry, Ann."

"It's alright, Alex. I spent a lot of time calling you 'creepy', so I can understand your hesitation."

"I won't call you 'Scary Annie' anymore. Peace?"

"Peace."

It was good to see them finally getting along.

Chapter Twenty-Seven
Todd's Point of View

Ann's parents and Ginny moved to Jamestown in August, and the harvest came shortly after that so I spent most of my time in the fields. Her father offered to help and seemed to enjoy the process. It was hard work, but it was work I enjoyed. I didn't miss sitting at a desk at the bank even though it meant regular work hours and weekends off. Besides, by the time the crop was taken care of, I had plenty of time to spend around the house getting things ready for the baby.

John gave us a bassinet he made, and Barbara, Ann and her mother sewed baby clothes. Whenever they discussed the details of giving birth and taking care of a newborn, I would find something else to do, even if her father or John wasn't around. I was happy and anticipated the birth of my child, but enjoyed my ignorance on the topics Ann loved to discuss. To her credit, she simply let me feel the baby kick and didn't say anything else.

It was late November when I woke up in the middle of the night and saw Ann sitting on the bed and staring out the window.

"Is something wrong?" I asked.

"I think the baby's getting ready to come."

I sat up in bed. "Why didn't you wake me?"

She smiled. "It takes awhile. I could be in labor for a day. There's no sense in both of us not getting much sleep tonight."

Now I was beginning to wonder if I should have asked for some of the details. "How long do you think it will be? When should I get the doctor?"

"The contractions should be five minutes apart when you get the doctor."

"Then I should probably keep track of them for you."

"You don't have to start yet. They're far apart. Besides, I'll keep an eye on the clock. I would like Barbara and my parents to also be here when the time comes. Barbara wants to help and I know my parents are eager to see their grandchild."

"Alright. Just tell me when I need to go." I wished there was more I could do for her, but I knew it was something she had to do alone. "If you need anything, will you let me know?"

She nodded. "I'm going to do some cleaning downstairs. Try to get some sleep."

"Shouldn't you be taking it easy?"

"If I do that, the night will pass too slowly. I have to do something." She leaned over and kissed me. "You're going to be a wonderful father. I hope your father will want to come here once the baby is born."

I sighed and squeezed her hand. "Even if he doesn't, I'll be alright. You and our baby is what I'm concerned about."

She left the room and I managed to go back to sleep. I didn't realize I had slept in so long until I went down to the kitchen after getting dressed. It was almost nine. I didn't usually sleep this late. "Ann? Where are you?"

She didn't reply.

I immediately ran through the house and breathed a sigh of relief when I saw her doing laundry in the small room off to the side of the parlor. Though I could tell she was in a lot of pain, she didn't scream as I expected her to.

When her face relaxed, I asked, "How far apart are your contractions and what are you doing in here?"

"I'm getting things ready. I've decided to give birth in here since it's the easiest room to clean. I have clean blankets, towels and clothes in the corner next to some clean water. It's really a matter of waiting. I already cleaned the downstairs. I got bored so I began washing some dirty clothes. I'm almost done."

"Ann, you're pushing yourself too hard." I didn't mean to sound stern but her actions worried me. I didn't want her to wear herself out.

"The work keeps my mind off the pain. I can manage it better if I concentrate on something else."

"I never realized how worrisome the whole process could be on the husband," I admitted, softening my tone. I took out my pocket watch. "So your last contraction just ended?"

She nodded. She turned her attention back to the clothes.

I couldn't think of anything to talk about, so I just stood there and stared at my watch. When she paused and gripped the sides of the wringer, I knew she was in pain again. I forced myself not to snap at her. "You're four minutes apart, Ann."

I didn't wait for her response. I simply grabbed my coat and boots and rushed out to Lightning. The horse was hungry but he'd have to wait. My first stop was at Barbara and John's house. Barbara immediately jumped on her horse and headed over so I could go into town to get the doctor and her parents.

"When did her labor start?" the doctor asked as he collected his bag and coat.

"Around four in the morning. She was supposed to tell me when her contractions were five minutes apart but when I got up, they were already four minutes apart."

"I hope I make it there in time."

He didn't say anything else, and I didn't feel like asking him if she was in danger because she waited too long. Again, I wished I had asked for the details but shrugged off the thought and went to tell her parents.

"We'll leave shortly," her father said.

Her mother was too excited to talk.

I rode the horse hard back to the house. I was anxious to find out how she was doing. Lightning protested when I didn't feed him, but I ignored him and went into the house. On my way from the barn, I shook my head at the sight of the clean laundry hanging on the line. I hoped Barbara had talked some sense into Ann. She really didn't need to be doing work when she was about to give birth.

Barbara ran out of the scullery room, looking irritated.

"Is she alright?" I asked, alarmed.

"Oh, she's fine. She's just stubborn, that's all. Did you know she was hanging up laundry when I got here? She nearly doubled over in pain when I came up to her. She kept saying that she needed to focus on something else, but I made her lie down. She really shouldn't push herself so hard. That baby is eager to come out. I don't know if the doctor will get here in time. I may need your help."

She grabbed a bucket of water and turned to go back to Ann.

I hadn't realized I beat the doctor in getting back. He probably didn't know about the shortcut. I wished I had told him because by this time, Ann wasn't holding back her screams, and quite frankly, I didn't want to go through this. But I followed Barbara into the room. I had never seen a woman in labor and from the look on Ann's face, I could see that the pain was intense.

"Here." Barbara handed me some clean towels. "I'll hand you the baby. Its head is starting to come out."

The room started to spin around me. I felt like I was going to pass out.

Fortunately, the doctor entered the room at that moment. "I'll take over from here," he told me.

I didn't argue with him. I handed him the towels and left the room. I hadn't expected it to be so hard to watch Ann like that. I wished I could take the pain for her.

"I see the head," the doctor said.

How could he be so calm?

"You're doing good, Ann. When I say to push, push," he told her.

I felt sick. I had to get outside. As soon as I stood on the porch, I took a deep breath. The cold air settled my stomach. Ann's parents climbed up the porch steps. I was thankful for the distraction from listening to Ann scream.

"I think this is a situation where we should be out of the way," her father said as her mother ran into the house.

He sat in the chair.

I was too nervous to sit. Ann had stopped screaming.

"It's not easy for us men either, though the women do all the work," he acknowledged. "Are there any chores that need to be done?"

It took me a moment to remember the horses. "I haven't fed the horses yet."

The sound of a baby crying interrupted my thoughts.

"Todd! It's a boy!" Barbara called out from the front door. She walked out. "Ann and the baby are doing fine. She practically gave birth all by herself. I can't believe she progressed that fast. I wish my labors were that easy."

I smiled, relieved and glad it was over but also anxious to see Ann and our son.

"Ann's mother is washing the baby and the doctor is taking care of Ann. We'll bring the baby out after the doctor says it's alright." She quickly went back into the house.

"I'll feed those horses for you," he offered.

"Thank you." Feeding the horses was the last thing on my mind. I wanted to see what the baby looked like and make sure Ann was feeling well.

After what was five minutes but seemed like forever, Ann's mother came out holding a swaddled tiny baby in her arms. "He's precious." She smiled as she gently placed him in my arms. "He has ten little fingers and toes and little bit of light brown hair on his head."

I was surprised that he was asleep after all the crying he had done just a couple minutes ago. He seemed small and fragile. He yawned. I laughed. It was an amazing experience to know I was holding my son.

"Did you and Ann decide on a name?" she asked.

I looked at her in surprise. "Didn't she tell you?"

"She said she wanted to wait until after he was born."

"Nathaniel Alexander Brothers."

"What a nice name."

The doctor came out of the house and shook my hand. "Congratulations! Mother and child are doing fine. Ann can have as many kids as you two want. She handles labor very well. In the future though, notify me when her contractions are about seven minutes apart. She gives birth faster than most women. Now I already talked to her about not waiting so long next time, so you don't have to worry about that. Ann is ready for you to see her. Good day." He nodded to Mrs. Statesman who smiled in return.

"I'm going to tell Ann's father the news," she said.

I walked into the house, careful not to disturb Nathaniel who was still sleeping. I couldn't stop smiling.

Barbara came out of the scullery room. "I just finished cleaning up in there. I'm going to take the dirty blankets and clothes to my home and wash them and bring them back so Ann won't worry about it. Knowing her, she'll probably try to do more laundry before the day is over. The doctor made sure she understood she has to take it easy for the next two weeks. I don't know if she'll listen, but between me, Mrs. Carson and her mother, we should be able to do enough of the work so she can relax and focus on the baby."

"I appreciate that, Barbara. I know she can be stubborn."

She laughed. "She wanted to see you right after the baby was born but kept telling us to wait until she was presentable. She said you looked like you were going to faint when you thought you were going to be there for the birth, and she wanted to spare you from seeing anything else. She really does love you, Todd. Anyway, would you tell Ann I'll be back this evening with a meal for everyone?"

I nodded.

After she left, I went into the scullery room where Ann was lying on a couple of blankets on the floor. I sat next to her and lightly tapped her on the arm. If she was asleep, I'd let her stay that way. But she opened her eyes and smiled at me.

"How are you feeling?" I asked her.

"Wonderful. Barbara was right. I don't even remember the pain. As soon as he cried, it was all worth it."

"I didn't think it was possible, but you are more beautiful than I've ever seen you."

"I'm a mess."

"You're my wife who just gave me a son. You're the most beautiful woman in the world." I leaned over and kissed her. "I love you."

Tears filled her eyes. "I love you too."

This time I didn't mind it that she was crying.

***

That Christmas, Ann wanted to have her parents and Ginny over so she could do the entertaining. The house was filled with a lot of warmth. The smell of ham, potatoes, and cake filled the air. Her mother held Nathaniel while Ann and Ginny took care of the cooking. Her father and I got the sleigh ready for a ride. Shortly before dinner was ready, there was a knock at the door. The women were so busy talking, I doubted they even heard the knocking. When I opened the door, I paused, stunned.

My parents stood on the porch.

My father cleared his throat. He had his hat in his hands. "May we please come in?"

For a moment, I couldn't speak. Finally, I stepped aside so they could enter the house.

"May I join the women?" my mother asked.

I nodded. "Of course."

Ann's father smiled and led my mother to the kitchen so my father and I could be alone.

Feeling awkward, I closed the door. "Would you like to sit?"

"Yes, I would."

He's as nervous as I am. I took a deep breath as I sat across from him. I couldn't think of what to say, so I waited for him to speak.

"I came to apologize," he slowly began. "I feel like a fool." He shifted in the chair. "Will you let me into your life?"

I fought back the swell of emotion that came over me. "You have always been my father. I would like to have you back in my life. I am sorry for the way I left. I was afraid you would talk me out of it if you knew."

He smiled. "Yes, I would have, but that would have been wrong. You were right. You have to follow your path, not mine."

"Thank you."

Ann and my mother stepped into the parlor. My mother held Nathaniel in her arms.

Ann smiled. "It's good to see you, Mr. Brothers. Will you be staying here for a couple of days? We have a guest bedroom."

My parents and Ann looked at me.

"It would be nice to talk," I replied.

My father nodded. "Yes, we will stay for three days. Thank you."

"His name is Nathaniel," she told Father, smiling at the baby. "May he see him?" she asked me.

"Of course," I softly replied.

"We'll leave you two alone," Ann said.

We nodded as they left.

Father grinned. "I remember the day you were born. I held you in my arms and you looked so much like this little one. Where did the years go?" He sighed. "In the end, it's family that matters. It's not what you do with your life, it's who you do it with. The job at the bank isn't worth losing my relationship with you."

"I appreciate that. And who knows? Maybe he'll want to be a banker. He might even want to work in Virginia. But it has to be his choice."

He wiped the tears in his eyes. "You are a good son."

We spent the next ten minutes talking about what I was doing and what was happening back in Virginia.

I noticed a movement out of the corner of my eye. Ann stood by the parlor doorway, smiling at us. When she realized we saw her, she announced that dinner was ready.

I waited until Father entered the kitchen so I could have a moment alone with her.

"How did it go?" she asked.

"Very well."

"I'm glad. We've all been hoping for a reconciliation. What a great Christmas gift. It makes the hat I gave you fail in comparison."

I hugged her. "The greatest Christmas gift I have ever received is your love. You have made my life complete. Merry Christmas, Ann."

"Merry Christmas, Todd."

We kissed before we entered the kitchen.

You've read Todd and Ann's story.
But Kent Ashton has a story to tell as well…

In *Falling In Love With Her Husband*, Kent Ashton was the villain… Or at least that is how Ann Statesman and Todd Brothers saw him.

But was he really? Why did he really end his courtship with Ann? Was his scandalous behavior with Rebecca Johnson the reason he became engaged to her? And what compelled him to go after Ann after she married Todd and moved to North Dakota?

This novella tells why he did what he did. And it paves the way for the book that will lead to his own happy ending.

Please note: This is the prequel to *Catching Kent.* It does not have a "happily ever after" ending. The happy ending comes in *Catching Kent.*

Kent Ashton finds his happy ending in…

Kent Ashton has returned to America in search of a new start, a chance to live a quiet and unassuming life. But fate has other plans.

After spending time in Ireland, Kent Ashton has returned to America. It's his chance at a new start, and he's determined to go all the way to California–far away from his past and the list of regrets he's left behind. But while in Omaha, Nebraska, thieves rob him and leave him for dead in the back of an alley. That's when Dave Larson finds him and brings him home so he can recover. As soon as Kent is better, he plans to continue his journey to California.

But Dave's daughter, Rose Larson, has other plans for him. She's bound and determined to make him her husband. Sure, he might protest, claim he's not the right one for her, that she's better off with someone else. But she's not one to give up lightly, and if she has to chase him to get him to the altar, then so be it.

48288359R00171

Made in the USA
San Bernardino, CA
21 April 2017